T0024582

Praise for

saving
beck

"Courtney writes poignant and emotionally driven stories that prove again and again why she's the best at what she does."

—Rachel Van Dyken, #1 *New York Times* bestselling author of *The Wager*

"[A] heart-wrenching, suspenseful tale . . . This riveting story highlights the unrelenting force of addiction and the havoc it can wreak on any family. Through accessible and absorbing prose, Cole tells an important tale full of complex characters and nuanced family drama. An intense but stunningly hopeful story about drug addiction, loss, and relationships."

—*Kirkus Reviews*

"With addiction being so pressing an issue for so many people today, *Saving Beck* is a must-read cautionary tale. It will rip your heart out but then leave you knowing there is a light at the end of the tunnel."

—Nikki Sixx, *New York Times* bestselling author of *The Heroin Diaries* and Mötley Crüe bassist

"Raw and timely."

—*Booklist*

"In her most compelling work to date, Courtney Cole lays open the soul of addiction with such compassionate precision it will take your breath, break your heart, and restore your hope in the strength and resilience of the human spirit."

—M. Leighton, *New York Times* bestselling author of *Down to You*

"From its visceral opening scene to the satisfying final twist, this story held me in its thrall. Courtney Cole's firsthand experiences make *Saving Beck* a raw, powerful, heart-wrenching read."

—Robyn Harding, international bestselling author of *The Party*

saving

beck

COURTNEY COLE

Gallery Books

New York   London   Toronto   Sydney   New Delhi

G

Gallery Books
An Imprint of Simon & Schuster, Inc.
1230 Avenue of the Americas
New York, NY 10020

This book is a work of fiction. Any references to historical events, real people, or real places are used fictitiously. Other names, characters, places, and events are products of the author's imagination, and any resemblance to actual events or places or persons, living or dead, is entirely coincidental.

Copyright © 2018 by Courtney Cole

All rights reserved, including the right to reproduce this book or portions thereof in any form whatsoever. For information, address Gallery Books Subsidiary Rights Department, 1230 Avenue of the Americas, New York, NY 10020.

First Gallery Books trade paperback edition March 2019

GALLERY BOOKS and colophon are registered trademarks of Simon & Schuster, Inc.

For information about special discounts for bulk purchases, please contact Simon & Schuster Special Sales at 1-866-506-1949 or business@simonandschuster.com.

The Simon & Schuster Speakers Bureau can bring authors to your live event. For more information or to book an event, contact the Simon & Schuster Speakers Bureau at 1-866-248-3049 or visit our website at www.simonspeakers.com.

Interior design by Alison Cnockaert

Manufactured in the United States of America

10 9 8 7 6 5 4 3 2 1

The Library of Congress has cataloged the hardcover edition as follows:

Names: Cole, Courtney (Novelist), author.
Title: Saving Beck / Courtney Cole.
Description: First Gallery Books hardcover edition. | New York : Gallery Books, 2018.
Identifiers: LCCN 2017052962 (print) | LCCN 2017056113 (ebook) |
   ISBN 9781501184536 (ebook) | ISBN 9781501184529 (hardcover : acid-free paper)
Subjects: LCSH: Mothers and sons—Fiction. | Drug addiction—Fiction. | Drug
   addicts—Fiction. | Domestic fiction. | BISAC: FICTION / Family Life. |
   FICTION / Contemporary Women. | FICTION / Literary.
Classification: LCC PS3603.O42825 (ebook) | LCC PS3603.O42825 S29 2018 (print) |
   DDC 813/.6—dc23
LC record available at https://lccn.loc.gov/2017052962

ISBN 978-1-5011-8452-9
ISBN 978-1-5011-9702-4 (pbk)
ISBN 978-1-5011-8453-6 (ebook)

To Gunner.
Because your demons don't control you anymore.

prologue

I PACE, BACK AND FORTH AND BACK AGAIN, BECAUSE MY intuition is buzzing but I don't know why.

All I know is that I'd woken up from a dead sleep two hours ago, and I had a heavy, heavy weight on my chest and Beck was in my thoughts.

I cross the faded red Oriental rug, stepping carefully over the shadows on the floor. I do it once, twice, three times before I pause.

The house is so quiet I literally hear ringing in my ears, and the darkness threatens to loom out of control and swallow me up. It's just my imagination, of course, but night does that to a person. Things come to life, and they're bigger than they normally are.

For that reason, my home is a bright safe haven, something that helps ward off the monsters. Soft rugs, elegant yet comfortable furnishings, soothing art adorning the walls. It's a tranquil wolf's den, and I'm the mama wolf, and God help anyone who fucks with my pack.

Except sometimes, things are out of my control.

Times like tonight, and every night prior for the past one year, two months, and seven days.

Yes, I know the exact moment our lives changed. Who wouldn't?

It was 1:21 a.m. on a Saturday that had just turned into Sunday.

In that one moment I learned that the human body has an endless supply of tears at its disposal.

What I didn't know at 1:21 a.m. that night was that it was just the beginning. I thought it was an ending. And it was, but how could I know it was a beginning too?

With a sigh, I sink into the office chair and study the monitor in front of me, watching the red dot pulse on the screen that gives me hope my son is still alive somewhere. His phone hasn't moved in days, not even an inch. That's impossible, unless he's . . . I can't even think the word. If I think it, it could make it real. So I won't do that.

If it still hasn't moved by morning, I'll go hunt it down in person. It's in a terrible part of town, and I'm sure that when I get there his phone will be lying in a dumpster covered in trash, and I'll have no more of an idea where he is and if he's alive than I do right now.

But I'll do it anyway. Because I always do. Because it's all I *can* do. That's what happens when things are out of your control. They spin and twist and all you can do is grasp at their pieces.

I stare at the clock. 12:11 a.m. 12:12. 12:13.

The minutes tick so slowly by I can practically feel them move.

I wrap my robe around my shoulders ever more tightly and pace again.

One, one thousand.

Two, one thousand.

Three.

A noise on the front porch interrupts my steps, the silence of the house amplifying the jarring sound. I pause in the middle of the rug and listen.

A rustling. The shuffle of a foot across the brick. A heavy thump.

My heart leaps into my throat, wildly slamming in panic. No one should be here at 12:17 a.m.

But someone is.

I don't even feel my feet hitting the hardwood floor as I fly through the hall toward the front door and peer out the side window. I don't feel my hands as I push the curtains back, and I can't feel my heart when I see him. I'm too numb.

But when I see that pile of clothing—the rumpled shirt I bought him for Christmas, the dark blond hair glinting in the streetlight—I know him.

I'd know my son anywhere.

I throw open the door, and he looks up at me, his eyes blurry, dark, hollow, sad.

He's in a heap in front of me, his legs crumpled beneath him, dried vomit on his shirt, foam bubbling from his nose.

"I . . ." He tries to speak, but there's more foam, and it's orange, and then it's red like blood.

It is blood.

I scream and drop to the ground, clutching him as his eyes close. The night is shattered with my screaming, and seconds pass, then minutes, and people arrive and his eyes still don't open. Red and blue lights flash across my lawn, and he's shaking and convulsing and EMTs mill around and take him from me.

It's 12:32 a.m.

one

NATALIE

H E'S FOAMING AT THE MOUTH AS THEY LOAD HIM ON THE
gurney, and he looks at me with wild eyes.

"Angel," it sounds like he says, but his voice is thick and gurgly and
it's hard to make out his words.

"What?" I ask quickly, trying to get through the EMTs to grab his
hand. "I'm not an angel. You're not dying, Beck. Do you hear me?"

Nothing feels real as I watch the paramedics slam the ambulance
doors closed. They latch with finality, sealing my son inside, and panic
erupts in my heart as red and blue flash against my skin. He can't be
alone.

"I want to ride with him," I hear myself say, and they shake their heads.

"We're sorry, ma'am. There's not enough room. Follow us in your
car."

I'm not sure how I find the front door to grab my purse and my
keys, or how I make it to my car. I can't even feel my foot as I press
the stiff accelerator. It doesn't occur to me that I should perhaps put
real clothes on, so I find myself chasing the ambulance in my bathrobe
through the Chicago streets.

It's not for five more minutes that I remember my other children, and with a gasp, I call my sister.

"Sam, you've got to come," I manage to say around the lump in my throat, a giant piece of terror that is stuck halfway down.

"What's wrong?" she says quickly, even though she was sleeping and I can hear it in her voice.

"Beck." My voice breaks, and I can't breathe. I try to inhale and it doesn't work. I can't speak. *It's Beck. Of course it's Beck.*

"Nat?" My sister is urgent and her voice is thin. "Nat! Talk to me! You're scaring me."

"We're on the way to the hospital," I manage to gasp. "Dev and Annabelle are at home. Sleeping. Please . . . go there."

That's all I can squeeze out.

"I'm on my way," she says, and I can hear her throwing her covers off and grabbing her clothes. "Vinny, we've gotta go," she tells her husband. I hear him mumble that he's asleep, but I can't think anymore.

All I can do is focus on the back of the ambulance, on the perfectly square doors and silver handles. My son is in there, and I can't lose him.

"Nat?" Sam asks, and she's hesitant. "Is Beck . . ."

"He's alive," I say limply. "Or he was when they took him. But barely. I don't . . . I can't . . ."

I hang up because saying any of those words out loud might influence the outcome. I might tempt fate and God might take my son if I doubt Him.

"Don't take him, don't take him, please don't take him," I plead under my breath as I weave in and out of traffic, trailing the ambulance like I'm attached with a tether. The siren wails and it's monotonous but it's good. It's good the siren is on. They would only turn it off if . . . if . . .

I can't think it.

Beck is in that truck.

He's okay.

He's breathing. I have to believe that's true.

The hospital is a beacon of light and hope as we pull in. I barely remember to put my car in park before I jump out and leave it in the middle of the lane, the tires wrenched haphazardly toward the curb.

"Ma'am, you can't park there," a guy in a security uniform says with his fake badge, but I don't answer. I toss him my keys and push my way to the doors, and *that's* when I see him.

My son.

They've pulled him out of the ambulance, and he's so still, so white. He's got the body of a man and the face of a boy, and he's got vomit in his hair. One hand dangles over the edge of the gurney, orange flecks dripping from his fingers to the floor, but no one notices.

"Beck," I breathe, but he doesn't open his eyes. "Beck," I say louder, as loud as I can. His mouth is slack, but he's not dead—he can't be dead, because someone is pumping his heart with her fists. She's running next to the gurney, and she's pounding on his heart, making it beat.

"Coming through," she yells at the doors, and there is a team of people working on him. They're frantic, and that's not good.

I chase after them, through the emergency room, through the people, but someone grabs me at a giant set of double doors, the gateway to the important rooms.

"You can't go in there," a nurse tells me.

"That's my son," I try to tell her, but she doesn't care. "Beck," I scream, and I try to see through the windows, but I can't because he's gone. "I love you, Beck. Stay here. Stay here."

The nurse grasps my arm, and I can't stand anymore. My legs are tired and the adrenaline . . . it numbs me. I collapse beside her and she tries to hold me up, but she can't . . . I'm on the ground.

My face is wet—when did I start crying?

"You have to save my son," I beg her, my fingers curled into her arm. I stare into her eyes. Hers are green, ringed with blue, and she looks away. Something about her seems so familiar, something about those eyes.

"We'll try, ma'am," she says uncertainly. It's the uncertainty that kills me. "We'll do everything we can. I'm going to take you to a quiet room and give you a blanket. Is there anyone I can call for you?"

I shake my head no. "I already called my sister."

"Okay," the nurse says quietly, and her name tag says Jessica. She takes me to a waiting room, a quiet private one, the ones they use when the outcome might not be good. I know that because I've been here before.

I swallow hard and she puts a cup of coffee in my hand.

As she does, she pushes a stray hair out of her face and her bracelet catches my eye. A simple chain with a silver dolphin on it.

"You were here the night my husband was brought in," I say slowly. "Weren't you? Do you remember me?"

It was over a year ago. Of course she doesn't remember me.

But Jessica nods.

"I'm so sorry about your husband," she tells me now, her voice quiet and thick. "I swear to you, we did everything we could."

"I know," I tell her. Because I do. The accident was so bad, there's no way anyone could've survived. Except for Beck. He lived. But Matt . . . his injuries were insurmountable. That's what the doctor told me that night.

I stare at the door, and this is the same room and that is the same door and this is the same blue-and-white-tiled floor. For a minute, I'm back in that moment and the doctor is coming in. I'd waited for hours and his face was so grave and I knew, *I knew*, before he could utter a word.

I shook my head because I didn't want to hear what was coming next, but he spoke anyway.

Matt's injuries were insurmountable, he'd said. *We did everything we could.*

But everything wasn't enough, and my husband died.

"Is it a different doctor tonight?" I ask suddenly. "I need a different doctor. One who can save my son."

I know it's illogical. I know it was never the doctor's fault, but it doesn't matter because Jessica is nodding. "It's a different doctor tonight," she tells me. "Dr. Grant, and he's very, very good."

"Okay," I whisper. "Okay."

"If you need anything, you tell me," Jessica says, and I can see that she means it. She likes me. Or she feels sorry for me. It doesn't matter which. I nod and she's gone, and I'm alone.

Just like I was a year ago, and just like that night all I can do is pace.

I'm a caged mama wolf and there's nothing I can do, but I know that if I stop moving, Beck might die. My energy is attached to his energy. I have to move. It all depends on me.

So I walk in circles.

I walk six paces, over the six white tiles, then I turn, taking three steps over the blue. I tread back six paces over the white, and then turn again, taking three more over the blue.

I will not stop, Beck. I won't fail you. I won't.

It becomes rhythmic, and I match my breaths with my steps. I'm a machine, a timekeeper, a being made of clockwork as I walk in circles, marking time. Every step I take, Beck is still alive. I feel it in my heart. It's all up to me.

I'm alone in the room, and the door is ajar. The lights in here are dimmed, but the lights out there, out in the hospital, are bright. A wedge of that brightness falls across the floor, across the line of blue and white tiles, and I step over it time and again, determined not to touch it.

I won't step into the light, Beck. I won't go into the light if you don't. Promise me.

They won't let me see my boy, but if I just think hard enough, if I *feel* it hard enough, he'll hear me. He'll hear my begging and my pleas, and he'll forgive me for everything, and he'll live.

Please, please, please.

I pause for just a second on the far edge of a blue tiled square. The tile is dog-eared here in this spot, standing out amid the other perfectly polished ones. This one is cracked, and I'd stepped on it a hundred times a year ago when I was waiting for news of my husband.

Kneeling now, I finger that crack.

Maybe if I hadn't paused then, if I hadn't focused so much on the imperfections of this one tile, Matt would've lived.

I hadn't moved enough that night. I didn't save him.

Bolting to my feet, I restart my pacing, furious now. I'm a woman possessed, and I don't care about being rational. I don't care about logic.

I care about saving my son.

I would do anything to save him. I'd offer my own life in trade. I'd make a deal with the devil.

"Tell me what I need to do," I whisper adamantly to God. "Just tell me."

Through a heavy fog, I hear the hospital sounds instead of an answer.

The beeps of machines, the squeak of nurses' shoes on the floors. I hear gurneys rolling and curtains being shoved back, the metallic rings scraping against the metal rods. I smell the waxed floors and the iodine and the sterility, and it makes me sick.

An overwhelming blanket of dread drapes me, wet and suffocating, covering me up. I feel so suddenly hopeless, so bereft.

"This can't be happening," I whisper to the empty room. "How can this be happening? What kind of God would do this to me again?"

But then I'm instantly scared. "I'm sorry," I tell Him. "I didn't mean it." But I kind of did. I just can't say it aloud. I can't have Him punish Beck for my doubts.

"Don't take my son," I say instead. "Please, please, God. Don't take my son. You took my husband. Please don't take my boy. I can't deal with that. It's been enough already. You know it's been enough."

I leave it at that, and I begin to pace again, because in my addled and illogical mind, my movement also has a direct correlation to how hard the doctors will work on Beck. My steps are frantic and fast, and that's good. It's something I can do. I can power the doctors with my energy; I can push the breath in and out of my son's lungs with my steps.

I've made two hundred laps around the tiles when the door is pushed open, and the light opens onto the floor and I look up, and I'm frantic, and I expect to see the doctor.

But I don't.

It's Kit, my husband's best friend, and he's filling the doorway with his giant shoulders. He's a Great Dane in a sea of Labradors. He always has been.

"You don't need to be here," I tell him immediately. "It's fine. I'm fine. Beck is going to be fine."

"Tell me how he is, Nat," Kit says calmly, unaffected. He steps inside the door and grasps my elbow in an effort to get me to pause. I shake him off because I can't stop. Not for anyone.

"I don't know," I say, and I'm helpless. "He overdosed, I think. He was on my porch and there was so much vomit, and he was . . ."

My voice trails off, because I can't relive that moment.

"What has the doctor said?"

"He hasn't been out at all. They were . . . Jesus, they were doing CPR on him, Kit. His heart wasn't working."

There are tears on my cheeks even though my heart is a block of ice. I don't know how that's possible. Kit tries to hug me, to pull me against his big chest, but I can't, I can't. I pull away.

"Kit, stop. I have to move."

The rejection and pain on his face cut me a little, but I can't worry about that. I can only worry about Beck, and I have to move.

I feel Kit watching me as I pace, and I know that I look crazy. But I don't care.

"Nat, is there anything at all I can do?"

I feel him trying to read my thoughts and I look away. I want to tell him to just leave me alone so that I don't have to worry about anyone but myself in this moment. I word it more delicately than that.

"No. There's nothing. I just want to absorb the quiet and pull myself together, honestly."

He pauses, unsure.

"I mean it," I insist. "You know how I get. I handle things better alone."

He finally nods, albeit reluctantly.

"Call me if you need me," Kit says before he turns to leave. I nod, and he's gone and I'm back to being alone.

I pace and time bends and blends.

Jessica brings me another coffee at some point, and I'm dizzy from pacing.

"Your friend wants you to drink this." She pushes the hot Styrofoam into my hand.

"My friend?"

"The big blond guy? He's out in the public waiting room."

I exhale. Of course Kit didn't leave. He wouldn't. He's the closest friend we have. He would never leave.

"Thank you. Is there any news?"

She shakes her head. "They're still working."

God.

I nod, and my head is a ball on a stick, bobbing like a bobblehead doll.

She starts to leave, but I stop her.

"Jessica? What time is it?"

She checks her watch.

"It's one forty-seven."

I exhale slowly with relief. Matt died at 1:21. Beck outlived him. I know it's illogical, but I don't give a fuck at this moment. It seems important.

"Thank you."

She nods and she's gone, and Beck outlived Matt.

It's important.

But I can't get cocky.

two

BECK

WHERE THE HELL AM I?

A heavy weight presses on my eyes and I can't open them.

What the fuck is that about?

My arms and legs are like concrete, too heavy to move, and my body is frozen in place. I'm in a state of complete stillness, and for a minute I'm pissed about that.

But then I realize something.

The itching . . . the horrible bugs-crawling-all-over-me feeling from earlier is gone. I don't feel anything now, actually. Just a slight warm sensation.

I feel calmer now, and I wait, listening.

There's a lot of movement, and then some prodding. Someone is poking me in the ribs, in the belly, but it doesn't hurt.

That's fucked up.

Maybe *I'm* just really fucked up.

Maybe this isn't real.

My thoughts aren't coming as they should. Instead, they feel broken, choppy. Like the water in Lake Michigan on a stormy day.

Lake Michigan.

I live in Chicago. That's a start. That's something.

My name is Beck Kingsley, and I live in Chicago.

"He's still tachycardic," a woman says next to my ear, and cold metal is pressed to my chest. "His arrhythmia is out of control. Someone get me droperidol. The lorazepam isn't touching him. Oh, son of a bitch. He's gonna seize."

I feel my chest rise off the table, breaking rank from the rest of my body, and I feel myself thrashing against my will, yet it doesn't hurt. My arms are restrained; there's something around my wrists. I don't know why I'm able to think calmly when my body is out of control.

My head slams against the table over and over, and then someone is holding it. I feel steady hands on each side by my ears. Their fingers are cool, my skin is hot, and yet my head doesn't hurt.

"His temp is one-oh-five," a man says. "We've got to bring it down."

"He's got blood coming from his nose," someone else says. "Shit, we've got cerebral edema."

Their voices blend together now in a frenzy of noise. My fingers are matchsticks and they are striking against flint, and I'm in flames and everything around me is cold, too cold. My teeth chatter together, slamming like ivory doors.

If this is real, I'm in the hospital. But with me, especially lately, I don't know what's real and what's not.

I don't know how I ended up here.

I can't think of anything. My mind is a fuzzy mess, and it's incapable of focusing. I try harder, trying to grab anything from it.

Anything.

So I do what anyone would do.

I focus on home. I mentally grab a piece of a memory and drag it to me. Anything is better than being here in this moment, even if the memory is from long ago.

———

"LET'S GO!" MY MOM called from the bottom of the stairs. I tumbled out of my room and found my mother with her hand on her pregnant belly, waddling toward the front door. She looked so top-heavy, like she'd topple over any second. She held my little brother's hand as he toddled with her. "Matt!" she called over her shoulder.

My father emerged from the kitchen with sports drinks in the crook of one elbow and a bat bag slung over his shoulder.

"You ready, kid?" he asked me, tapping the bill of my baseball cap. I nodded.

"Yeah, Dad." Dad knew I didn't like baseball nearly as much as football, but he was the coach for our Little League team, so I played and I did the best I could.

The ride to the diamond didn't take long, but my mom groaned every time we went over a bump, her hand on her giant belly.

Dad smiled at her. "You okay, there, USS *Natalie*?"

She scowled at him. "I assume you're saying I'm big as a ship?"

He opened his car door. "I would never."

Other parents were already there, but that was nothing new. My dad was always running late. We jogged to the field and warmed up with everyone else, and before I knew it, we were playing.

I sat in the dugout with my best friend, Tray, as we waited our turns to bat. I glanced out at the stands, and my mom was perched in the bleachers, my brother, Devin, nestled into her side. She looked like she'd swallowed a watermelon. I still wasn't sure what I thought about having a new sister. What the heck was I supposed to do with a sister?

My dad was standing behind home base, whispering words of encouragement to the batters, and when he caught my eye, he winked.

Pride swelled up in me. My dad was the head coach because my dad was awesome. Everyone knew it. I worried about letting him down, though. My dad was perfect. He never messed up. Not ever.

I wiggled on the bench, adjusting my cap and then tying my shoe. When I sat back up, Mom and Devin were next to the cage.

"Your brother wanted to give you something, sweetie," Mom said, smiling. I looked down at Devin, and he was holding out a grubby hand, one of his green marbles in his palm.

I scowled. "What am I gonna do with that?"

Devin's face fell, and my mom frowned.

"He wants you to have it for a good-luck charm. We know you can do this, sweetie."

"A marble is gonna make me have a good game?"

Mom's smile was forced. "Honey, he's trying to be nice. He loves these marbles. We want you to know that even though you don't love this sport, you can do anything you put your mind to."

I sighed and held out my hand. Devin gave me the glass marble happily.

"Thank you," I told him dutifully. I promptly handed it to Mom. "Can you keep it right now? I don't have pockets."

She nodded, and my dad called my name.

"Kingsley, you're up!"

I sprinted out and got into the stance, my butt wagging and my feet spread, just like I'd been taught. My dad leaned in.

"Aim for center field," he whispered to me. "Their shortstop isn't good, and their center fielder is even worse. You've got this, kid. Swing high!"

I nodded, focused on the ball.

The stadium lights were on already, though, and I was disoriented for a minute. Why were they on in the middle of the day? I stood staring into them, and I felt a weird sense of peace overwhelm me.

"Clear!" someone yelled from the stands, and what did he mean? Clear away from what? Shouldn't he have said *strike*? I missed the pitch because I wasn't paying attention.

"Again!" that person shouted. My chest lurched, and I must have been nervous. I wanted to stare at the lights more for some reason, but my dad was whispering to me.

"Focus, Beck. It's not time for that. Swing high!"

The pitcher aimed, threw, and this time, my bat connected with a loud, metallic thunk and the ball swept into a mighty arc, up and over the field.

"Run!" my dad called, and I threw the bat and ran with all of my might. I cleared first base, second, then third. My dad was screaming, motioning for me to come home, so I did.

I ran for everything I was worth.

I felt the other team closing in on me, I felt them throwing the ball to get me out, and I skidded. My hip hit the dirt, and I sprawled across the base.

"Safe!" the umpire called. "We've got a pulse again. Good job, everyone."

I shook my head because that wasn't right. I was pretty sure that wasn't what he was supposed to say, but I was safe, so that was all that mattered.

I stood up and walked into the dugout so that my friends could slap my back.

It was my first infield home run.

My dad beamed at me. I'd made him proud.

Maybe that old marble was good luck, after all.

three

NATALIE
MERCY HOSPITAL
2:51 A.M.

"M RS. KINGSLEY?"

I'm in the middle of my 330th lap around the room. My hands shake uncontrollably and I pause, scared to turn.

But I do.

The doctor stands there, tired and pale and sallow, a surgical cap on his head.

"Your son is alive," he says simply, and my ears roar in disbelief and shock. I realize suddenly that I wasn't expecting to hear this news. I was expecting the worst because that's what happened a year ago. The worst. The doctor had said *Matt's injuries were insurmountable; we did everything we could.*

But this is a different doctor, and this different doctor says different things.

"He's alive?" I'm afraid I heard wrong. I search his face. There's something there, something else, something yet to know. I tremble all over, from my fingers to my toes and everything in between. Behind the doctor I see Kit looming in the doorway, listening.

The doctor's eyes are tired but kind, and he nods.

"He is. We were able to bring him back. But I'm going to be frank. He's in bad shape. He's in extremely critical condition. His brain is swollen and we've had to put him in a medically induced coma to relieve it. He suffered a stroke from the overdose, which we believe was from a combination of heroin and methamphetamines."

"No," I say slowly. "That's impossible. Beck doesn't use meth."

I argue even though I don't know that for sure. I've been clinging to the boy he once was. I don't know anything anymore; I haven't seen him in two months.

"We believe he was, at least tonight," the doctor says gently. "He's touch and go right now, Mrs. Kingsley. His heart stopped for around sixty seconds. Be strong for him. He needs it right now. These first twenty-four hours are the most critical. If he makes it through, we'll have reason to be hopeful. I'd like to bring him out of the coma in twenty-four hours."

"*If* he makes it through," I repeat in a whisper, and I'm frozen. His heart already stopped for an entire minute. This was what I was expecting, because this is what happened to Matt; *he died*, and doesn't history repeat itself?

"You said he suffered a stroke," Kit interjects in his calm way. "How bad was it?"

"We can't know yet," the doctor answers. "Not until it's safe to bring him out of the coma. For now, we have to treat the brain bleed and the swelling. They are paramount."

I nod and I'm limp.

"Can I see him?"

The doctor pauses. "He's in ICU, and he won't know you're there. I suggest you go home and get some rest, change clothes. Tomorrow will be a long day."

I remember now that I'm in my bathrobe, but it doesn't matter.

"You say he might not survive the night," I manage to say. "So I'm not leaving."

"I thought you'd say that," the doctor answers, and in his eyes I see a thousand other situations like mine. He has seen them all, an endless combination of other boys and other mothers. "Come with me."

At the door I pause with Kit. "Can you call Sam?" I ask him. "Let her know?"

"Yeah," he says. "And I'll go get you some clothes."

"You don't have to," I answer, but I'm already walking away.

I follow the doctor through the halls, and we stop outside of a room with glass walls. The curtains inside are drawn, and on the door KINGSLEY is written on a dry-erase board.

My son is in there.

I push past the doctor, and I'm stunned as I stare at the boy in the bed.

He seems so small and pale, not my six-foot-four tanned boy, the strong boy who led his football team to a district championship just last year. This boy is frail. This boy is skin and bones.

I gasp, and the doctor's hand is on my shoulder.

"There's a chair over there," he tells me. "You should rest."

I slide into the pink vinyl chair and find Beck's hand amid the tubes. His arm is so thin. He's lost so much weight in just two months. He's skeletal. It's unfathomable. I clasp his hand inside of my own, and even though his is technically bigger, it's so bony it feels like it will break.

My head slumps to the bed rail and the plastic is cool against my forehead.

"Please, Beck," I say aloud, staring at the floor because I can't stare at him. It's too terrifying. "Please. Come back to me. Fight through this. Everything will be better if you just wake up."

I know he can't right now, that it's not his choice. But I want him to know that when it's time, *it's time*. That *not* waking up isn't an option.

Picking my head up I stare into his face, steeling myself.

Someone has cleaned him up. The vomit is gone from his face; the bloody scrapes are bandaged. There are dark bags beneath his eyes, eyes that I know are a mossy green just like his father's. His cheeks are sunken and I know he hasn't eaten. There's no way he's eaten.

Guilt snakes around my heart, slithering in, and it steals my breath. I should've done something more. There had to be something else to do. I should've found it.

"Beck, baby, I love you," I tell him. "Nothing else matters. You're okay. I'm okay. And after all of this, we're going to go home and fix everything, you hear me?"

I squeeze his hand, but he doesn't squeeze back, because he doesn't hear me. Because he can't. But that doesn't stop me. I have to speak. If I don't . . . I'm afraid of what will happen.

So I talk.

Behind me, I hear the hospital moving on with life, saving people, clattering and clamoring. But in here, it's just me and my boy in the dark silence.

"Remember Boy Scout camp when you were eight?" I ask him. "You were so homesick. Daddy didn't want me to come get you, he said it was character building, but I came anyway. I picked you up in the middle of the night. And then Daddy took you back the next morning. He knew best, I suppose. You ended up having an amazing time, and you made me that green dream catcher out of Popsicle sticks. I still use it, you know."

It hangs from the headboard of my bed. It doesn't keep the nightmares away, but I'll never tell him that.

"If Daddy were here now, he'd know the exact right thing to say," I tell him, and that lump is back in my throat. It's exactly the thing I'd told him the night of the accident. When he was yet again lying in a hospital bed, and Matt, my beautiful Matt, was on his way down to the morgue.

"I told you that night that Daddy was okay," I remember aloud. "You were unconscious, and I lied to you. I didn't think it would matter, but I feel guilty about that. I just wanted you to wake up without being afraid. But that was wrong. Honesty is best, Beck. Always. And the truth is, I'm scared right now. I'm scared you won't wake up, and God, baby, I can't lose you too."

I drop my head and sob, and my ribs rasp and wrack, and I keep his hand inside my own. My tears splash onto our skin in fat drops and it doesn't matter, because Beck isn't awake.

The similarities between that night and this one are too much to think about. My baby is once again in a hospital bed, only this time . . .

I refuse to think of it. I change the subject instead.

"Your lips are so dry," I tell him, and I reach for my purse, only putting his hand down for a second. I dig through the loose change, gum wrappers, and Kleenex. I also see one of Annabelle's Barbie shoes. I find my tube of ChapStick.

I examine his face as I apply the balm to his chapped lips, and he's still impassive. His hand is exactly how it was, his thumb bent. His hair slants across his forehead, and I push it back. The skin on his forehead is soft and smooth in his sleep. It's as though he has no idea of the terrible danger he's in.

He probably doesn't.

He's in a coma.

My kid is in a coma.

I exhale again. I reach over, putting my thumb in the cleft of his chin. My eyes well up when it still fits perfectly. It's sharper now, though, my thumb wedged between the edges.

I think about the last day I saw him, two long months ago. The anger and the yelling, and how I'd watched him drive away and I couldn't do anything about it.

I was helpless then, and I'm helpless now.

"Take me instead," I pray to God. "Take me instead."

It would almost be a relief.

I close my eyes and the machine beside me beeps, loudly and rhythmically, with the sound of my son's ventilator. With it, he breathes.

At the moment, it's all that matters.

After everything that's happened, I have to focus on the hope that he will keep breathing, so that the gravity of my present doesn't drown me like my past.

I WAS SOUND ASLEEP when the phone rang, jolting me awake.

Nothing good ever came in the middle of the night, and I struggled to find my phone on the nightstand. Matt and Beck still hadn't gotten back from their campus visit to Notre Dame. The clock numbers glowed red in the dark: 1:21 a.m.

"Hello," I said thickly after I pulled the phone to my ear.

"Mom!"

Beck's voice was so desperate, so terrified. "We need help!"

"Beck! Honey, what's wrong?" I was instantly awake now.

"Mom, he's not breathing."

"Who? Beckitt, what's happening?" My heart pounded and I sat straight up.

"Oh my God, Mom. He's bleeding so much. What do I do?"

He was screaming, and I was trying to comprehend, to make sense out of his words.

"Your dad?" My words were a rush. "Who, Beck? Where are you?"

There was a muffled noise from the background and I was saying his name. He didn't even hear me.

"I think he's dead," he said instead, and he was moaning. "Oh my God, oh my God. What do I do?" More muffled noises, a cracking. "Dad, open your eyes. You're okay, you're okay. Talk to me. Open your eyes. Jesus, Mom. What do I do?"

"Is your father breathing?" I managed to ask, and my chest was very, very tight, adrenaline spiking everywhere.

"No. Oh my God."

"Stay calm, Beck," I instructed, fighting my own panic as I tried to remember what to do. "Feel for the bottom of his sternum with your fingers. Keep your elbows locked and press on that spot. Measure two fingers in, interlock your hands, and start beating his heart for him with the heel of your hand. Beck, are you hearing me?"

"Yes. I might have to put the phone down."

"Put it on speaker. Have you called an ambulance?"

"I don't know where we are. On the highway somewhere."

"Did the car's emergency system talk to you?"

"Yes. It said help was on the way."

"Okay, good. Is your dad talking?"

"No. Mom, he's dead. Jesus, he's dead. His bones are . . . I can hear his bones."

"Don't stop CPR," I cried out to him, and fear pulsed through every beat of my heart. Please, God, please don't let this be real. "Don't stop, Beck."

"I'm not," he assured me, and his voice was broken.

"Are you okay? What happened?" I was trying to make sense of it all with my sleep-addled brain.

"I'm not okay. But I'm better than Dad. Jesus, I'm sorry, Mom. This isn't working. It isn't working."

"Don't stop," I instructed him with a shaky breath.

"Dad, I love you. Please breathe. Please breathe. Dad, please," Beck begged, and his voice cracked and I was helpless. They were there, and I was here, and there was nothing I could do.

"Tell him I love him," I practically shouted as I heard a siren in the distance. "Help is coming, Beck. Hang on."

"It's too late, Mom," my son said wearily. "It's too late."

"Don't say that," I snapped. "It's never too late, Beck. He'll be okay. He'll be okay."

But he wasn't.

When I arrived at the hospital an hour later, I found out he wasn't. I screamed, collapsed, and threw up.

Then I sat beside the love of my life and said goodbye, stroking his hair out of his broken face, my hands bloody from his skin.

"I love you," I whispered. "I love you. Don't leave me."

But he did.

four

BECK
MERCY HOSPITAL
3:12 A.M.

I MUST'VE DRIFTED AWAY FOR A MINUTE, BECAUSE ALL OF A sudden I'm awake but I don't know where I am. I have to listen again, and there are voices.

My mom is here. I hear her talking, but it's like it's through a tube and my ears are stopped up. I can't understand what she's saying; all I know is that I'm not ten years old anymore. I don't know how I know it—I just do. I also know that I've done something terrible, something reprehensible, and I wonder if I'm better off not remembering.

I listen to the muted noise for a while, just soaking it in. I can't see my mother, but I know she's here. That's enough.

I try to move, to say something to her, to apologize for being here, but I can't. I'm still frozen, still too heavy. I'm concrete, I'm rocks. Why won't my brain work right? My thoughts are like mud, slow to move and thick like sludge.

There is a ringing, accompanied by a buzz. Slowly, I realize it is my mother's cell phone. Her voice is low and hushed as she greets someone, and I focus hard, hard, harder, and something clicks into place, like the gears of a clock, and I finally understand the words.

"How are the kids?" she asks.

"They're fine," a female voice answers, and the room is so quiet that I can hear through the phone. "Don't worry. How is Beck?"

The voice . . . I know it but I can't place it. Like everything else in my head right now, it's a puzzle and the pieces don't fit.

"Sam . . . he's . . ." Mom touches my hand. I try to squeeze her fingers, but my hand won't move. It's like my appendages are broken, only I don't feel any pain.

Sam. Sam. My aunt. I picture her face. She looks like my mom, only younger.

"Nat, tell me," Sam says, and she's scared. I hear it in her voice.

"He suffered a stroke," Mom answers. Is she talking about me? That's impossible. Strokes are for old people. That's when they can't talk anymore, and their mouths droop on one side of their face. That's not what's wrong with me. Is it?

Internally, I wrench around, trying to thrash, trying to fight, but my body is a prison and I can't break free.

Help! I think, as loud as I can. *God, Mom, help me!*

But no words come, and she doesn't know I can hear her. "The doctors don't know how extensive," my mom says, her words laced with so much pain. I did that. I can taste the guilt in my mouth.

"He's strong," Sam tells her, and I love her for saying that. I *am* strong. Or I was. Whatever is wrong with me, I'll fight it. I wish I could tell my mother that.

A chair scoots across the floor and the legs grate on the tile.

"I need you to remember something," Sam says, and I strain to hear. She's talking so low and everything sort of sounds like I'm underwater. "This is not your fault. You did everything you could to help him, Natalie. You tried, you fought. But in the end, it was his decision to make. He had to get help. You couldn't make him. No one could."

"You don't understand," my mom almost whimpers. "When I see Beck in my head, I don't see the person he is now. I don't even see the person he was a year ago. I see the boy he used to be, the one with the sticky chin and red Kool-Aid mustache. It's not his fault either, Sam. He was forced to deal with a situation that even adults can't deal with sometimes. He's a good boy. This is all . . . this is all just wrong. I should've tried harder. I fell apart, and you know it."

She's crying now, and a pang nails me in the gut. I've hurt her. She's the only one who loves me no matter what, and I hurt her.

"Natalie." Aunt Sam is calm. "You love your son. You've always loved him. What you need to do now is focus on your inner strength. The thing that got you through the entire past year, the thing that keeps you going every day. You're strong too. You've got to use that strength now."

"What if he dies?" my mom asks, her voice paper-thin, and I want to scream at her. *No, I won't die. I won't. I won't do that to you.*

But I can't promise that. My head feels funny, like rock or wood. It's foreign to me, like something that isn't mine. Is this what it's like to die? *Am I dying?*

"Don't think that," Sam answers, and she's so confident that even I almost believe her. "They're doing everything they can medically do. He has to do the rest, and I think he will. He has fire in him, Natalie."

"That's the problem," Mom answers. "That fire. It was anger that ate him up. It's anger that made him run, and anger that put him here now. It might destroy him, Sam. We tried to contain it. We tried—you know we tried."

She's crying again, and Sam is murmuring in soothing tones, in words I don't understand and can't really hear.

But what she said . . . I focus on that.

I have fire in me. Anger.

That's definitely true.

It burned and burned, and maybe Mom is right. Maybe it's just gonna burn me up.

But what am I so angry about? Why did I run?

I'm muddled again. But then pieces come flooding back, and I grab more of them so I can make them fit, so that something, anything, makes sense. Life isn't what it once was. I do know that.

————

I STAYED IN THE weight room for hours after school. Our coach was relentless about staying in shape during the off-season. When I finally collapsed into my car, drenched in sweat, I almost didn't have the energy to drive home. I was starving and thirsty but didn't even have enough in me to stop at a drive-thru. All I wanted was my bed.

When I trudged up the driveway to my door, my bag slung over my shoulder, I noticed mom's car parked in front of the garage. Good, she was home. Hopefully she'd cooked something.

When I opened the door, though, I wasn't met with the smells of dinner.

I didn't know why I was surprised. She hadn't cooked in a while. I guessed I was just hoping.

The house was quiet too. Too quiet.

"Devin?" I called for my little brother as I dropped my bag on the floor inside the door. "Anna-B?"

No answer.

I poked my head into the dining room where I found Devin at the table, his schoolbooks in front of him. He looked up, his glasses off-kilter. He shoved them up his nose to straighten them.

"Hey, Beck," he said, greeting me.

"Where's Mom?" I asked. He looked away.

"In bed."

Again. Son of a bitch.

"Have you eaten?" I asked, and my muscles were so tried they were shaking.

Dev shook his head.

Damn it.

"Okay. Where's Anna?"

"She was in her room playing with her Barbies last time I checked."

"I'll find something in the kitchen to eat. Can you go get her?"

I was resentful as I yanked open the fridge and looked inside. There was nothing in there but orange juice, and I was pretty sure it was expired.

My mother should be doing this. I got it—she was sad. We were all sad. My dad had been dead for six months, though, and Jesus Christ. I was *there* when he died, and you didn't see me lying in bed every chance I got.

But that's what she did. Every damn day.

She did the bare minimum around the house and stayed in her darkened bedroom as often as she could. It was getting fucking old.

I grabbed two frozen pizzas from the freezer and punched buttons on the oven.

Annabelle burst into the kitchen and grabbed me around the waist. "Beck!" she sighed into my sweaty shorts.

Her hair was tangled, and I wondered if she'd gone to school like that.

"You hungry?" I asked. She nodded, releasing me.

"I'm soooo hungry, Becky."

"I'm making pizza."

She grinned happily, because she'd eat pizza for every meal if we let her.

"Go wash up," I added. She trotted away to the nearest bathroom, and the phone rang.

I grabbed it.

"Hello?"

"Beckitt," my aunt Sam said. "Why haven't you been answering your cell phone?"

"I was at football," I told her, sliding the pizzas into the oven and holding the phone under my chin. "Why? Is something wrong?"

Pause.

"No," she answered after a moment. "I just couldn't get ahold of your mom, so I thought I'd try your number."

"She's in bed." I tossed the empty boxes in the trash and ran a sponge under the water so I could wash off the table. "Again."

Another pause.

"Do you want me to come over?"

"No, I've got it. I'm making frozen pizza for dinner. That's all we have."

I tried hard to keep the resentment out of my voice, but she heard it.

"I'll go grocery shopping tomorrow," she promised. "I'll get all kinds of stuff. Don't worry."

"Are you going to make her cook it?" I asked next, and I regretted it as soon as the words left my mouth.

"She can't help it," Aunt Sammy reminded me. "She's depressed, Beck. She's trying."

But she wasn't. That was the problem.

"I've gotta go," I told her. "I've got to make sure Dev and Anna get their homework done, and then I've got to make sure they're bathed before they go to bed. You know, because Mom is *sad*."

A third long pause.

"It's going to be all right, Beck," my aunt told me, although she didn't sound so sure.

"Okay."

We hung up, and the kids and I ate. I listened to them talk about their days, even though the only thing I wanted to do was take a shower and wash off my grime.

"Go take baths," I told them once they'd each eaten three pieces of pizza. They bounced up the stairs, and I put the dishes into the dishwasher.

This isn't my job, I thought to myself. And it pissed me off.

When I went up to check on the kids before I took my own shower, I poked my head into my mother's room.

She was curled on top of the covers, fully dressed and fast asleep. She had bags under her eyes. I could see them from here. She looked vulnerable, and against my will, my anger at her slipped away.

She was in this situation because of me in the first place.

I tiptoed in and grabbed a blanket from the foot of the bed, pulling it over her. She didn't stir. As I turned to leave, I noticed a pill bottle on her nightstand.

I picked it up to read the label.

Natalie Kingsley, Xanax.

Stunned, I stared at the words. She was taking Xanax? I had no idea.

I unscrewed the top and put a few in my pocket. If it helped her, it might help me too. I was miserable too; the difference was I hid it better. I slipped back out so I could check on the kids.

I had to get up at four a.m. to go to the gym if I had any hope of getting that scholarship from Notre Dame, if I even still wanted it. After everything, I didn't know anymore. Plus, if I went away to college, how would my mom stay afloat here? I didn't know. I didn't know much of anything anymore.

five

NATALIE
MERCY HOSPITAL
3:42 A.M.

MY HANDS ARE SHAKING.
The doctor checking on Beck notices the same time I do as I reach over to touch Beck's face. My fingers convulse and my nail grazes his cheek. I snatch my hand back, gripping it with my other one.

"Take a deep breath, Natalie," he instructs in an efficient, yet sympathetic voice. My eyelashes flutter closed, and I do. I inhale deeply, then push all of my breath out of my lungs, like I'm breathing through a straw. When I've done that a few times, I look at my hand again.

It's still shaking, and with a sigh, I reach for my purse, fishing out the Xanax bottle. I'd never taken anything in my life until Matt died. But then everything changed. God. My head falls back against my chair, the lousy pink vinyl chair, and I stretch my legs out in front of me. They're falling asleep and I shake the pins and needles from them.

One pill won't do it. Two would do it under normal circumstances, but tonight . . . no way.

Three it is.

The doctor raises one eyebrow in a silent question, peering over the edge of his clipboard.

"Don't judge me," I tell him. "My son could die. I'm entitled to whatever I need to get through this night." I don't have to mention just how much Xanax I've taken this past year.

He shakes his head, puts the chart down, and checks Beck's pupils, lifting up one eyelid, then the other.

"I wasn't judging," he answers, and his voice is calm. "I just wanted to make sure you have everything you need. This is a difficult time, I know. Are you having trouble breathing?"

I assess myself, taking a big breath in.

"Not right now. My chest feels tight, though. Heavy."

He nods. "I want you to sit up straight, and don't worry so much about breathing deeply in, but focus on blowing out. Pretend your lungs are deflating balloons."

I do that, following his instructions. I close my eyes and envision my lungs being two bright red balloons. In my head, I watch them empty until they are limp, their rubbery sides clinging to each other.

"Good," he tells me. "The more deeply you can breathe, the less constricted your chest will feel. Often when a person is anxious, they forget to breathe."

"Thank you," I say simply. He finishes his examination of Beck.

"Is there any change?" I ask him.

"Not yet. But he's not worse. So that's good news right now."

"I'll take what I can get."

He nods, and pauses at the door.

"If you need anything, page me. My number is on the table." He gestures, and I see the paper—I didn't even notice him writing it down. I must be seriously out of it.

"Thank you."

He's gone and I'm alone with Beck again.

My son's face is tranquil from the drug-induced coma, and to look at him you'd never know that he's fighting for his life. The machines beep and breathe and monitor, and Beck just lies there, so calm, so peaceful.

For a minute, I wonder if this is what he would prefer. To slip away from all of this ugly pain, to go in his sleep and to never have to worry again.

I shake my head hard. No. I lean forward and hold his hand.

"What you don't realize is that you can get past this," I tell him. "All of this pain . . . it's temporary. You just have to make it through this part, and then it's smooth sailing for the rest of your life. You'll get past the grieving, and one of these days, you'll think about your dad and you'll smile, not cry. I swear."

At least, that's what they tell me.

The clock on the wall ticks the seconds relentlessly.

The first twenty-four hours, the doctor had said. It's so short a time to determine someone's life.

What if he doesn't have enough time to fight?

I grip Beck's hand, and it's icy cold. I rub it, trying to get some life into it, but his fingers stay curled and limp.

"Can you squeeze my hand, baby?" I ask, and I'm practically pleading. "If you hear me, squeeze my hand. Even just a little."

I wait, and his hand is lifeless in mine.

My soul folds in on itself, the fear too heavy to carry.

I try to think of the last time I'd held his hand when he was healthy, and it takes me a minute. At his age, he didn't let me do it often.

———

THERE HAS NEVER BEEN anywhere more peaceful than here.

I sat on my husband's grave, my back against his headstone, and stared around me. The trees were always rustling here, as though an unseen hand were moving them. It was quiet, it was serene, and here, in this place, I could just be.

I didn't have to pretend that I was okay, because I wasn't. A part of me was missing, and it was never coming back.

I let my head rest against the stone and I stared at the sky. The evening clouds swirled and I wondered where Matt was.

Idly, I pulled at the newly growing grass around me. Surprisingly, grass takes a while to grow on new graves. It had been months now, and it was just starting to sprout through the mound of dirt. I hated that, though. It was just an emphasis on how much time was passing, how long it had been since I'd seen my husband.

I was just glad I had the flexibility to come here when I wanted. As a Realtor, I could make my own schedule. This morning, I'd gotten up, updated my listings, and since I didn't have any showings today, I had the rest of the day free.

Like always when that happened, I came here.

"I gotta say," I told Matt aloud. "I don't think this is prime real estate. I'm sure the noise level is fine, but I bet the nightlife sucks."

God, I missed making jokes for someone who could laugh at them.

I closed my eyes, and allowed myself to think about the fact that Matt was literally a few feet below me, down where the ground was cool and dark. Unbidden, though, I started wondering what he looked like now, today. Was his skin turning gray? Had the smooth texture begun to get eaten away by decomposition? Was my husband rotting? My stomach lurched at the thought, and my eyes popped open.

That's when I saw someone walking toward me, over the graves.

My son, tall and lanky.

Behind him, his black car sat parked, with Devin and Annabelle in the back seat. Confused, I reached for my phone to check the time, only to realize that I'd left it in my car.

"Mom!" Beck called. In a few more strides, he reached me.

"You shouldn't walk on the graves," I told him. "It's disrespectful." He was quiet.

"Do you know what time it is?" he asked me quietly, and he knelt down next to me. The sun was starting to dip lower into the sky, almost at the horizon, and I swallowed hard.

"It's later than I thought," I answered. "I'm sorry. Time got away from me."

He sighed, and he smelled. He was in sweaty workout clothes.

"You weren't home when the bus got there," he said now. "Annabelle was scared, Mom. She thought something happened to you."

"I'm sorry," I whispered, and he grasped my hand, holding it. His fingers were getting so long, like a man's. When did that happen?

"I understand," he said, and he was so sympathetic. "I do. But can you . . . maybe . . . make sure you come home by the time the bus does? Maybe come here in the mornings instead?"

I didn't tell him that I'd been here since this morning.

I nodded instead. "Of course I will."

"You're okay," he insisted, and I wasn't sure if he was trying to convince me, or himself.

"Have you eaten?" I asked, and the guilt was creeping up.

"Not yet. There wasn't anything at home."

"Okay." I squared my shoulders and got to my feet, releasing his hand. "Let's go somewhere."

"Annabelle wants waffles," he said as we made our way back to the cars. He was careful this time not to step on the graves.

Dev and Annabelle waved at me happily from Beck's back seat. They loved riding with him. It was a rare treat—he seldom let them. Beck waited until I got into my car, then he followed me to the restaurant.

When we arrived, Annabelle bounded out into my arms. Her pigtails were uneven because she'd been practicing them herself. One was ear level, and the other at the nape of her neck. At eight, she was still bouncy and happy, loving and unconcerned by who knew it. Devin, my solemn twelve-year-old, followed at a cooler pace.

"Hi, Mom," he said, greeting me. He was wary because he knew that something wasn't right with me. The hostess showed us to a table and gave Annabelle crayons.

"Mommy, why didn't you answer your phone?" Annabelle asked curiously while she drew a picture of a bunny. "We tried and tried to call."

Beck's eyes met my own. He hadn't mentioned that part. Son of a bitch. What kind of mother was I?

"I'm sorry, sweetie," I answered, guiding her hand to help her with the ears. As I did, I remembered when Matt taught Annabelle how to tie her shoes. *Bunny ears, bunny ears, playing by a tree. Crisscrossed the tree, trying to catch me. Bunny ears, bunny ears, jumped into the hole, popped out the other side, beautiful and bold.* I swallowed. "I left my phone in the car on accident."

"Ohhhhh," she answered in her singsong voice. "How was Daddy today?"

My chest constricted. "He's fine, baby."

Devin looked away. He never liked it when we talked about "visiting" Matt. He thought it was delusional, and maybe it was.

Beck sat across from me, the scruff on his jaw a testament to how old he was getting. It made me uncomfortable that time was passing so quickly when Matt wasn't here to see it. Thank God, though, he was still here when Beck needed to learn how to shave. I wouldn't have had the first clue. Quickly I glanced at Devin. He didn't have peach fuzz yet, but he would soon. I'd get Beck to show him.

We ordered and our meal came shortly after.

For just a little while, we felt almost normal. We ate, I listened about their days, and if anyone had looked at us without knowing us, they'd have thought we were a regular family. They wouldn't know that I felt like wood inside, that my smile was fake, that my emotions were frozen.

They wouldn't know any of that.

Even when we got home a while later and I walked in through the front door, I marveled at how normal our home seemed. A cozy Cape Cod, with an updated kitchen and built-in shelves, and stacks of books and nice rugs.

Anyone would think a normal family lived here. People who were untouched by tragedy, people who didn't have a care in the world.

It just went to show that perception isn't anything but a lie.

I managed to help Annabelle with her bath and put her to bed for the first time in a week or so. She was delighted when I read her a story, and closed her door behind me.

I poked my head into Devin's room to say good night, and he was studying at his desk.

"Good night, honey," I told him. "Don't stay up too late."

He nodded, and I continued to Beck's room. I knocked, but there was no answer. I eased his door open to find that he was already sound asleep.

He was hanging over the side of the bed, his dark blond hair unruly. He slept like he did everything else, all sprawled out. One of his long legs was kicked up against the wall, his toes enclosed in a sock. His other foot was bare. His hands were long and manly, and sometimes I had to do a double take. He wasn't a little boy anymore. It continually surprised me.

I pulled a blanket up over him, and as I did, his phone buzzed. Glancing down, I saw a text from his girlfriend.

What do you mean everything?

Curious, I scrolled upward just a little.

Beck had texted, *I'm sorry.*

She had answered, *For what?*

He had replied, *For everything.*

With a small grimace, I put it back down. I was too exhausted for teenage drama. Quietly, I made my way out of his room and down the hall to my own.

For now, our home—and my bedroom in particular—was a mausoleum. My husband's clothing still hung in the closet, his dirty clothing still sat in the hamper, his razor lay next to his sink. I couldn't move it. I literally couldn't.

My heart constricted like it always did when I thought of him, and I swallowed hard. A lump had been in my throat for months, and maybe, just maybe, one of these days I'd be able to swallow it.

But today wasn't that day.

My phone rang on the desk beside me, vibrating against the wood, and I jumped. It seemed so loud in the stillness. My sister's picture was flashing on the screen, like it had every night since the accident.

"Hey, sis," she said. "What was going on earlier?"

"What do you mean?" I played innocent as I pulled off my shirt and stepped out of my yoga pants.

"The kids couldn't find you," she answered, and there was a little judgment there, barely masked.

"I forgot my phone," I replied. "It's okay. Beck found me and we went to IHOP. What's up in La-La Land?"

Sam had married into an Italian family, last name LaRosa. It was so much more colorful than my own.

She talked just a little bit about her day and then announced, "You sound tired. You should get some sleep."

"I couldn't agree with you more," I answered. We hung up, and my room was quiet once again.

The bed was too big; the room was too dark.

I reached out a hand to feel Matt's empty side of the bed, where his body should be, where his head should be indenting the pillow.

Don't do it today, I encouraged myself. *Be strong. Take a step forward. Don't do it.*

For a while I didn't.

But then . . . when the silence and quiet and solitude became too much, I caved.

I dialed my husband's number just to hear his voice. I hadn't been able to bring myself to cancel his service yet. If his phone was still on, then it was almost like he was coming back someday.

"Hey, this is Matt. I can't get to my phone right now, but leave a message and I'll get back to you."

I paused, reveling in the husky, deep voice that I loved so much.

"I miss you," I whispered before I hung up. I was exhausted now, physically and mentally. My bed called to me, and I went straight to it, dropping onto the softness eagerly, into the bed I'd shared with my husband for so many years. I covered myself with a blanket, blocking out the real world.

I missed Matt so much that I didn't think I could stand it. I didn't know if I could continue to move through each day. But I had to.

I had three kids who needed me.

I sighed and closed my eyes, immediately regretting the split-second thought that sometimes I wished I didn't have anyone else relying on me.

six

BECK
MERCY HOSPITAL
3:59 A.M.

"BECK, JUST MOVE YOUR FINGERS," MY MOM WHISPERS, AND her voice is right in my ear. I can smell her perfume.

I try to move. I really do.

I focus on my index finger, my pinkie, and my thumb.

None of them will even twitch.

They don't even feel like a part of my body anymore. They aren't attached.

I'm a shell.

Everything I was before seems to be gone.

I'm fading away.

I feel it. My energy, my thoughts, everything is dimming dimming dimming. I'm going to fade away into nothing. And all of a sudden, I'm not sure that's so bad.

What did this life ever do for me? I mean, really?

"Where were you, baby?" my mom whispers, and I think I've broken her. Her voice has something in it I've never heard before . . . absolute fear. She's afraid for me. She knows she can't protect me.

I can hear all of that in her voice.

I can't open my eyes, so I have to listen.

They were right—all of those people who said that when you lose one sense, your others get heightened. I'm hearing everything now. I hear the bustle in the hall outside of the room, and I hear the low hum of machines. I hear my mother's raspy breaths; I hear her when she quietly cries. I hear my mother's pain, and I know I did that to her.

I shouldn't be here.

But I don't know where I *should* be.

I lost any sense I had of myself two months ago when I left home.

I'm a stranger now. I don't know who I am.

———

"WHERE'S MOMMY?" ANNABELLE ASKED me, her lips caked in thick layers of lipstick. Mom was gonna flip out when she saw that my sister had raided her makeup. I was supposed to be watching, but I had my own homework to do, and how could I watch them every single second?

"She had an open house." Which I was happy about. It meant she had to get dressed and leave the house for once.

"But why are you watching me?" she asked as she stripped off her pink striped T-shirt.

"I told you. Mom's got an open house."

Annabelle wrinkled her nose. "I hate her job."

"She's just doing what she has to do," I told my sister as she climbed into the tub. "I'm sure she doesn't like it much either. She'd rather be here with you."

Or in bed.

"Want to play unicorn with me?" Anna asked hopefully, already thinking about something else. I rolled my eyes and said no, but then dipped my hand into the bubbles, putting them into a horn-shaped mound on my forehead.

"Look at me," I demanded. "I'm Sprinkles, and I grant wishes and piss dreams."

Annabelle giggled, then paused, her eyes narrowed suspiciously. "What's *piss* mean?"

Oops.

"It means to pee, but don't tell Mom I said that," I told her. "It's a bad word."

She started to sing it then, of course.

"Piss, pissing, pissing, piss." She was cheerful, and I was annoyed.

"Stop," I told her. "Before you get us both into trouble."

"You shouldn't have said a bad word," she told me indignantly.

"That's true. But you shouldn't be saying it either. Santa won't come at Christmas."

That shut her right up and I didn't even feel guilty. I shouldn't have been the one in here doing this. I should have been studying for the Spanish test I had the next day, and instead, I was putting kids to bed and then hunting for the utility bill to make sure our power didn't get turned off.

It was ridiculous.

But as soon as the anger started to bubble, I remembered a key thing.

This was all my fault.

That was sobering enough to extinguish the fire of resentment and stoke the flames of my patience.

I deserved this. I knew it.

I sat on the toilet lid and messed around on my phone, trying to think of anything but that, while Annabelle played with her dolls in the tub. Eventually, I got a text.

Dude, where are you?

Son of a bitch. I was supposed to meet Tray at eight.

It was 8:39.

I'll be late, I answered. *Babysitting.*

Sucker, he replied.

He'd been getting annoying lately, because all he wanted to do was smoke weed, when he should be worried about his scholarship. But at the same time, he was the only one who didn't judge me when I had meltdowns. His parents divorced last year, and while it was different from my situation, it was close enough.

He understood me.

That alone was priceless.

Want me to save some for ya?

No thanks, I answered.

I slid my phone into my pocket.

"Come on, get out," I told Annabelle, standing up and holding out her towel. She puckered her lip.

"No. I haven't had enough time." Her curly blond hair was twirled on top of her head, and I couldn't imagine what she still needed to do.

"Time for what?"

She stuck her chin out. "Time to talk to Daddy. I talk to him in here so it doesn't make Mommy sad."

I stood frozen. Suddenly I couldn't breathe.

She dropped down onto her little knees in the middle of the water and clasped her sudsy hands, squeezing her eyes closed. She moved her mouth silently, and she was praying . . . to God, to our dad, to God about Dad?

I sucked in a breath and it was like rats were chewing on my trachea and the holes were letting out the air. I couldn't get enough in.

I dropped heavily back onto the toilet and the bathroom was spinning, my face hot.

"Beck?" Annabelle asked me from somewhere outside of the fog. "Becky? What's wrong?"

She was alarmed, and so was I. This had never happened before.

I thought my heart might be exploding. Was I too young to have a heart attack?

"Becky!" I heard my sister shrieking, and I tried to act calm, I really did, but it was impossible because the world was closing in on me. I gasped and clawed at my neck, and then . . .

Nothing.

Just blackness.

I woke up and Annabelle was kneeling over me, crying. Devin was with her, slapping at my face.

I'd passed out.

Shakily, I pushed up onto my elbows. "I'm all right," I told them, although I couldn't be sure. I could breathe now, and nothing was broken when I'd tumbled from the toilet to the tile floor.

"Are you sure?" Dev asked, like he didn't believe me.

"Hey, Mom has a bottle of medicine on her nightstand," I told him, and it was still a little hard to speak. I had the baggie in my other pocket, but I didn't want Devin to know that. "Go get me two of the pills inside."

He didn't hesitate. He ran.

When he came back, he handed me the pills and I swallowed them immediately, slumping against the toilet.

They were bitter.

And then . . . I lay back against the tiles and waited. Within a couple of minutes, a warm, safe feeling flooded my body. It was subtle, not obvious. It felt a little like when I fell asleep on the couch, and my mother would cover me up with a blanket. A little bit comforting, and it sort of covered up the anger seething in my belly. It didn't take it away, but it soothed it a little bit.

I liked it.

"Are you okay now?" Devin finally asked. "Beck?"

I felt dizzy. A little disoriented. A lot strange.

"I'm fine," I told them both. "It's fine."

"I was afraid you died," Annabelle said, sniffing, and her hands were shaky. "Everyone said you could've that night, during the accident. I was afraid you died tonight instead."

"I wasn't dead," I told her, and I got to my feet. "It's all right, Devin." He eyed me, and then finally nodded.

"Don't tell Mom I took her pills, okay?" I said. He hesitated.

"I'm serious," I told them both. "She's got enough to worry about.

It's nothing bad. I think I had a panic attack. I'm sure it won't happen again. I've never had one before. Promise me you won't tell Mom."

Devin was uncomfortable, but he finally nodded and left the bathroom. He was such a rule follower that this kind of thing killed him. He wanted to get as far away from it as possible.

"Becky, we've gotta call Mama," Annabelle told me, and she was grabbing my phone.

"No." I snatched it away. "It's all right, Anna-B. It was just a panic attack. At least I think that's what it was."

She was still now, watching me warily. "Like Mama had after Daddy's funeral?"

I remembered that, how Mom had collapsed and Kit and Vinny had had to pick her up. Aunt Sam had whisked her off to wash her face and get her some water, and when we saw her thirty minutes later, she was better.

"Yeah," I told her. "Like that. That's why Mom's medicine helped. I'm okay. Don't worry."

My sister wasn't sure, but I tightened the towel around her shoulders.

"Run and get into your pj's," I instructed. "I'll be in to read to you in a little bit."

She did as I asked, and I tucked her into her bed. I still felt dizzy and weak. I sat down heavily on the edge of the bed.

"Are you sure you're not going to die?" She was suspicious now.

"I'm okay," I assured her as I reached over to turn on her nightlight. It was pink and it made ballerinas dance around the room. "I'm not gonna die."

"Not ever?"

"Not any time soon," I promised. "I cross my heart."

She held out her pinkie, and I hooked it with mine. To her, pinkie promises were the ultimate foundation of trust. She nodded her head in satisfaction.

I covered her up and tried to tiptoe out, but she whispered from beneath the blankets.

"Becky, will you stay with me 'til Mom comes home? I'm scared."

She looked so small and pitiful, and I was the cause of that tonight.

"I'll stay," I said, sitting back down on the bed and propping my head on my arm. "There's nothing to be afraid of. Go to sleep."

It took her a long time to fall asleep, her hand tucked tightly within my own. Every time I moved or breathed loudly, her eyes popped wide open to make sure I wasn't going anywhere, so eventually I settled in for the long haul.

She was resting now, but my thoughts were racing. What the fuck just happened to me? Why did it happen? I was stronger than that, damn it. Pussies had panic attacks. I was no pussy. Something was gonna have to give. This couldn't keep happening. I'd have to do something.

I pulled my phone out and texted Tray.

Save me some.

Something had to give. Something had to change. Maybe Tray's dumb weed would mellow me out enough to handle all of this shit. I'd been smoking cigarettes for a couple of weeks now to calm my nerves. Surely weed was no worse than that.

Annabelle stirred and grasped my hand tighter, and I forced my thoughts to calm. My restlessness was keeping her awake.

I don't know what time she finally fell asleep, because I fell asleep too, watching the pink ballerinas dance around her room.

seven

NATALIE
MERCY HOSPITAL
4:19 A.M.

"N AT?"

My sister pokes her head back in the door, and she's got a bag on her arm. She's younger than me by two years, but tonight she looks younger by a million.

"When did you get here?" I ask, not letting go of Beck's hand. Sam puts the bag down next to me and bends to kiss Beck's forehead. That tender gesture clenches my stomach.

"Just now. I brought your clothes," she says, her voice thick. She's trying not to cry, I realize. That scares me because she never cries. She says it's because her heart is a block of ice, but I know she just doesn't like to be vulnerable. "Vince is still with the kids. Don't worry."

"I wasn't," I tell her. She'd never leave the kids alone. I'd trust her with my life. "Thank you for the clothes."

Sammy sits on the bottom of Beck's bed, careful not to disturb him. "Has he woken up?"

I shake my head. "No. He's not going to until they *wake* him up. They say the first twenty-four hours after a massive overdose is the most critical. They'll bring him out then. If he . . . that's when we'll know. If he's going to make it. And if he makes it, if he'll be the same."

My voice cuts off and Sam grabs me tight. I bury my head into her slender shoulder. My beautiful sister, who has helped me so much in the past nightmarish year.

"Don't say *if*," she demands. "It's *when*. When he wakes up, we'll know that he's going to be okay. He will, Nat."

"Okay."

"Jesus, he looks so peaceful," Sam says in wonder. She stares down at Beck, worry etched on her face. "He's so skinny. Where the hell has he been? Do you know?"

I shake my head. "He wasn't really conscious when he fell on my porch. I don't know where he's been, what he's been eating, *if* he's been eating. The doctor said he was on meth today, and God. I don't know anything, Sammy."

She hugs me tighter.

"We know he's here now," she reminds me gently. "And that's the most important thing. He's safe in this bed, and it's the best place for him to be."

"He's in this bed," I agree. "But he's far from safe."

Sam looks away because she knows I'm right. She grabs Beck's other hand, and together we stand vigil, two sentinels with one priceless thing between us.

Minutes pass before she speaks again, and when she does, her lips are white from being clenched together.

"Go get dressed, Nat," she tells me. "I'll wait with him. Wash your face, and go down to the cafeteria to get some coffee. You need to move around a little bit. You need a break."

"No," I say immediately. "I'm not leaving him."

"Now is the best time to go," Sam tells me softly. "He's not going to wake up until they *wake* him up. I'm here. He's fine. Go get dressed. It will be daylight soon, and you're still in your pajamas."

I look down at myself and my robe is faded and old, and I'm so tired. More coffee would be helpful. My eyes burn.

"Okay," I finally agree. "But I'll be right back."

"And we'll be right here," my sister says, still holding my son's hand. I nod and grab the bag.

"I'll bring you back a coffee," I tell her. She nods and I hurry to the bathroom down the hall, change into my favorite jeans and a plaid shirt. I pull the shirt on, but try as I might, my fingers shake too badly to fasten the buttons.

"Son of a bitch," I mutter, and try again. But my limbs are jelly and my fingers won't obey.

I pull my jeans up, leaving the fly open, and sit limply on the toilet.

I feel the cool of the seat, the rigidity of the tiles beneath my feet. The ghastly fluorescent lights tint my skin, and I am numb.

I'm in a hospital and my son could die.

I try to absorb the gravity of that.

But he's not dead yet.

I suck in a breath, and with determination, I manage to first button my shirt, then my jeans. I throw my robe into the trash. I never want to be reminded of this night, no matter what happens.

I yank a comb through my hair, splash water on my face, and head down to the cafeteria.

I rush because if he somehow wakes up on his own while I'm gone, I'll never forgive myself. I know it's impossible, but still. Beck has always been headstrong. If anyone can do it, it's him.

I rush to the line, in such a hurry, but then I have to wait. I'm jittery, and I can't stand still. I shift my weight from one foot to the other. Rocking to and fro.

The woman in front of me turns around. She's got puppies on her scrubs.

"You can always tell a mother . . . She rocks when she stands."

She smiles, and I try to smile back.

As I wait, I can't help but watch the people around me. Doctors, nurses, X-ray techs, all coming through on their breaks, as part of their routine. They see this stuff all the time; this is their *job*. It's not personal.

But there are other people like me here. People who are tired, people who are scared. People who don't know if their loved one will live or die. It's hell on earth, and in this moment I'm somehow connected with them. It's unspoken, but it's there.

There's a woman at a table near the line, and her face is so drawn and pale, her shoulders so slumped, I think someone she knew has already died. She glances up, and her eyes are dark and empty, and I nod ever so slightly at her.

I'm sorry for your loss.

She looks away, her eyes fixed on an imaginary spot on the wall.

Lord, the hospital can be a depressing place.

The line moves a little, and I'm antsy because I need to hurry. My son needs me. He's not gone yet, and I am not that woman.

Not yet.

Over the loudspeakers, there's a chime, a small, quick melody from "Rock-a-Bye Baby."

"What the heck?" I mutter to myself. The nurse in front of me turns again with a smile.

"They play that every time a baby is born," she explains. "It's cute, right?"

I nod, and she turns back around, and I think about that.

Life and death happen all the time. Does one balance out the other? If too many babies are born, will Beck have to die?

I'm being irrational but I don't care. Maybe life isn't as rational as we all like to think.

We inch forward again, and now I can see another table with a teenage boy. He's eating a hamburger at four thirty in the morning. He picks off all the toppings, the lettuce and the tomato, and I can't help but smile just a little because that's something Beck would do. In fact, I've seen him do it.

I can't help but stare at this boy, and as I do, I pray.

"Please don't let him die. Please, God. Please, God."

It's not until the nurse in front of me turns back around that I realize I was praying aloud.

"MOMMY."

I opened my eyes and found Annabelle standing next to my bed. She was wearing a nightgown, and it was almost two a.m.

"Sunshine?" I murmured, feeling for her little arm and pulling her to me to breathe her in. At eight, she still had the little girl smell, like sunshine and hope. Her eyes were brown and scared.

"Mommy? I had a dream."

I stroked her blond hair away from her face. "What was it, baby?"

"I dreamed that Daddy was gone."

"He *is* gone, sweetheart," I told her, and a lump formed in my throat. "He's in heaven, remember? He's with Gramps and Gran."

"I know. But I dreamed that he was just gone. That he was nowhere and that I'd never see him again. That he was in a black abish."

"Abish?"

Her eyes were large as she stared at me. "Yeah. A place that has no bottom. Devin taught me. It's a spelling word."

"Abyss?"

She nodded.

"That's not true, honey," I assured her. "Your daddy is *not* in an abyss. We'll see him again, someday. When it's time to go to heaven."

"Promise?" Her eyes were so big and innocent. I nodded.

"Promise. You can stay in bed with me."

She nodded seriously against my cheek. "I like it in here with you, Mommy," she confided. I hugged her tight. She fell instantly to sleep, feeling safe in my arms.

We slept until Devin poked his head in to wake us a few hours later. "We've got to go to school," he told us. "Come on, Anna."

Obediently, she rolled out of bed and disappeared down the hall and I sat up, rubbing my eyes. I felt awful because I didn't know what day it was. Tuesday? Thursday?

I'd better get up and find out.

Dev was already at the table finishing a bowl of cereal, his polo neatly tucked in.

"Were you born as a thirty-year-old?" I asked, rumpling his hair as I passed. He glared at me for mussing his hair, and fixed it before he picked up his dish and washed it in the sink.

He immediately went to the pantry and pulled out things to make lunches, and got two brown bags from the cupboard. One for him, one for his sister.

I couldn't stop my eyes from welling up. He was making lunches because I so often forgot.

Oh my God. The realization caused my shoulders to quake, and before I knew it, I was sitting at the table and Devin had his arms wrapped around my shoulders.

"It's okay, Mama," he whispered. "It's okay. Don't cry. I'm here."

My little boy was comforting me, doing the thing that I should be doing for him.

"I'm sorry, sweetie," I told him. "I'm sorry. I know I've been a mess lately, but I'll do better."

He seemed confused as he looked up at me, his eyes wide.

"You're okay, Mom," he said softly. "It's okay to be sad. I'm sad too."

God. My chest constricted and constricted until it couldn't possibly get any tighter.

"Let me check your homework," I finally managed to tell him. He looked pleased that I remembered, and scampered to get his bag.

I checked his math, and he'd gotten every problem right.

"You're my genius," I told him. He smiled.

"Anna-B!" I called up the stairs. "Let's go! The bus is coming!"

I could hear it rumbling up the road. She raced down the steps, and I escorted them out to the stop. My daughter waved from the bus window as it drove away.

I was walking back up the sidewalk to the front door when I caught a whiff of cigarette smoke, and something rustled on the side of my house. The distinct sound of the rose branches scraping against the siding.

Curiously, I stepped across the dew-covered grass, turned the corner, and promptly found my eldest son leaning against the house, his hair rumpled, a cigarette dangling from his lips.

The look of surprise on his face almost certainly matched my own.

"Beckitt Matthew Kingsley, what the hell are you doing?"

For a split second, he had the "oh shit" look on his face, the one he used to get when he was afraid of getting caught. But that quickly hardened into a blasé devil-may-care face.

"I'm smoking," he said calmly. He took another drag, then dropped it on the ground, twisting his foot to stamp it out.

I was stunned. "You can't smoke," I told him indignantly. "You'll get cancer."

"We all gotta die sometime," he said, shrugging. Anger flared up in me.

"Maybe. But *not* on my watch. Give me the rest of them." I held out my hand. "You're not going to smoke in my house. I can't believe you. You're an athlete. You know better."

"I used to think I knew a lot of things," he said, and his words were laced with something I couldn't place, something unlike him. "But I was wrong about most of them."

He dug in his hoodie pocket and fished out his smokes. He handed them to me, and there were only three or four left in the pack.

"Don't buy any more," I warned him. "I'm serious. If I catch you smoking again, there will be hell to pay."

He was rolling his eyes as he started to walk away.

"Since when would you even notice?" he asked, and I was startled and guilty and pissed. He'd never spoken to me that way before. I was taken aback. His voice seethed with anger, and the venom was directed at me. This wasn't like him at all.

"Trust me, I'll notice," I told him. "Straighten up."

He stomped away, and I was left shaking alone on the side of the house, cigarette butts surrounding me on the ground, a million warning signs that I couldn't bring myself to face.

eight

THE ANGER IS BACK.

I don't know why, but it bubbles up within me like a raging sea of ugliness.

What am I so pissed about?

I try to think, I try to remember, but the memories aren't obedient. They are random, and when they come, I just hold on.

I'm vulnerable here, though. I'm in a bed, and I can feel everyone staring at me in judgment. I know there's judgment. There has been for a long time.

Nothing I did was good enough, but don't they know I tried my best?

I seethe silently because I can't move my tongue.

The beeps come from nowhere and everywhere, and I start to realize that they are attached to me somehow. The more pissed I am, the faster they get. I know I should try to control that, but I don't know how.

"His heart rate is so erratic," my aunt whispers, and I think she squeezes my hand.

My mom murmurs in agreement. "I know. It's scary."

Why? It's my fucking heart. It will do what it wants. Right?

If anything scares me, it's the anger. It feels like it came out of no-where, and I don't know why; it feels like it might burn me up. It's bigger than I am.

Now I suddenly realize what my aunt was talking about earlier when she said there was fire in me. I can feel it now, burning bright and brighter, big and bigger. It's an inferno and it's spreading everywhere. As it spreads, the beeps get faster and faster.

———

I ROLLED THE TOWEL up under my bedroom door, blocking the smell from reaching the rest of the house. I lit up the joint and sucked it in.

Blessed relief.

Through the door, I heard Annabelle downstairs, watching an annoying kid's show, one of the ones with the ridiculous songs and dancing animals.

I'd skipped school today with Tray because we'd had to meet his dealer to get more weed. With two of us smoking, his stash had run out quicker than usual. I bought my own today, though, so I was set for a while. If I smoked it in combination with my mother's Xanax, it helped.

It calmed my nerves, and it gave me the sense, if only temporarily, that I was going to be fine. There was nothing to worry about.

I lay on my back in the middle of the bed and stared at my ceiling fan. It was always the first thing I saw when I woke up in the morning, including that morning. The morning Dad and I went to Notre Dame.

If only I could go back in time and change that day. We'd never have gone.

But I couldn't do that. It was impossible. All I could do was deal with the fallout now.

I sucked in another drag.

My phone rang, but I ignored it. It rang again and again, insistently, but whoever it was could wait.

I was doing something important here. I was saving my sanity.

I closed my eyes and rested. I was floating on a cloud of smoke, away from here. If I imagined hard enough, that was where I was.

But then there was a knock at my door, and anger flared.

"Go away," I called irritably. But there was another knock, and before I could do anything, my door was pushed open, the towel forced away.

My brother stood there, glaring at me as he sniffed the air.

"Beck, oh my God. What are you doing?"

But he was a smart kid, and once he saw the joint in my hand, he knew. His eyes widened.

"Beck, you're being stupid."

He was afraid now, and I was pissed.

"It's nothing," I told him. "Mind your own business, Devin. You aren't even supposed to be in here."

"I'm not supposed to use the oven," he reminded me. "I wanted you to put a pizza in."

"Go ask Mom." I snapped this, and it was ridiculous because she hadn't made dinner in months and we both knew it.

"Oh, I'll go talk to Mom," he assured me, and his face was determined. "About a lot of things."

He turned to leave, and I called his name to stop him, but he didn't. Whatever.

I shrugged to myself.

Mom wouldn't do shit.

She wasn't present enough for that.

I opened my window to air out my room, sprayed a few squirts of cologne, then banged down the stairs to leave. Anywhere but here.

I turned my key and started driving.

nine

NATALIE
MERCY HOSPITAL
5:01 A.M.

I HOLD MY SON'S HAND, AND AS I DO, I EXAMINE IT. IN BETWEEN his fingers, there are strange bruises. It occurs to me, all of a sudden, that they are needle marks.

"He was injecting into his fingers," I say, and I'm stunned, frozen. If only I could fix this. If only I could fix *him*. God.

"You can't," Sam tells me, as though she can read my thoughts. "You can't change anything. All you can do is be what he needs now, Nat. He needs you here, and he needs you to support him when he works through this."

"When he wakes up," I answer.

She nods. "When he wakes up."

She doesn't say *if*, and I am grateful.

I sit back in my seat and watch while the door opens and the doctor comes back in. He assesses Beck, scribbles in his chart, and starts to leave. I stop him with my hand on his arm and a pleading look.

He shakes his head. "There's no change, Mrs. Kingsley. Keep talking to him."

"I thought you said he can't hear."

The doctor looks away. "It can't hurt."

He leaves, and I lay my head against Beck's arm.

"Stay with me, sweetheart," I tell him firmly. "I'm here now."

I won't leave again.

———

MY BEDROOM WAS DARK, just the way I liked it, when Dev came in. He was hesitant because he didn't want to disturb me. Out of all three of my kids, he was the one who was born considerate. If he could've, he would've apologized in the delivery room for being two days late.

"Mom?" His voice was quiet now.

"Yeah, honey?"

Devin walked to the side of the bed, and I could see that his face was worried. I sat up, alarmed.

"What's wrong?"

"Beck. He's smoking, Mom."

Oh. That. I already handled that.

"It's okay," I answered him, relief spreading through me. "I already took care of that."

"No, you didn't," he answered simply. "He was just smoking pot in his room. Just now."

Pot?

I stared at him for a long time.

"Honey, he wouldn't do that." He knew I couldn't deal with that. He wouldn't do that to me.

Devin nodded, though. "I caught him."

"How would you even know what pot looks like?" I asked him, trying not to be patronizing.

Devin shrugged. "Everyone knows, Mom. Trust me, Beck had it in his room. Can you do something?"

This was ridiculous. Beck was the one who had been feeding the kids for me; he even paid the utility bill for me yesterday. He'd come in and asked for the bank account information. He couldn't be that responsible and also smoke pot on the side.

"You're mistaken," I told Devin plainly. I lay back down, comfortable in my answer. "I'll talk to him about the cigarettes."

"Mom," he said firmly, unwilling to let it go. "Come down to his room. You'll see for yourself. You've got to do something. They aren't cigarettes."

All I wanted was to bury my face in Matt's pillow again, and this conversation was delaying that.

"Devin, let it go," I told him irritably. "You're mistaken."

"I'm not, Mom . . ." he tried to argue. "You've got to listen . . ."

"Devin!" I snapped, and I hadn't spoken to him like this in . . . I'd never spoken to him like this. "Go out. Go to bed. Quit trying to make trouble for your brother."

Devin closed his mouth, and the expression on his face was so, so injured. I felt bad, but the pain in my heart . . . it was bigger than that. I couldn't deal with this. Not right now.

"I was just trying to help," he muttered as he walked out.

I squeezed my eyes closed and tried to go to sleep, to escape this. When I was asleep, nothing hurt anymore, and sometimes, when I was lucky, I dreamed about my husband.

But now I was bothered. I tossed and turned, and finally, about an hour later, I got up. I padded down to Beck's room and knocked on the door.

No answer.

I pushed the door open and went in.

Everything looked normal. There were books on his desk, his bed was rumpled, his book bag was on the floor with books spilling out the top. I could taste thick cologne in the air, and if he'd really been smoking pot in here, I'd be able to tell, wouldn't I?

Of course I would.

I turned and went back out, while his curtains from the open window fluttered in the night breeze. I caught a whiff of something, probably cigarette smoke.

When I got back to my room, I texted my son.

I warned you about the cigarettes. If I catch you smoking again, you're grounded from your car.

He didn't answer.

I went back to bed.

ten

BECK
MERCY HOSPITAL
5:12 A.M.

They speak in hushed whispers.

My mom, Aunt Sammy, the nurses. They talk like they don't want to disturb me, and that itself is disturbing.

A while ago, I heard Aunt Sammy ask my mom, *Where has he been for the past two months?* It's a really good question.

I don't know. My mind is messed up and I can't remember.

I've been thinking on it, though. My memories are coming back in layers, and it's frustrating.

Someone picks up my arm and a finger runs down my skin.

"Lord, Nat. The track marks. There are so many."

Track marks.

Needles.

Fucking-A.

I love my aunt but I want to tell her to shut the hell up. The last thing my mom needs right now is to look at fucking track marks. Jesus.

At the same time, I think on those words. Track marks. I have track marks. How did I get the track marks?

"Hush, Sam," my mom snaps, and I can hear the scowl in her voice.

Good for you, Mom, I think. *Don't listen. I'm not all bad. I did bad things, but I'm not all bad.*

Mom takes my arm out of Aunt Sammy's hand and folds my hand next to my cheek. I feel instantly comforted. It's how I like to sleep. My belly feels warm that she knows that.

"Vinny will call when the kids wake up," Sam says. "Should he bring them here?"

God, no, I want to shout. They can't see me like this.

"They can't see Beck like this," my mom says, as though she read my thoughts. "They'd be devastated."

"But what if . . . what if . . ." Sam doesn't finish her question, but Mom and I know what she meant. What if I don't wake up, and Devin and Annabelle never see me alive again?

My mouth tastes like guilt. It's salty and tastes like rotted metal.

Dev used to look at me like I was king of the field, a hero. Even after he caught me smoking. There's only so much they can forgive, though. They can't know everything I've done. I don't want to see what it does to them.

"We'll see what happens when they bring him out," my mom finally says, and is she giving up on me? *Don't!* I want to shout.

But I can't.

I can't make a noise at all.

All I can do is listen.

"It'll be okay," Sam assures my mom, but if I don't know, then she can't possibly know. "It'll be okay."

Someone is crying. The sobs echo throughout the room. It's my mother. Her breath sucks in over and over, as though time and time again, she can't draw another. I saw her like this only one time before. At my father's funeral when his mahogany casket was lowered into the ground. She'd clung to me then, and we'd stood there watching my father sink into the earth.

She's crying the same way right now. It's alarming.

"The thought of him being alone this whole time kills me," Mom says, and her voice is wet.

"You don't know that he was," Aunt Sammy reminds her. "We don't know anything. When he wakes up tomorrow, we'll ask him."

"Later today," my mom corrects her. "Tonight."

Sammy is quiet and I have no idea what time it is. How much time do I have? I don't know and it's fucking ridiculous.

Because as I understand it, they've sedated me now and God knows what else. But when they bring me out . . . we'll know if I'm going to live or die.

I don't know if I'm ready . . .

Ready to wake up, *or* ready to die.

Do I have any reason whatsoever to live?

I think on that. And when I do, a name forms in my head.

Elin.

———

THERE WAS NOTHING LIKE Friday-night lights in October.

The air was crisp, the sky was dark, and our home bleachers were full of red and white shirts, of devil horns and face paint. The electricity was in the air, the amazing energy of football, the smell of sweat and blood and freshly torn-up field.

In the distance behind me, the cheerleaders were screaming, and I knew Elin was among them, her slender arms straight as arrows while she jumped and cheered.

"Red and white! Red and white! Go, Red Devils!"

In the crowd, people were chanting my name. "King! King! King!"

I was a superhero here; I could do no wrong. It was transcendent.

As I was carried off the field, someone dumped a cooler of Gatorade on me, and I shook the yellow liquid off like a victorious dog, the flecks flying. Everyone laughed, everyone was happy. Of course they were. We won.

In the showers, Tray turned to me, tossing me soap.

"Good game, my man," he said. "I saw a recruiter for Alabama in the stands. I swear to God. Roll Tide, dude."

I rolled my eyes because I could afford to. I knew I was being recruited, but that was a given. I was only a junior in high school and could throw seventy yards in my pads. I had a God-given talent, and I wasn't going to waste it.

I lathered up and got some slaps on the back and a couple on the ass. The locker room was hot and steamy as I washed away the grass and blood. Not my blood, of course. My guys protected me on the field like I was precious cargo.

Once I was clean, I emerged to find Elin waiting for me, just like I knew she would.

"Your parents said they'd see you at home," she told me as I pulled her in for a kiss. The energy of winning came through my body and channeled into the kiss, electric and hot. She squirmed against me, her body slender. "They said you could stay out 'til one," she added against my lips.

I smiled.

"Good."

"You hungry?" she asked when we broke apart and headed for my car. I shook my head.

"Only for you."

She smiled under the streetlight, and she looked like a fantasy, the fuel of every man's red-blooded dreams.

We'd talked about it, discussed it, planned it.

After dating for almost two years, tonight was the night.

I'd barely made it out to the bluffs and put my car in park before Elin was in my arms. The smells swirled together—my letter jacket, the leather of the car seats, her perfume, her strawberry shampoo. It was a smell I'd remember forever.

Her hands clutched at me as I pulled her closer.

Everything was fluid, like we'd rehearsed it a thousand times.

We kind of had. We'd gone to the edge a hundred times before, but never over it.

Tonight was different.

I wasn't sure how we made it to the back seat, but we did. Her mouth was on mine, and we were breathing together, our heartbeats synced.

I traced the ridges of her rib cage, and she whispered in the night, "Are you scared?"

"No," I answered truthfully. "Are you?"

"No."

She smiled, her lips curved against my skin, and I knew in this moment that she was all I wanted. She was all I'd ever want.

"I love you," she told me after I slid inside of her. "You're mine, Beck."

"I'm yours," I breathed into her neck, and Jesus, she felt like heaven. "I'm yours."

Losing our virginity together was always the plan, but we never knew it would feel like this. That it would seem so momentous, so important.

Afterward, we were sort of in shock as we lay together, curled up in the car. Elin's hand was on my chest, and my fingers were in her hair. She had a faraway smile on her lips, and I'd never been so happy.

I told her that, and she smiled again.

"I know," she agreed. "Me either."

There was another scent in the air now, musky and warm, and I realized that it was sex. I'd remember that smell forever too. Sex, letter jackets, and strawberry shampoo.

"I should get you something to eat," I told her, but I was reluctant to move, and so was she.

"Wait," she whispered. "Let's just . . . one more time, Beck."

She reached for me and she was so soft, and I'd never get enough of her.

I barely made it home by one.

After dropping Elin off and grabbing a hamburger at a drive-thru, I literally opened my front door at 12:59.

My dad was waiting for me, reclined in his favorite chair.

"Good game tonight," he said, eyeing the fast-food bag in my hand. "You didn't eat with Elin?"

I shook my head and dropped onto the sofa, wolfing down my burger and fries. "No. We weren't hungry."

Dad chitchatted a little bit, but he was yawning. He was starting to get up when I just had to tell him. I had to tell someone because it was so huge.

"I had sex with Elin tonight," I said.

And the living room went quiet.

"Did you use protection?" Dad asked calmly, staring down at me. His face was unreadable. Was he mad? Was he proud? I couldn't tell.

I nodded. "Of course."

"Do you have any questions?" He was uncomfortable now but still doing the fatherly thing.

I shook my head. "No."

"Okay. Good. Well, if you do, you can ask me. It might be awkward, but still."

I nodded again. "Thanks."

"Things will be different now," he said, and I knew he was right. They already felt different. "Your emotions are going to be even more involved, so be aware of that. Elin's a good girl, and you need to treat her right. But I know you will."

I nodded because of course I would.

"I trust you to always do the right thing," he added. "You're a good kid, son."

Yeah, I knew that.

"Thank you."

"We don't need to tell your mom this particular thing," he added, and I physically recoiled at the thought of her finding out. Dad laughed. "Good to see we're on the same page. Some things don't need to be announced. Night, bud. I love you."

He gripped my shoulder.

"Night, Dad."

I didn't say I loved him back, because that was corny, but I was pretty sure he knew.

When I went to bed later, I fell asleep with visions of blond hair and long legs wrapped around my hips, and I knew nothing would ever be the same.

eleven

NATALIE
MERCY HOSPITAL
6:21 A.M.

"KIT'S STILL OUT IN THE WAITING ROOM," MY SISTER SAYS. She watches me, but I don't look. I can't.

She waits for me to say something, but I don't. She sighs.

"I told him to go home, but he won't," she adds.

"I told him that too," I tell her. She eyes me, and she's curious.

"Am I missing something?" she asks, and I'm annoyed.

"Now isn't the time," I tell her abruptly.

She's quiet because I'm right and she knows it. Even still, her curiosity lingers in the air, thick and palpable.

"Still. It's not fair to just leave him out there," she answers stubbornly. "He should be able to see Beck. It's only right. He loves that boy too, Nat."

I think on that . . . about all the times Kit helped with Beck and how he'd stepped in when I was a mess and didn't know what to do.

I do owe him.

"Fine," I say, nodding.

She slips out of the room and returns within minutes with Kit in tow. He's apologetic but concerned, and he immediately starts talking to Beck.

"Hey, buddy," he says soothingly, and he grasps Beck's arm. "Hey. You're doing good. Really good." His voice is grave, though, and his shoulders are tense.

It's telling. He's worried.

My head drops.

"How are you holding up?" he asks me, and my heart clenches.

"I'm okay."

But I'm not okay.

And he knows that.

He nods again with his big head, and his blond hair brushes his shoulders. "Have you eaten?"

"I'm not hungry," I answer. "I had coffee, though."

Kit is silent, Sam is silent, and the three of us look at our boy, because even though he's mine, he's *ours*.

All of ours.

"Did anyone call Elin?" Sam asks suddenly, her head snapping up.

I feel awful because I didn't think about it. Beck is hers too, and I'd totally forgotten.

"No," I answer simply. "I'm sorry. I forgot."

"Of course you did," Kit answers soothingly, and he pats my shoulder. "Don't worry about it, Nat. You have a lot going on. I'll go call her for you."

I start to nod but then shake my head instead.

"No, I should do it," I tell him. "Can you sit with Beck?"

"Of course."

So I leave Beck with Kit and Sammy, and step into the hall. I stare at my phone and ponder what to say.

Things are complicated with Elin and Beck right now because he'd left and he'd broken her heart, like he'd broken all of ours.

But still she loves him.

And there's no good way to make this call.

I dial her number.

She's sleepy when she answers, groggy.

"Mrs. Kingsley?"

"Elin . . ."

Eeeeelin. Who names their kid that? Not Ellen. Eeeeelin.

I focus.

"Sweetheart, Beck is in the hospital."

She snaps to attention, her voice immediately clear. "You found him? How bad is it?"

"It's not good," I say slowly.

"I'm on my way."

"Wait, honey," I tell her. "We don't know what's going to happen. They've put him in a coma. His brain is swollen and could be damaged. We don't know what's going to happen when they bring him out. He could be different. Or he could . . ."

I can't say the words, and she doesn't wait to hear them.

"It doesn't matter," she says stoutly, and I love her for that. "Are you at Mercy?"

"Yeah."

"I'll be there in twenty minutes."

"Okay."

"Wait," she says, and there is hesitancy in her voice, fear. "Do you think he'd want me there?"

"I do, sweetie. I do."

"I'll be there shortly," she says immediately.

I hang up and slump to the floor, my phone still in my hand.

The fluorescent lights swirl above me, and no one seems to think that me lying on the floor outside a room is odd. Everyone continues with their business, stepping around me.

I remember when I used to think that Beck and Elin were puppy love. That was back when they were sophomores and had stars in their eyes. They were the cliché cheerleader and quarterback, and everyone thought it was a passing phase.

But they've been together for years, and the things they feel for each other are very adult things. In fact, when he started pushing her away, that was when I knew something truly serious was going on. It was one of my first real warning signs, even though I didn't quite realize how big it was at the time.

Regardless of that, he loves her. I know he does.

If anyone can get through to Beck, it might be Elin.

"WHAT COLOR IS ELIN'S prom dress?" I asked my son.

He looked up from the TV, and he was confused.

"I don't know. She didn't say. Should I know that?"

I sighed. "I'm ordering her corsage," I explained. "It'd be nice if it matched."

"Oh." He picked up his phone and punched some buttons, in the lightning-fast way that teenagers do. "Pink."

"Hot pink? Pale pink?"

He rolled his eyes. "Just pink, Mom."

"Okay. I'll just text her myself." I started to do that very thing, but Beck snapped at me.

"Don't. Leave it alone."

Startled, I stared at him. "Why in the world not?"

"Because I don't want you to. Just let me handle it."

Confused, I narrowed my eyes, but he looked away, returning to his video game. He rarely played those things, and it was weird that he was so into it tonight.

"Fine. A white corsage it is." I clicked the Order button and closed my laptop.

"I don't want to go to prom," he told me for the twentieth time. "It's dumb and a waste of time."

"I don't want you to regret it later," I told him. "You need to have all of these experiences, all of these memories. One day you'll thank me."

"I doubt it."

I was beginning to doubt it too. Lately Beck hadn't shown much interest in anything, and he'd even been slacking with Elin.

She was honestly the prettiest, smartest girl in his senior class, and if he was losing interest in her, then what was I supposed to do with something like that?

"Well, I know Elin definitely wants to go, so you'll have to suck it up. Besides, you're gonna look so handsome in your tux. Everyone does."

He barely grunted.

"Where are you taking her for dinner?" I asked, trying to get details. "I'm going to pick up your tux tomorrow. Is everything all set with the limo?"

He'd gone in with a group of his friends to book a party limo. None of the parents wanted the kids to drive on prom night, so we'd all contributed to the cost.

"Yeah," he said, without taking his eyes from the screen. "It's all set."

"Okay."

"Mommy, if Beck gets to ride in a limo, what do we get to do?" Annabelle asked, and she had her teddy bear dressed in overalls. "I want to wear a princess dress."

"Okay. You can wear a princess dress and I'll take you and Dev out to eat. We'll have our own party."

She was satisfied with that. "I've got to find my tiara," she decided, and ran for her room. That wouldn't be hard. She had at least four of them.

"You should take Aunt Sammy," Beck mentioned, still playing his game. "She's bored lately."

"How do you know that?" This was interesting.

My son shrugged. "She texts."

"She texts you," I repeated.

He rolled his eyes. "Yeah. It's the twenty-first century, Mom. People text."

"I know," I answered as patiently as I could. "But do you text her back?"

"Of course. It'd be rude if I didn't."

"You don't answer *my* texts," I told him, leading him down this path all along. "Why can you text Aunt Sammy but not me?"

He glanced at me, unconcerned. "Because you're my mom and you don't get offended."

I was speechless, but reasoning with a teenager was an exercise in futility.

"Whatever," I muttered.

"You're not seriously upset," Beck said, phrasing it like a question but still not looking away from the television.

"Of course not," I answered. "I'm a mom. I don't have feelings, apparently."

He huffed and shot someone and I shook my head.

"If we were hamsters, I'd eat you," I announced as I headed out of the room.

"You would not," he called after me. "You wouldn't want the fur in your mouth."

He was chuckling, which actually made me smile.

He didn't laugh much nowadays.

I could still hear him chuckling as I ducked into Devin's room. I found my younger son quietly studying his spelling words, without even being asked.

"You take after your dad," I told him, and that made me so proud. There wasn't a thing that Matt didn't prepare for.

Dev smiled up at me, such a serious little man.

"He liked to do my spelling words with me," he said quietly, flipping the card. I felt a rush of guilt. Matt had been gone six months and I hadn't thought to sit down and work out spelling words with Devin.

What the hell was wrong with me? I was like a robot. I was able to do the basic things but unable to see everything that I actually needed to do.

"Want my help?" I offered now because it was better late than never. Devin's freckles stood out on his pale cheeks. I brushed his hair back with my hand, and his lamp, the one with the spinning lamp-shade, was throwing shadows of the seven continents on the ocean-blue walls.

He shook his head and it kind of hurt my heart.

"That's okay, Mom. I know you don't like studying."

"I like studying with *you*," I corrected him. He grinned.

"Okay. How do you spell *pterodactyl*?"

He cocked his head and waited, because he knew that Matt was the speller.

"Well, Mr. Smarty Pants, you're the one who needs to spell it, not me!"

I yanked the card away and waited for him to spell it out, which of course he did perfectly. The silent *p* didn't trip him up at all.

"Good job," I told him, pulling out a fresh card. "*Peninsula*."

He paused, and I thought I'd tripped him up, but his eyes looked sad. I lowered the card.

"What?"

"Mom, you're not Dad."

His words stung.

"I know, honey. I just thought . . . I could help you too. What did Daddy do differently?"

"He made up dumb songs to make things easier to remember."

Honest to God, I tried. I did. I started singing, but it didn't come out right and I couldn't think of what to say. I just wasn't as goofy as Matt, and I never would be.

"It's okay," Dev told me. "It's fine. You have other things to do, Mom."

"Wait, I can do this. Just give me a minute to think on it. We have to do things differently now. We have to adjust."

"I don't want to," he said simply, and he was so small to have to deal with such a big thing.

"I know," I agreed. "I don't want to either. But we don't get to choose."

He took the card from my hand.

"I'll just practice alone," he told me. He didn't hear the sound my heart made as it broke. "It's easier that way."

I saw it in his eyes. He didn't want me to take that place in his memory of his father. I had to respect that.

"Okay," I said, relenting. "But if you need help, just yell."

He rolled his eyes. "I'm a better speller than you, Mom."

"You're twelve going on twenty," I answered. I paused to pick up his dirty laundry.

"Date night on Saturday," I told him when I got to the door. "While Beck is at prom, you, me, and Anna-B are going out."

"He's going?" Dev looked up, his brow furrowed. "I heard him talking on the phone yesterday. He said he wasn't."

"He doesn't *want* to," I corrected him. "But he's going. There are memories to be made."

"When I'm eighteen, will you make me do stuff too?"

"Yeah. It's my right as your mother to make your life miserable."

He scowled, but it was too adorable to have his desired effect. I rumpled his hair and headed out, just in time to see Beck disappear into the bathroom. He took three long showers a day, and I didn't like to think about what went on in there.

It was when I was walking past his room that I heard his phone.

Text alert after text alert, like rapid machine-gun fire.

I paused.

Don't do it, I told myself. I always said that I wouldn't snoop in my kids' business unless there was a reason.

But something felt different this time.

Glancing over my shoulder, I made sure he was still in the bathroom. Then, I stepped into his room, picking his phone up off his bed.

Twenty-nine texts from Elin.

How could you do this?

Prom is in two days.

This isn't you.

You love me. I know you do.

Startled, I scrolled upward into the conversation, to Beck's last text to her.

I can't do this right now. You should be with someone who can. I don't deserve you, E.

I was so stunned that the words blurred together.

What in the world prompted this?

You're all I want, Elin answered. *What are you talking about??*

I scrolled through the words, and Beck's answers just didn't make sense. *You deserve better.*

Better than my son?

I was so involved in reading that I didn't hear Beck coming back down the hall, and when he came into his room, I still had his phone in my hand.

"Mom, what the hell?" He grabbed it from me, his gaze furtive.

"Why did you break up with Elin?" I demanded. "You love her. You've been together for so long. This doesn't make any sense."

"Why are you reading my texts? All you do is lie in bed, and the second you get up you snoop in my phone?"

"I . . ." I didn't have a good answer. Telling him my gut told me to wouldn't fly. "I just heard your phone blowing up and I thought it might be important."

Beck scowled at me, not buying it, and I couldn't blame him.

"I didn't mean to intrude on your privacy," I said carefully. "I'm sorry. I'm so worried, though, Becks. What is going on? This is so . . . unexpected."

In this moment, he was a little boy. *My* little boy. He was hurting and I couldn't fix it.

"Nothing," he insisted. "People break up, Mom. It's not like we were going to get married. We're probably going to go to different colleges, so breaking up was gonna happen anyway."

He tried to sound so nonchalant, but I heard the sadness in his voice. I could see it in the way he stood, in the way his shoulders slumped.

"Do you really feel like she deserves someone better than you?" I asked, my voice thin. "Because there's no one better than you, Beckitt."

He didn't answer. He just looked at me, his eyes dark and almost forlorn.

"Mom, I'm in a towel. I need to get dressed."

I nodded, taking the not-so-subtle hint.

I headed for the door, tripping over his discarded pants. As I did, a pack of cigarettes slid out of his pocket.

I was stunned and turned back around to find Beck already scowling.

"Don't say it," he told me, bending to reach for the pack. "I'm an adult and this is my decision."

"You're *deciding* to get lung cancer?" I raised an eyebrow. "Do you think if your father could have chosen, he would've chosen to die? He wouldn't. But smoking . . . *that's choosing.* That's choosing to do something very risky, something that will kill you. Give them to me."

Beck was defiant, his eyes flashing.

"No. Mom, you can't control me. Smoking helps me cope."

"Smoking will help you die," I insisted. "This is ridiculous. Give them to me. You're grounded from your car for two weeks."

"No," he argued again. "It just takes the edge off. It helps with the anxiety."

"You're not smoking in this house, Beck. I mean it."

"You're being stupid," he railed at me, pulling a shirt over his head, then yanking on pants. "This is the least of the things you should be worrying about. You should be worrying about yourself, not about my girlfriend or my smoking."

"*You* are the most important thing," I answered slowly. "You, Annabelle, Devin . . ."

"Then show it," he screamed, slamming out of the room. "Act like you give a shit about someone other than yourself. Get out of bed, comb Annabelle's hair, pack their lunches. Worry about yourself."

"Come back here," I demanded. "You can't talk to me like that! You still have to follow my rules. As long as you're under my roof—"

He interrupted me, pausing on the stairs.

"Maybe I won't *be* under your roof," he snapped, and then he stormed out, out of my house, out of my sight.

I was frozen on the staircase, and from there I could see out the window. I saw Beck's taillights disappear down our street.

He was gone. What if he really didn't come back?

"Mommy?"

Annabelle's little voice interrupted my panic, and she was at the bottom of the stairs, her thumb in her mouth. She had a Kool-Aid stain on her shirt and her hair was rumpled. I really hadn't combed it today.

"It's okay, punkin," I told her. I took her hand and led her down to the kitchen where I combed the snarls out. There were so many of them. Had it been combed all week?

"Why is Becky mad?" she asked me, and she was so worried, so innocent. I had to protect that. I couldn't tell her that her brother was slipping away.

"He's okay, honey," I lie. "He and Elin are fighting, but they'll be all right."

"But he sounds mad at you," she pointed out. "Is he going to move away?"

She was worried, and I was appalled. Surely not. He didn't mean that.

"He's fine, honey," I told her. "Sometimes we say things we don't mean."

"But Becky does everything," she said, and she was mournful now. "He feeds me and gives me baths. He can't leave, Mama. He can't!"

What have I done?

"That's all my job," I said. "Mommy hasn't been feeling well, honey. But I'm getting better. I promise."

She looked up at me doubtfully and it broke my heart.

"Let's get you some apple juice; then I'll read you a story," I suggested. Being read to was her favorite thing, so she agreed immediately, her fears about Beck forgotten.

Not for me, though.

Long after I'd tucked Dev and Annabelle into bed, I worried about Beck. I texted my sister and Kit, and neither had heard from him.

I watched for his car, I texted him.

No answer.

I texted him again. *You were right. I've been pathetic. I'll do better. Starting now. Come home.*

Still no answer.

If Matt were here, he'd know what to do.

It was after midnight when I gave up. I turned off all the lights downstairs, then locked the door. I jiggled the handle to make sure, then checked the lock again. I was never paranoid before, but like everything else, now that Matt was gone, everything had changed.

Things that go bump in the night had become a little scarier.

The night had become a little darker.

As I brushed my teeth, I noticed that my hand was shaking.

Damn it.

I was never one to get anxious before. But now . . . well, now the anxiety consumed me in ways I'd never imagined. On my darkest days, it took my breath away.

Once I rinsed and spit, I went for the Xanax. I usually tried not to take it until my fingers started to shake.

I'd become so good at suppressing the anxiety that I only noticed it when my body literally manifested it in a physical way.

I dumped a pill into my hand, and the bottle seemed low. It was startling.

Had I really taken most of the bottle?

Holy shit.

That was another problem. Sometimes I'd forget things now. Memories were blurs, complete chunks of time missing. I knew it was just a by-product of coping with grief, but still. Maybe Beck was right. Maybe *I* was the reason things were falling apart.

I swallowed the bitter pill and climbed into the cold bed.

I still hadn't gotten used to the vastness of it, the loneliness of being the only one in the bed.

Out of habit, my fingers reached out for Matt, but they grasped at air. I sighed and tried to sleep, but sleep was elusive for once.

I was wide-awake, staring at shadows, when Beck finally came home. It was after three in the morning.

Only then could I close my eyes and rest.

twelve

"OH MY GOD. HE LOOKS SO . . ."

"Yeah," my mom agrees. "He looks bad. I know."

How bad do I look? Is my face smashed in?

Someone new picks up my hand, someone with smooth, slender fingers.

"I think he's been in a fight," she says. I know that voice. It's sweet and clear. "Where has he been?"

"We don't know," my mom whispers. "We don't know anything."

"Here, Elin," Aunt Sammy says quickly. "You can have my seat."

Elin. *Oh my God.*

All of my feelings whoosh out of my body, like my breath has been knocked out. She's here. Right now. After the way I left, after everything I've done.

Only of course she doesn't know what I've done.

I don't deserve her, definitely not. She just doesn't know it.

Lips are next to my ear. Soft and full. *Elin.* I recognize her scent, flowery and feminine. She is everything good in the world, and she always has been. I picture the way her nose crinkles when she laughs, and it hits me hard, right in the gut.

"Where've you been, babe?" she asks, and her voice is so tender, so sweet. Her hand brushes my cheek, and it must make my mom uncomfortable, because she speaks up.

"We'll give you a little privacy," she says awkwardly, and then there is rustling, and the door opens, then closes.

"Oh my God, Beck," Elin whispers, and her hand is squeezing mine so tightly. "I've been so scared. You can't leave me. Not ever again. You're mine, and I'm yours. Remember?"

I remember breaking things off with her so I didn't hurt her. That's what I remember.

I want to tell her everything. Everything I've done. But I can't force my lips to move. It's maddening. I have to lie here and let everyone believe that I'm worth it. That I'm worth their pain. I'm not.

Once upon a time, I was. I was everything they thought me to be. I was good and kind, considerate and thoughtful, and fuck, I was a gentleman, just like Mom raised me to be.

But I'm not that person anymore.

———

TRAY AND I HID in the locker rooms, standing on a toilet with our joint poked out the slanted open window.

I sucked in slowly, letting the herb reach my lungs and then my bloodstream, then breathed out. I handed it over to my friend, and he did the same.

"Did you break it off with Elin?" he asked in the weird voice that potheads use when they're trying not to let smoke escape their lungs.

I nodded. "Yeah."

"I assume she didn't take it well?" He sucked in again.

"No."

"Well, she's just gonna have to suck it up. What did she think? That you'd stay together when you leave for college? That's stupid."

But it's exactly what she had thought, and me too. We had planned on going to college together. But she deserved someone better. I knew that now. Now that I was spiraling, I couldn't pull her with me. I felt myself get a little more out of control every day. Elin deserved better.

"Let it go, dude," I told him, reaching for the joint. I hated today. I hated most days now. My mom had been getting up and doing things around the house, but surprisingly it didn't help. She was just in my business now, and I wasn't sure what had sucked more—her sleeping all the time, or her being nosy.

There didn't seem to be a lot to live for—nothing that mattered anyway.

Tray glanced at me. "Whatever, man. But you'll be fine."

Would I? I wasn't so sure about that.

"Dude, we're smoking too much of this shit," Tray told me, his face screwed up. "It's getting fucking expensive. I'm gonna try something different tonight. Something better. You in?"

The bell rang before I could answer, and he dropped the last bit of the joint into the toilet and flushed it.

I opened the door, and even though it was the handicapped stall, it looked weird with two guys coming out of it. Some kid was washing his hands at the sink, but he didn't look at us twice. He probably smelled the weed.

"Later," Tray said over his shoulder as he ducked out the door.

I followed but turned in the other direction. And that was when I saw her.

Standing in the middle of the hall, amid all of the students rushing to class, Elin Fisher stood still among the flurry of movement. She watched me, her big blue eyes frozen on mine, and it took everything I had not to rush to her and beg her to forgive me for being so stupid.

But then I remembered what I'd done.

And Elin deserved someone far better than me.

I turned away, but not before I saw the tears streaming down her flushed cheeks, and the guilt. God, the guilt. I'd fucked everything up. Everything.

I texted Tray as I walked into my next class. I wasn't sure what his "something better" was, but if it helped me handle all of this shit . . . I punched at my phone.

I'm in.

thirteen

BECK

Come over before prom, Tray texted.

I knew why. I was nervous, I was scared, I was excited. I was all of those things, but I was going anyway.

I showered, got dressed, and went to find my mom to tie my tie.

I found her in the kitchen with Aunt Sam and the kids.

They all oohed and aahed when I walked in.

"You look beautiful," Aunt Sam breathed, and I rolled my eyes.

"Dudes don't look beautiful," I reminded her.

My mom was nervous and didn't really know how to act. She didn't seem to know where to look. I pretended that nothing had happened.

"Can you tie this?" I asked. She nodded quickly.

Reaching up, she looped the knot, and her fingers were shaking.

"You look so handsome," she told me quietly. "So much like your dad."

God, if she'd said anything but that. Those words clenched my stomach. I nodded.

"Thank you."

"I'm gonna take a picture of you two," Aunt Sammy announced. I

barely had time to turn her way before she snapped a picture of Mom
tying my tie, then another of the two of us standing together. Mom
threaded her arm behind me hesitantly, as though she wasn't sure if I
would snap at her or not.

"Perfect," my aunt declared as she examined the picture.

My mom's head snapped up. "Wait," she called over her shoulder,
rushing out of the room. Annabelle chased behind her, curious, and I
waited obediently.

She was back within a minute.

"Here." She held her hand out and dropped a pair of cuff links into
mine. "Your dad's. He'd want you to wear them."

Jesus.

I exhaled as my mother helped me with them.

"Now you're perfect," she decided. They all walked me to the door
and waved at me when I drove away. I saw them in my rearview mirror
as I turned the corner. Mom was wiping at her eyes, and I was happy
to get away from that.

From the heaviness.

From the guilt.

I drove straight to Tray's.

His mom was gone, and he was waiting for me with a baggie in his
hand.

"Dude, you won't believe what I scored," he crowed. "Take two of
these. I'll give you more later tonight. You'll forget every problem you
ever had."

He handed me two unmarked tablets. I examined them. "What are
they?"

"I told you. Painkillers. They will kill every pain you ever had." He
was so proud of himself and handed me an energy drink. "Wash them
down with this. There are parties tonight, man."

I decided not to overthink it.

I wanted to have a night where I felt normal. I tossed the pills into
my mouth and swallowed them.

"Let's go," he said, grabbing his tux jacket. "We've got women to screw and parties to drink."

I rolled my eyes and let him drive. I waited for the pills to take effect, but I didn't notice much difference. I told him that and he laughed.

"Whatever. These are for the refined palate, man. They dull your pain without you even realizing."

I stared out the window at the blurred trees and clouds, and forgot about it when we reached the first party.

I had a drink, then two. The music was loud; the chattering voices were garbled.

Time flew by, and before I knew it, I had missed the actual prom.

"Let's head over to Davis's house," Tray told me as the moonlight shone in the room. I shook my head clear. The pills had sped up time.

I went with my friend because I'd already missed prom anyway. What difference did it make at this point?

In the car, Tray offered me two more pills.

"How did you get these?" I asked curiously.

"I know a guy," Tray answered, and I wasn't sure if he'd been drinking. "He's setting me up. I'll be able to get more if you want them."

"What are they?" I asked again. "Specifically?"

Tray glanced at me at the red light.

"Heroin."

I'd already swallowed them.

"What the fuck, dude?" I grabbed a soda bottle from the floor and drank it hard, as though it would flush the drugs out of my system. Tray laughed.

"Chill out. They're oral form so they're weak, man. They'll just take the edge off. They're no worse than Percocet. Trust me, you needed it. You've been a dick lately."

I pondered that. I honestly didn't feel much different than normal. Only . . . mellower. Calmer. That couldn't be a bad thing, right? I thought back to all of the *Just say no* campaigns I'd seen over the years, and I compared the bad things I'd heard to the way I felt right now.

I felt harmless.

This couldn't be a bad thing. I'd know it, wouldn't I?

"I thought you were supposed to inject heroin," I mentioned as we got out of the car at Joel Davis's house.

He nodded. "Usually. I can get that for you if you ever want it."

He was acting like someone else, like someone I'd never seen. Since when was this Tray? Was he a dealer? Had he been guiding me down this path all along?

But I didn't care about much of anything tonight, and I followed him into the party.

fourteen

NATALIE
Mercy Hospital
7:17 a.m.

"H E THOUGHT I WAS AN ANGEL," I say to Sammy as we watch Elin and Beck through a crack in the door. "When they were loading him up in the ambulance. He thought he was dying."

"Jesus," Sam chokes before noticing my wet eyes. "He's *not* going to die, Nat," she insists.

"Okay." But she's not sure and neither am I. Every second with him is weighted, important.

"How did we end up here?" Sam asks, and her hand rests against my shoulder. She's cold and clammy, and I'm pretty sure she's in some sort of shock. "Why didn't we see it coming?"

"There were signs," I tell her, my heart like a rock. "But I always explained them away. I didn't want to believe them, you know? I was so wrapped up in my grief, in *poor me*, that I couldn't see anything else."

"You're being too hard on yourself," my sister says defensively. "You were struggling, Nat. Like anyone would've been. This is not your fault. Not at all."

I know differently, though. That will always be my cross to bear, I suppose.

"The smoking, and then prom night . . ." I ponder. "I should've known then."

Kit shakes his head from where he's leaning against the wall. "I was the one who told you not to worry on prom night," he reminds me. "That was my fault."

"Jesus, it's not your fault either," Sam snaps. "It just *is*."

The passing of blame, the talking—it's starting to eat at me, to wear what little patience I have left into a tiny nonexistent nub.

"Can you guys go get some coffee or something?" I ask them. "I want to talk to Elin alone."

My sister hesitates, but Kit immediately stands up, and for that I'm thankful. "Of course."

He guides Sam down the hall and I hesitantly push the door to my son's room open. I don't want to intrude, but time with him is precious right now and I can't miss out on any more of it.

Elin looks up at me with red eyes and a tear-streaked face. She's gripping his hand like there is no tomorrow, and I can't help but wonder if there will be.

"I'm scared, Mrs. K," she murmurs. "I'm so scared."

I cross the room and I'm numb as I hug her. Beck loves this girl, and she loves him, yet how do I tell her that her fears are founded?

I don't say anything.

I just hug her for a long time; then I let go.

I sit next to Beck on the other side of the bed.

The clock ticks on, marking the seconds before I finally speak.

"Did you suspect he was using?" I ask. "Before you guys broke up?"

She shakes her head immediately.

"No. He was hanging with Tray Jackson more and more, and I hated that because Tray's a jerk. He's funny, and he used to be a good guy, but then he changed. He's just got an edge to him now, you know? I don't trust him. I thought he just smoked weed, but apparently he's into other stuff too. I didn't know that at the time, though."

I nod because that's exactly what I figured. Beck wouldn't have let Elin know. He would've hidden it.

"On prom night . . . when he got arrested," I say hesitantly. "I feel like that was a turning point, somehow, for him. I just didn't realize it at the time. Do you know what happened?"

Elin tenses and she stares at the wall, her hand still clenching Beck's.

"Yeah. We went to the same after-party. Brody Brown wouldn't leave me alone and Beck got in his face. He'd been drinking—they both had. And Beck lost his temper. I think that's why the police were called."

"Beck broke up with you and still protected you?" That doesn't surprise me, but still. He hadn't told me.

"He still loves me, Mrs. K," she says firmly. "I know it."

"I have no doubt," I assure her. "Drugs make people do strange things. He wasn't himself."

———

SAM AND I PROPPED our legs up on the coffee table at the same exact time, collapsing into the leather couch cushions, shoulder to shoulder.

"Lord have mercy, your kids wore me out," she sighed, pushing the hair out of her face. Sam and I looked alike, with our blond hair and blue eyes, just like our mom, but without the resting bitch face.

I leaned over and wiped silver glitter off my sister's forehead. "Annabelle got to you."

She smiled. "Either that or I'm a stripper in my free time."

"Your boobs are too small," I announced, grinning.

She glared at me. "I'm wounded."

"Don't be. You'll be happy when you're sixty and your nipples aren't in your waistband."

"Well, that's a visual."

"I thought the kids were never going to sleep tonight," I groaned. "They get so wound up when you're here."

Sam chuckled. "Well, with dinner, a movie, ice cream, candy . . ."

I lifted an eyebrow. "Candy?"

Sam had the grace to look sheepish. "I might've given them candy. It's only fair, Nat. Beck's at prom. Dev and Anna-B deserved candy."

I shook my head, but I couldn't really be mad. She's such a bright spot in their lives.

"We need wine," Sam announced. "Because *we* deserve it."

"We do," I agreed. "It's in the kitchen, though. And we're in here. You're younger. You go."

Sam rolled her eyes. "Only by two years, but fine. Lazy ass."

I grinned, and she humphed off as I closed my eyes.

Sam and Vince never had kids. It was weird, since he was Italian and came from a big family, but he never wanted them and she was okay with that. She spoiled the dickens out of my kids instead.

When she reemerged from the kitchen, she was holding two giant glasses of red.

She settled back into the couch and we shared a blanket.

"I love you," I told her after a while. She gave me side-eye.

"You haven't had enough wine yet for the 'I love you' stage," she observed. I giggled.

"I know. I just thought I should tell you."

"Well, I love you too." She paused, took a sip, then another. "It's so good to see you up and about. How are you feeling?"

I glanced at her.

"You mean, how am I doing?"

She blinked. "Well, I know you're tired of people asking that . . ."

"So don't ask it," I suggested.

I thought about the long, lonely nights and the empty bed. The aloneness. Matt's razor sitting unused on the bathroom counter. But then I thought about Devin's grin over dinner, and how he stuck two straws on his front teeth to look like walrus tusks. And how Annabelle had marched right into the restaurant in her princess dress and told them in the third person that her majesty was ready to be seated.

"I'm getting there," I decided.

Sam studied me, checking for sincerity, and decided to believe me.

"Good. I'm here if you need me."

"I know."

She put her head on my shoulder. "I miss him too."

"I know."

"He used to let me tell him anything," she added. "I miss that. He was like my big brother, my confidant."

"Yeah." Everyone thought of him that way. He was the best listener.

We were quiet for a while, and before I knew it I'd finished my wine and it was midnight.

"What time is Beck going to be home?" Sam yawned, glancing at her watch.

"It's prom night, so he doesn't really have a curfew."

"That was generous," Sam said. "Remember our proms? We had to be home by midnight."

"Yeah. I wasn't going to do that to him."

"How did he take it when Elin told him she didn't want to go with him at all after he broke up with her?"

I shrugged. "Like he does everything else lately. With very little emotion. He doesn't show a reaction to anything."

"Yeah, I noticed that. Don't worry. It's his age. He'll figure out that it's okay to be responsive."

"I hope so."

Sam yawned again.

"Seriously, go home," I told her. "It's late. You're tired. I don't want you getting into an accident."

Sam's head snapped up because she knew why I worried about that.

"I can sleep over here if you want."

I shook my head. "No, there's no need for that. Seriously. Thanks for going out with us tonight, though."

She kissed my cheek. "Always a pleasure. Get some sleep, sis."

"As if."

She laughed because she knew I'd stay up until Beck dragged himself through that door. She grabbed her keys. "If you need me, call."

"I won't need to," I assured her. "Drive safe."

She nodded and left, and I cuddled into the blanket. I wouldn't go to bed, but I could rest here. The blanket was so cozy and the couch was comfortable.

I didn't mean to fall asleep. Really, I didn't.

But the warmth and the softness and blackness behind my eyelids just lulled me into it.

When my phone rang, it jolted me awake—I must've been out for a few hours.

I sat straight up, flailing about out of instinct, blindly grabbing for my phone. My heart was pounding. The phone shouldn't be ringing in the middle of the night. Not unless something was terribly wrong. My mind was fuzzy as I punched the Accept button, and I mumbled a feeble hello as I tried to wake up, as I tried to stay calm.

"Mom?"

Beck's voice was low. I was instantly awake.

"Beck, what's wrong? Are you okay?"

"I need you to come get me."

His words were solemn, slow. I rubbed at my eyes, trying to see the clock.

"It's two thirty," I pointed out. "Are you okay? Jesus, Beck. Just tell me."

"I'm okay."

I exhaled slowly, trying to still my racing heart. He's okay. He's okay.

"Where are you? I'll come right away."

"I'm in jail, Mom."

There was silence as I digested that, because I thought he would say he was with Tray or even Elin. My panicky feelings were fading as I wrapped my mind around this new thing.

Jail?

That was impossible.

"What do you mean you're in jail? Are you hurt?"

"I'm fine. But can you come?"

"Yes. What are you there for?"

"Underage drinking. I was at a party; everyone got busted for it."

Son of a bitch.

Okay. Okay. This is normal teenage behavior. Kids do this. It's okay. He's not hurt.

After I took another breath, I answered. "I'll be there right away."

"Thanks, Mom. I'm at the station on LaSalle."

"Wait—Beck?"

"Yeah?"

"You weren't driving drunk, were you?"

"Of course not."

He hung up, and my son was in jail, and I was stunned, but I stumbled to my feet.

I crept upstairs and into Devin's room. Even though he was twelve, I didn't leave him alone often because of Chicago's crime rates and I was paranoid now. But it was necessary tonight.

"Dev," I whispered, shaking his shoulder lightly. He stirred immediately.

"Yeah?"

"I've got to go pick up your brother." I didn't mention from where. "I'm locking the door and turning the alarm on. You'll be here alone for just a little while."

"Okay," he mumbled. "No problem."

I knew he was asleep again by the time I reached the bottom of the stairs.

Chicago was strikingly quiet at two thirty in the morning. Not as quiet as the country, because I could still hear a little traffic in the distance, but still eerie. The sky was dark, and there were barely even any stars.

I climbed into my car and pushed the button and . . . nothing.

I tried again.

Absolutely nothing. Not even a click.

"What the fuck?"

My car was dead and I didn't know why and I had to get to the police station.

Out of habit, I started to call Sam, but she wouldn't be able to help with my car and I didn't want to upset her anyway. So I did the only other thing I could think of.

I called Kit.

He answered on the second ring, his voice gravelly from sleep.

"Nat?"

"Kit, I'm so sorry. I know it's late but Beck just called. He was arrested, and my car won't start."

"I told you not to get a Land Rover," was the first thing out of his mouth.

"Kit."

"I'll go get him," he replied. "You stay at home with the kids. I'll bring him home."

"I can't ask you to do that," I protested. "It's the police department, Kit. It's . . . humiliating. I don't know what happened. He was drinking and . . ."

"Don't worry. I'll bring him home."

I tried to argue one last time, but he shut it down.

"Natalie, it's not a problem. I'll be there shortly."

"He's at the one on LaSalle."

"Don't worry."

He hung up and I was still stunned as I headed back inside and sank into the couch. My legs were jelly. My mind was racing and of course I was worrying. I was a ball of worry, actually, tightly wound.

Adrenaline spiked through my blood because my son was in jail and the phone woke me at two thirty in the morning.

The last time this happened . . . it was . . . the impossible had happened.

But that's not tonight, I reminded myself. Beck was fine. He was fine. He was fine.

Even still, I took a Xanax and paced the floor for the next hour and forty-five minutes as I waited for him to come home. I counted my steps on the Oriental rug. I was a gatekeeper in the quiet room as I waited. Every step made me agitated. How could Beck do this? He had to know what a call like that in the middle of the night would do to me.

It was so thoughtless.

So inconsiderate.

By the time the door creaked open, my fear had completely been replaced with anger. I was pissed at my son for putting me in this position, for scaring me. As soon as my son's mussed-up head poked into the room and I had made sure he was safe, I pounced.

"What the hell, Beck?" I hissed instantly. "What in the hell were you thinking?"

This was the appropriate response to underage drinking. This is what a good parent did. He didn't have to know that I was beyond relieved that he was okay, that the driving force behind my rage was actually relief, that all I really wanted to do was gather him close and smother him in a bear hug.

Kit stood behind him, tall and quiet. Beck was rumpled and his eyes were bloodshot and he was apologizing and his big hands were curled at his sides.

"I'm sorry, Mom. I'm really sorry. There was a party and . . ." I looked down and noticed he was missing a cuff link. I grabbed his hand.

"Do you know where it is?" I asked quickly, because it was Matt's.

Beck looked surprised, then stricken. "No."

"Just go upstairs," I told him icily, dropping his arm. He'd lost a piece of Matt and I'd never be able to get it back. "I thought something had happened to you. When that phone rang and it was the middle of the night, I thought . . . thought . . ."

His eyes glint because he knew what I thought.

"I'm sorry," he mumbled. "I really am."

I watched him trudge up the stairs, and he glanced at me as he turned the corner, his dark eyes soulful. I didn't blink. I didn't soften. He needed to know this wasn't okay so that he would never do it again.

My son looked away and disappeared, and I turned to Kit.

"Thank you," I told him, my anger and worry draining out of me almost instantly. None of this is his fault. "I'm so embarrassed. I don't know what he was thinking."

Kit chuckled tiredly. "He *wasn't* thinking. That's what most teenagers do, from what I've heard. It was prom night, Nat. Kids go nuts. Lord knows, you, me, and Matt did. Let him sleep it off and then lecture him in the morning. Don't worry. He's fine."

I blinked and my eyes were hot.

"Yeah. Until I kill him tomorrow."

Kit chuckled again. "Valid. And it *is* tomorrow."

"You want some coffee?" It was four fifteen, and I doubted either of us would go back to sleep at this point. It was Saturday, though, so thank God we didn't have to work today.

"I'd love some."

He followed me to the kitchen, and I bustled about brewing the coffee as he sat at the table. When I turned back around, he was tracing a deep scratch with his finger.

"Remember when I did this?" he asked, looking up at me. His eyes were very blue. I nodded.

"God, I was pissed at you two."

Kit laughed and looked into the distance, remembering. "You were waiting up on us. You guys hadn't been married long, and we were out playing poker."

"You didn't call," I told him. "And when you came stumbling in at three in the morning, you literally passed out facedown on the table."

"I still don't know how my belt buckle scratched it," he said wryly. "If we hadn't been so young and poor, I would've bought you a new one."

I shook my head. "It's okay. It gave it character."

"That's not what you thought at the time," he remembered, and I laughed.

"No, I was having murderous thoughts that night."

"But Matt never stayed out that late again, especially without calling," Kit told me. "So, lesson learned."

"I guess."

The coffee maker beeped and I got us both a full cup. As I handed Kit's to him, his hand paused on mine. His fingers were rough from hard work.

"Thank you," he told me softly, and I knew he was talking about more than coffee.

"For?"

"For sharing your husband with me for so long. He was the best friend a man could have."

A pang went through my heart because I'd been so focused on myself that I'd forgotten how Kit must have been feeling.

"Are you doing okay?" I asked, sitting down across from him.

He nodded. "Yeah. It's been tough, to be honest. But you know how that is."

"You were a good friend to him, Kit. The best."

"I'm still yours, you know," he reminded me. "I lost him, Nat. But I haven't lost you. You're still here."

"I know I've been checked out, and I'm sorry. But I'm coming back to life now."

Kit drank his coffee and his hand was so large around the ceramic handle.

"Don't be too mad at Beck," he said finally. "He was blowing off some steam. It was prom night. It's nor—"

I interrupted. "I realize it's a normal thing to do. He just scared me."

"Of course he did," Kit answered, his voice soft. "But every phone call isn't going to be catastrophic, Nat."

I nodded. "Tell my heart that. It seems to be the first conclusion it jumps to."

"That's understandable," he answered. "Anyone would be the same."

"Thank you for going to get him," I said, and my voice sounded small. "I'm sorry for calling you so late. I just didn't know what else to do."

"You can call me any time, day or night." His answer was firm. "Always."

I smiled and he smiled back, and it felt good to know that I wasn't alone. I still had people in my life who knew me, who had known me for a long time. It was a good feeling.

We drank the rest of our coffee in silence, comfortable in the quiet that comes from two souls familiar with each other. After he finished with his, he got up and put his cup in the sink.

"I'm going to come over later today," he told me. "And I'm going to clean out your gutters. Don't argue."

I was scared of heights and he knew it.

I smiled. "Thank you."

"You're welcome. It won't come free. I expect a home-cooked meal as payment."

"Definitely. Don't be surprised if Annabelle makes you wear a tiara, though."

"That's fine. I look awesome in rhinestones."

I laughed and he left, and I realized with a start that that was the first time I'd been truly amused in a long, long time.

It almost felt like a traitorous act, as though I were betraying my husband's memory by smiling. I shouldn't feel anything good, should I? Matt was gone, and he could never laugh again. Maybe I shouldn't either.

My brain knew this logic was flawed, but my heart seldom listened to my brain anyway.

I put it all out of my mind as I loaded the dishwasher and prepared to meet the day.

I had a lecture to give, and a dinner to prepare, apparently.

Just another day in Casa Kingsley while we learned to deal with our new normal.

fifteen

T HE DOOR OPENS AND CLOSES—I CAN HEAR IT. IT HAS A
significant click when it latches.

"Nat," Kit says, greeting my mom. I'm annoyed with him, but I
don't remember why. It's frustrating, but I'm learning to deal with that.
If I'm patient enough, it might come back to me.

"Kit. You don't have to wait here."

"That's ridiculous," he tells her. "Where else would I be?"

He has a good point.

They sit in silence for a while, until Kit speaks again. "Natalie, I'm
sorry. For what happened. I feel terrible. If I hadn't been there that day,
maybe Beck wouldn't have left. It was my fault."

"Oh please, Kit. It was not. He was mad at the world, but mostly
me. I failed him. I let him shoulder the burden around the house while
I grieved, and that wasn't fair. It's *my* fault."

So I left home and it was everyone else's fault? Somehow that
doesn't seem right.

I remembered slipping, and floating, and feeling like I was falling
apart.

Oddly enough, I don't remember what pushed me over the edge. It's a black hole in my jagged memory. But I do recall what happened after I left.

————

I WAS DRIVING.

The heroin pumped pumped pumped through my blood now and it tamed the wild fury that boiled just beneath the surface. A minute ago my heart felt like a bird flapping its wings against my ribs, trying to get out.

But now my heart had slowed.

The heroin lulled me into a warm place, a safe place, and I wanted to close my eyes, but I couldn't because I was driving.

I liked this feeling.

For the first time in a year, it felt like everything might be okay.

How had I lived for the past year without this?

This is for me.

After I'd woven in and out of traffic and driven across town, I pulled over onto a dark side road and just sat, sprawled in my seat, and stared at the clouds and skyscrapers.

The clouds moved in artistic ways, in ways man never could. They bent and melded and morphed, and I wished I were among them. I'd float away and never come back.

That was the dream.

Did everyone have it?

I didn't know how long I sat pondering that.

I only knew that I'd drifted off, in and out of a warm haze. My fingers were relaxed, my legs were liquid, and my lungs filled with soft air. It came and went in velvet breaths, puffing from a dragon's nose, and I'd never felt so fucking good.

I lifted my hand and stared at it because it felt so weightless. I needed to make sure it still existed, that I was still here.

I was.

I traced the outline of my fingers and they were there and I was real.

I rested my hands on my legs, and the feel of the denim beneath my skin felt like heaven, so textured, so striated, so perfect. I stroked at it, and it was soothing.

At some point, though, my phone buzzed on the seat next to me, disrupting my serenity. I scowled at it, at that vestige of reality, but it persisted, buzzing again and again.

It used to be that when it called, I answered. I was glued to it, a prisoner. It was my master, and I was its slave. But now . . . now . . . things were going to be different.

By ignoring it, I felt like I was snipping a leash that used to keep me tied to the earth, tied to pain. It was an iron chain, and it was attached to an anchor and the anchor was me. But the thing about being an anchor, the thing that people forget, is that if you're an anchor, you drown.

I was not going to drown.

I was not an anchor anymore.

Fuck anyone who thought otherwise.

I drifted away and imagined that I was on a raft in a dark, dark sea. I shoved away from shore, and I was floating and then gone, lost in the middle of the calm, my fingers dangling in the water.

I didn't know how long I floated.

When I finally decided to sit up, it was dark.

I'd been there awhile.

A long while. I'd been parked in the same place for too long, because there was a two-hour parking sign right in front of me, glinting in the dim streetlight. I had to move, even though rules felt so far away, distant things that applied to other people but not to me.

I started my engine and pulled farther down onto the side street to park again. I thought perhaps I'd just sleep there. I was soft and warm and this was as good a place as any.

First, though, I looked at my phone because I *chose* to, not because I *had* to.

My mother had called four times and sent seven texts.

Where are you?

Beck!

Beckitt!

Answer your phone!

Please come back.

I'm sorry.

I love you.

If I weren't high, I'd be annoyed, but honestly, I could barely remember what I'd been angry about in the first place. It seemed like a faraway land, a distant time.

Elin's texts were next.

Beck, we're worried. Your mom thought you were here, but I don't know where you are.

Please, babe. Call me.

I know you love me. I know you do. Call me.

You love me, I love you. That's the way things are. Call me. Please.

That was the way things *were*. Nothing would ever be the same again. I let my phone fall out of my hand, onto the seat.

I curled up, one hand beneath my cheek, and slept.

When I woke, it was light again.

And there was a guy sitting next to me.

I startled because the heroin had worked out of my system and I'd turned jumpy.

The guy had a longish beard tied with silver beads at the bottom, and he looked at me as though being in my car were the most natural thing in the world.

"Hey," he said in greeting. "Welcome to the neighborhood."

I nodded. "Uh, thanks."

"Of course," he said, smiling. "Want me to show you around?"

I started to shake my head, to politely decline, because something told me not to, that he wasn't the kind of person I should be around. But he held up my empty baggie between two fingers.

"You're my people," he said simply, and somehow, somehow, that changed everything.

Because I knew right then and there that I wanted another hit.

I wanted to feel what I felt last night . . . a warm nothing.

So I found myself nodding.

"Sure," I said.

He smiled. "Come on," he said, and he opened the car door. "I'll show you."

I followed him down the alley, over broken bottles and trash littering the pavement.

He paused outside of a broken-down building.

"You have money? If not, I can take you to an ATM."

I thought on that. I had three hundred dollars in my wallet. "I'm good," I told him.

He nodded and opened the door and gestured me inside.

I stepped over the threshold into another world.

In that moment, I thought . . . *Things are gonna change now.*

People sat in the dingy building, on boxes, on broken chairs, on the floor. Some were talking, some had the vacant and empty expression of the truly high, and I even saw a pair of people having sex in the back corner. Two men, actually. One young and one old. My head snapped back because I wasn't expecting that.

The boy, who was maybe my age, stared at me with wide-open eyes as the guy behind him had his way, and the boy's expression didn't change. He wasn't into it, but he wasn't *not* into it. He was just . . . there. Enduring it? I didn't know.

"Welcome to the neighborhood," the guy said again, pulling my attention back, and he was amused at my expression. "I'm Dan."

"Nice to meet you." I didn't give him my name, and I still felt the boy watching me, the boy who was getting ass-fucked in the corner. His gaze was on my skin and I felt dirty with it.

"Come here," Dan said, gesturing, and I followed, mainly to get away from the boy's stare. I didn't know why I was there in the first place, other than the fact that I had a driving need to disappear.

That was a startling thought.

I wanted to disappear.

I wanted to be nothing.

Dan led me to another guy in another corner, a guy with a black duffel bag.

"What's your fancy?" he asked, and he was deadly calm and casual. His index finger had a ring on it, a plain silver band, his hand resting on the top of his bag. I assumed the bag contained his precious cargo.

I didn't want to say what I wanted out loud.

I paused.

"Well?" the guy asked. "I can't read your mind, friend."

That's when I reminded myself . . . They're all into this. Not just me. I was one of them now, and they wouldn't judge me.

"Uh. Heroin," I muttered, fast and jumbled. "The pill kind." The guy rolled his eyes.

"I don't carry that pussy-ass crap. I got the real shit, though."

I stared at him. "Okay. I'll take that."

"How much, newbie?"

That, I didn't know.

I didn't know the going rate and I didn't know what to ask for.

I pulled out a hundred dollars.

"This much."

He nodded and dug in his bag and pulled out a baggie with tiny rocks inside. "You need a rig?"

"I, uh. Yeah, I guess."

He dug around again and handed me a shiny spoon, a lighter, and a needle sealed in a medical wrapper.

My heart pounded as I took it, and he said, "That'll be an extra ten bucks."

Of course it was. I handed him the money, but I only had a twenty.

"Sorry, I don't have change," he said, shrugging.

Right. I didn't challenge him. He was surrounded by his people here, and I was alone. I knew they'd accept me, but only if I played by their rules.

I backed off, away into the room. There were hallways and other rooms, not one of them empty and not one of them with an electric light. There were battery-powered camping lanterns scattered here and there, casting LED light over the dirt.

There were people everywhere and they weren't the kind you would take home to Mom. Most were dirty, although some weren't. They all had the same expression in their eyes, a hardened, jaded expression. They knew what was up. I could tell that. They were like a family. A new family. It was a comforting thought, actually.

I was alone, but not really.

I found a dark corner in a back room because I felt self-conscious.

I was new, and if they watched me shooting up, they'd know. It was a dumb thing to worry about.

I examined the rocks in the bag. It seemed to me that I should've gotten more for a hundred dollars, but there was no way for me to know for sure. So I didn't say anything. I put one in the spoon, heated it up, and then drew the amber liquid into the needle.

I looked at my arm.

I could see the veins on the inside of my elbow, branching out like a tree with small purple limbs and no leaves. I wasn't quite sure how to do it.

I held my mouth firm and positioned the needle above the biggest purple branch.

Without giving myself time for second thoughts, I pushed it in.

I didn't hit a vein.

I pulled it out, repositioned, and tried again.

Again, I missed.

"Dude, you're doing it wrong," a guy said next to me—he'd come from nowhere. "Here."

He helped me insert the needle at an angle, and I pushed the plunger in.

Lord God Almighty, I felt it immediately as it slid into my vein, fucking bliss. I released the plunger and it stung it stung it stung, even as it was warm and soothing. It was that blessed place between wake and sleep, that nameless place where you hover and are weightless.

That was heroin.

My vision blurred and my head dropped back and I thought I saw the guy smile.

"You got some for me?"

I pulled out my baggie and offered it without opening my eyes. He took it and I allowed the warmth to swirl around me, and the warmth felt like it had a color.

It was orange.

Everything was orange.

"Don't hit the same vein twice in a row," the guy told me through the orange haze, and everything smelled yellow. "And don't let anyone use your needle."

I nodded, but I couldn't open my eyes at this point. My eyelids were too heavy, and I didn't want to.

Reality was too heavy now and I laid it down. It had no place here among the orange weightlessness.

I put it away and it ran and hid and I hoped it never found me again.

sixteen

NATALIE
MERCY HOSPITAL
8:31 A.M.

THE MACHINES BEEP AND BEEP, BUT I DON'T TRUST THEM. I don't trust that they'll keep Beck alive, because every once in a while, they stumble. The beeps become erratic, and his cheeks get flushed. His forehead is clammy, and even though he looks peaceful on the outside, I know there's a storm raging on the inside.

There has to be.

He has to be fighting in there. If I don't believe that, I'll fall apart.

"You're stronger than you think, Nat," Kit tells me, and I hear him from a distant fog. I'd been so focused on thinking about Beck's struggle that I forgot Kit was even here.

"I'm not," I tell him without looking up. "Trust me."

"I know you," he reminds me. "And after everything that has happened, you're still standing."

"Barely."

"Nat . . ."

"No. You know I fell apart. You know Beck held everything together. If I'd been better, he might not be here right now."

"I don't think that would've mattered," Kit finally answers. "He had many other things that were tormenting him, Natalie. You know that."

I want to blame myself. I *need* to blame myself. Because if something is my fault, then maybe I can fix it.

"A few days before he left . . ." My voice wavers, and then I try again. "We had a huge fight. The most terrible things were said. I got sucked down into the depression again that day, and I was curled up into a ball, and . . . It was bad. So, see? It wasn't just you that last day. It was a lot of things."

Kit tries to say something, but it doesn't matter what he says. I know the truth.

I know I drove my son away.

———

I HADN'T FELT LIKE eating in two days.

I didn't know why the grief came in waves. For days, I was able to cope, then suddenly, BOOM. It was back and it was debilitating.

Today, I had managed to get the kids off to school before I'd crashed onto my bed. I'd sprayed Matt's cologne onto his pillow, and I'd hugged it to me until I'd fallen asleep.

That was how Beck found me hours later.

I woke to find him standing in the doorway, his eyes red, his face tired.

"Mom, you've got to get up."

He was firm, tired, angry.

I rubbed at my eyes, glancing blearily toward the clock.

"Can you just . . . can you wait at the bus stop for the kids? It's not that big of a deal, Beck."

He glared. "It is a big deal, Mom. You need to stand outside for them. You need to put clothes on and comb your hair and act like a goddamned adult."

My head snapped back.

"Don't swear at me," I told him quickly. "Use some respect."

"Then earn it," he snapped. "This is getting ridiculous. I've been patient. You told me you'd be better. And here we go again. You're in bed *again*. I can't do this again, Mom. I can't!"

I stood up and pulled a robe on. My hair was mussed, and I knew he was right. But the tone he was taking infuriated me. This wasn't the kind of son I'd raised him to be.

"I don't expect you to understand," I told him tiredly. "But I'm your mother, and I'd like for you to respect that at the very least."

"Then give me something to respect," he retorted. "Please, I'm begging you."

But he wasn't begging—he was screaming.

The anger came raging out, and I raged back.

"Do you think I asked for this?" I screeched, and he was startled. "Do you think I asked to be left alone with three kids? Do you think I wanted this?"

"All you've wanted is to sleep all day, every day," my son answered. "You've left me to do everything in this house, to sign permission slips and pay bills and take care of the kids. Your kids. You checked out and it wasn't fair, and I hate you for it!"

I saw red, and words tumbled out before I could stop them.

"Do you think I don't hate you too, sometimes?" I demanded. "If it hadn't been for your stupid college visit, your dad would never have been in the car that night. He'd still be alive."

As soon as the words were out and I saw the look on Beck's face, I wanted to take it back.

"I'm sorry," I fumbled, reaching for him. "I didn't mean that. It wasn't your fault, Beck."

He wrenched away from me, heading toward the door.

"Wasn't it?" He paused, turning to me. "I know it was my fault. And now I know that you feel that way too."

He turned to leave, but paused.

"Do you know what today is, Mom?"

I stared at him blankly. I never knew the date anymore.

"It's October 12. The one-year anniversary of the accident. It kills me what happened. It kills me that it's *killing you*. I know it's all my fault. That's why I understood when you didn't get out of bed for my graduation. That's why I tried to understand that you needed me, so I haven't complained that I can't go to college yet."

I started to protest, but Beck's face twisted in anger.

"I can't leave," he practically spits. "You can't even comb your fucking hair. I have to stay here to babysit you, and to make sure the kids are okay. My life is slipping away, and while it's mostly my fault, maybe you should realize that there's a part of it, a part that's growing bigger and bigger, that's your fault too."

I was stunned, and silent, and he left, his tires squealing as he drove away.

I'd never hated myself more than I did in that moment.

seventeen

BECK
MERCY HOSPITAL
8:37 A.M.

"MA'AM," A NURSE SAYS, COMING IN AND SPEAKING TO MY mother. "We'd like to empty your son's catheter and check some of his reflexes. Would you like to use this as a chance to get some fresh air or coffee?"

Even I can tell she is politely asking my family to leave the room. They apparently do, because in a moment, I'm alone with what I can only assume are two nurses. I have hands on me from both sides of the bed.

I am poked and pulled, and my eyelids are pried open, a light shining into my eyes. Then darkness again.

"What's his story, Jessica?" one of them asks the other.

"God, it's tragic," Jessica answers, her voice hushed. "His dad died a year or so ago. I was here. He and his dad were in a terrible car crash—it's amazing this kid lived. But he did, and then apparently he started using drugs after."

"That's awful," the other one clucks as she picks up my elbow, her hands cool.

"He comes from a good family," Jessica continues. "His mother is as sweet as pie. His dad was some important attorney. It just goes to show this crap can happen to anyone. I don't know what she's gonna do when she loses her son."

The other nurse agrees. "Yeah. I doubt he's gonna make it. The stroke, his injuries . . ."

"Maybe it's for the best," Jessica decides, her voice right next to my ear. "He's an addict. It's going to be a struggle for him to survive even if he does live through the day. He might be permanently damaged, even. It'll be hard on him, hard on the family. They've all been through enough."

"That's a terrible thing to say, Jessica," the other one says, and I agree.

"Hey, I just call it like I see it. I've seen a thousand other kids like this one, and this family doesn't deserve it."

"Does any family?" the second nurse asks, and she sounds indignant. Good for her.

"No, I guess not," Jessica answers. "I'm just tired. I feel sorry for the mom. Don't pay attention to me." She laughs tiredly, but her words weren't a joke. They stung.

"I would imagine the mom wants her son to live no matter what," the other one replies, her voice dry. Jessica falls silent, and they push and pull me some more.

When they are ready to leave and I'm waiting on my family to come back in, I think on the conversation.

It can happen to anyone, but this time . . . this time it happened to me, and I have a horrible, heavy pit of guilt in my chest whenever I think on it.

I'm to blame. I don't deserve to live. I don't deserve to live when my father died.

Jessica is right. Everyone has been through enough already.

———

I'D BEEN DREAMING.

About the twisted red wreckage of my father's car.

When I came to that night, I'd been hanging upside down by the seat belt. The OnStar had been talking to me. *Don't worry—help is on the way.*

I'd pushed the release button and fallen onto the roof of the car. I'd pulled myself through the broken window, and I was alone.

My father was nowhere to be found, and the car. It was mangled past the point of recognition. All I could see in the dim reflection of the streetlights were flashes of red paint twisted among the metal.

But I wasn't there now. I was here.

The abandoned building shimmered with the wintry sun and I thought for a minute as I sat up.

How did I get here?

My thoughts were mushy, but I found them.

I'd spent a long time in the first building. Maybe a couple of weeks. I'd gone through my money, and I'd traded my car for more H.

H was what my new friends call heroin. I'd picked up some lingo, tricks of the trade.

Then I'd left.

The first building had hardened me, educated me. I saw what was what, and what people do. The boy in the corner? He regularly had sex with older men for drugs. He didn't have any money because he never needed it. He pimped himself out.

I stood up, and dizziness swirled around me from lack of food and from coming down from my last high. I was low now, in a pit. I crunched across the trash in the building and emerged into the cold air, sucking it in like a drowning person.

There was a cigarette butt in the street and I knelt to examine it. Even though it was tattered and dirty, there were a couple of puffs left on the thing. Someone might've even run over it, but I wasn't choosy.

"Dude," I called to a stranger passing on the sidewalk. He was young with his ball cap on backward. "You got a light?"

The guy paused, examined me, his eyes flicking up and down, and

I saw the questions in them. Was I safe? Was I an addict? Was I going to rob him?

Yes, yes, and probably not. I was too fucking tired.

The guy dug in his pocket and tossed me his lighter.

"Keep it," he said curtly and continued on his way. It was a red plastic Bic, half-full. That was good, because I had somehow lost my other one.

I lit the butt and stuck my new treasure into my jeans pocket, next to the piece of hot dog bun I'd found this morning. I wasn't hungry now, and I wouldn't be later, but I knew I had to eat. If I didn't, I'd die. I was probably already on that path; I didn't need to rush it along.

A bell ringer collecting money for Christmas stood in the doorway of a nearby store and watched me with a pinched mouth. Behind her, I saw my reflection in the window, illuminated by the streetlights, and I knew why she was suspicious.

God, I was getting skinny. I looked like hell because I hadn't had a haircut or a real shower in weeks, and I was tall. So even though I was skinny, I was big from sheer height. I guessed I was intimidating, particularly since I had deep circles under my eyes. You couldn't even tell what color my eyes were. They just looked dark and hollow.

It was fitting, because that's how I felt.

Digging in my other pocket, I pulled out every bit of money that I had to my name.

One nickel and three pennies.

I dropped the eight cents into the woman's red bucket and I swear to God she flinched.

"Uh, thanks?" she said, and she was sort of snotty.

I guessed to some, eight cents wasn't much. In fact, once upon a time, it wasn't much to me either. I used to actually vacuum pennies off of the floor of my car because I was too lazy to pick them up.

A lot of things annoyed me then.

Long football practices, giggling cheerleaders, gossip, calculus, college applications, my mom nagging me to clean my room, my little brother hogging the shower.

All of those things didn't matter anymore.

Real life arrived with a vengeance, and a year had passed, aging me ten years in the process. I was eighteen and while I looked twenty-eight, I felt a hundred and eight.

I looked into the window and studied my eyes. They might have looked black, but they weren't.

They were moss green.

No one noticed that anymore, though. What they noticed now was what the uppity woman noticed . . . what everyone noticed. I heard her whisper "junkie" to someone next to her and they both stared at me.

It was a stage whisper, meant for me to hear. I didn't know if it was meant to shame me, or humiliate me, or what.

The joke was on her—I didn't feel anything at all.

Heroin took my feelings weeks ago. It absorbed everything in my life and became everything and took everything.

My conscience.

My emotions.

My heart.

My wit.

My drive.

They were all tucked in heroin's handbag now, and it happened so fast and I didn't know if she'd ever give them back. I said *she* because I'd decided heroin was a woman. She had to be. I didn't know if a man would be able to plan such a multifaceted attack. Men weren't good multitaskers, and men simply weren't so vicious.

Pausing, I stared up at the black sky. The stars were hard to see here in the city because the Chicago smog masked everything. The city light swirled upward, ran together, and faded into the clouds. It bent and swayed, and was it real?

I thought so.

I rambled around the streets, walking in and out of traffic. I didn't hurry, and people honked and swerved but I didn't care. Their headlights turned into stars and the stars turned into streetlights, and I didn't even know if the bench I eventually sat on was real.

I sprawled on it and the wood was cold beneath my ass, so I was pretty sure it existed.

Someone sat on the other end, and I couldn't tell if it was a man or a woman because it was dark and my vision was cloudy from heroin.

"You been here long?" I asked the shape. It nodded.

"All night."

"You gonna rob me?" I asked it. "If so, you're outta luck. I don't have anything."

"No worries," it told me, and I still couldn't tell if it was a man or woman. I guessed it didn't matter. "I'm just resting, man."

"Me too."

I closed my eyes, and the honks and traffic noises blended into silence and black.

"I'll watch out for you while you sleep," the voice told me, and I didn't know if I could trust it, but honestly nothing even mattered at this point. The heroin had dulled every waking thought I had, every nerve ending, every emotion.

This was where I loved to be, in the abyss, and if something happened to me in reality while I was gone, then so be it.

Nothing mattered.

I drifted into sleep, into unconsciousness, into the dark, dark ravine, and when I woke, I thought maybe days had passed.

The reason I knew that was because my back hurt from the bench, from the wood.

There was a small tree at the other end, and I decided that the person I was talking to was never real.

It was the tree all along.

Go figure.

eighteen

NATALIE
MERCY HOSPITAL
8:47 A.M.

I POKE AROUND IN THE WHITE PLASTIC HOSPITAL BAG THAT holds Beck's possessions.

"That's the stuff he had in his pockets," the nurse tells me while her fingers rest on Beck's radial pulse.

I nod.

There's the marble that Devin gave Beck long ago, two quarters, a gunky penny, and his driver's license.

How could an entire life be reduced to this?

"I tried so hard to find him," I whisper, and I'm not talking to Elin or Sam or Kit. I'm talking to myself. "He didn't want to be found."

"We know." Sam soothes me, her arm wrapping around my shoulder. "We know, hon."

"It wasn't enough," I tell her. "There isn't anything that parents can do. Once their kid is past eighteen. Calling the police doesn't help. If the kid left home willingly, the police won't look. It's a broken system."

Elin looks away, and Sam nods. "It is," she agrees.

"Normal people . . . we just aren't equipped to know what to do.

Everyone thinks they can do it better, but trust me, if you're in this position, you don't know what to do. You don't have a right answer."

"*Is* there a right answer?" Sam asks, looking sadly down at my son. I have to shake my head. "I don't think so."

———

"MA'AM," THE VOICE ON the other end of the phone explained patiently, "I've told you. We can't send anyone out to look for him. He's not a runaway. He's of legal age."

"But he's on drugs. He's a danger to himself," I argued. "I can't find him. If I can't call the police to help, who can I call?"

I'm frustrated, the helplessness closing in.

"We suggest that you call all of his friends," the voice said helpfully. But it wasn't helpful. Of course I'd already done that. Many times over. "If he gets picked up, you'll be called."

"Thanks." I hung up. This wasn't getting me anywhere.

I walked up to his room and sat on the bed.

It was exactly as he'd left it, like a tornado had hit it. Football gear on the floor by the closet, notebooks scattered. I opened his nightstand. Big mistake. A big box of condoms was in there, and I closed the drawer quickly.

"Where are you?" I whispered. "Please come home."

I texted him yet again, and I scrolled up through the thread. It was completely one-sided as far back as fifty messages. I'd asked him and asked him where he was and to come home.

He hadn't answered.

I dialed his number and it rang twice. I wasn't expecting him to pick up, but he did.

My heart leapt.

"Hullo," he said woodenly, his voice slurred.

"Honey? Where are you?" I asked. "I'm sorry about what happened. Please let me come get you. We'll sort everything out."

He laughed and it was a scary, mirthless sound.

"That's ridiculous," he slurred. "You've gotta stop calling me, Mom. I'm where I belong."

"But where is that?" I demanded. "Beck, you're scaring me. Please."

"Love you."

There was a bunch of muffled noises, and then the phone went dead.

"Beck? *Beck?*"

But he was gone, and there wasn't a thing I could do about it.

nineteen

BECK

M Y EYEBALLS FELT LIKE THEY WERE GOING TO EXPLODE right out of my head from the pressure, because they weren't used to being sober, and my hands weren't either. They shook hard enough to vibrate the leg of my jeans.

Whrrrrr. Whrrrrr. If vibration could make noise, that's what it would sound like. *Whrrrrr.* But wait. It *was* making noise.

I was sober, so I knew it was real.

I was sober, but I wished I weren't.

To that end, I waited beneath the bridge while the L clattered above me, the old train cars bouncing along the track, click, click, clack. I waited quietly and impatiently, a crumpled ten-dollar bill in my hand.

I'd stolen it this morning, lifted it right out of a lady's wallet at the grocery store.

Women were bad about wandering down the aisle to look at products, leaving their purses unattended. This was something I'd learned in the crack house, tricks of the trade. I didn't want to steal, but my mistress was demanding, and I had to had to had to have a hit.

My time came when a hooded man strolled up. He went by the name

Weezer, and I'd dealt with him before. Sometimes he gave me credit, sometimes he didn't, but the further I'd fallen down this hole, the more my credit with him was denied. He was a master at addicting people.

"What do you have?" he asked me in a throaty rasp.

"Ten."

"Good." He slipped me a little plastic bag and I handed him the cash. I could've used the cash for a meal, but I didn't want to eat. I didn't need to eat. What I needed what I needed was the bag. Give it to me give it to me.

I practically ran to the nearest dark alley and pulled my spoon out of my pocket. It was bent and blackened now, but it worked. I held the lighter beneath the belly of the tarnished metal, lighting it up, heating what I needed.

I needed it.

I needed it.

My hand shook and I could hardly wait, but I did I did I did. My veins pulsed and waited and pulsed, and they were caving in, waiting waiting waiting.

When it was liquid, I took the syringe out of my pocket and slid the barrel back, drawing the thick oblivion in, farther, farther, until it was full.

I injected it between my toes, where it wouldn't show, not that it mattered anymore. It was just a habit, and the twinge of pain felt so good so good so good, a blessed relief. I could feel the warmth spreading through my foot, through my leg, pulsing up toward my heart, clearing my head, then clouding it.

Thank God.

Thank God.

Thank God.

My vision blurred and bent and contorted, and I was back where I belonged. I was where reality wasn't real, and the things I saw might have been pretend. That was fine, because real things were hard. So hard, too hard.

I felt limp and soft, and my legs didn't want to hold me up, so I lay down, right in the alleyway, slumped against a dirty brick wall. I curled onto my side, my hand against my face, and I stared at my fingers.

They were dirty, they were smudged, they needed a shower and smelled slightly of sex that I didn't remember having. My eyelids slid slowly lower, and I saw my knuckle, then a sliver of my fingernail, then blackness.

It was where I liked to be.

Nothing could reach me here.

Behind the darkness my eyes moved. I saw things, things I couldn't turn off, even though my eyes were closed. Images, faces, shapes. The thing with being high was that the emotion usually attached to those things was gone. My heart was cleared of worry, of pain, of fear. It was a blessing.

Because the things I saw were awful.

The fear.

The blood.

The shriek of tires and the screech of metal.

The headlights in my face, the long honk of a horn, the wail of a siren, the red and blue flashing lights, like beacons in a shattered night.

It came back to me every night, high or not, but when I was high, it was bearable.

When I was high, I could deal with it.

No one understood me. No one could. I was alone.

My thoughts faded, and my legs became numb. I thought I felt my cell phone vibrating, and I was startled for a minute because I thought it was turned off, but that thought must not have been real. It was ringing now, and I thought about not answering it, but suddenly I was so lonely.

I moved my tongue as I pushed the button. It felt like a lump of wood, hard and restraining, but it did the job.

"Hullo?"

My voice didn't even sound like me anymore. But I was on the nod now, in a place of relaxed wakefulness, in a place where I was floating through the air, and the air was black, and I was breathing breathing breathing it in. I had time before I passed out.

"Honey?"

The voice sounded like a bell, clear and melodious, and I focused on it. It was my mother. "Where are you? Tell me, and I'll come get you. You need help. I'll help you."

"I can't," I murmured. "I can't."

She cried and I could hear it, and I didn't feel bad, because that was a benefit of H. It carried that burden for me.

"Don't go anywhere," she told me. "Stay put."

I knew she was going to track my phone, so I had to turn it off and run.

"Love you," I muttered, and I powered it off. I heard her cry out for me before I ended the call, but I couldn't focus on that. I had to run. I couldn't let her take me. She'd put me in rehab, and then reality would be mine, and everything that had happened would surround me day in and day out, and I couldn't do it.

I couldn't.

I tried that, and I failed, and I don't want to go there again. This was better. This was my road. I'd chosen it and it was mine. *I owned it.*

My feet pounded on the pavement as I put distance between that alley and me.

My legs wobbled and wavered and protested, but they carried me, as good legs should.

I collapsed somewhere far away, in a park, I thought. I was at the top of a twisty slide, a tornado. It was metal, and it was red and blue and yellow, and the colors the colors—they swirled.

Kids went around me, sliding down, shrieking and laughing, but I was out of sight from their parents. Parents didn't come up this far, so I was safe. Someone stepped on my ear, but it didn't hurt. It should've, but it didn't.

I heard the rush rush rushing of my blood, pulsing through my membranes and cells and pores, and it lulled me to sleep.

I was lost I was lost I was lost.

It was where I wanted to be.

twenty

BECK
MERCY HOSPITAL
8:59 A.M.

M Y BRAIN ISN'T WORKING RIGHT. IT'S FUZZY. AM I HIGH? I am poked and prodded. Am I being stepped on? Am I hiding up in the slide again?

I focus.

No. I'm not there. I'm here.

Something rubbery drags on my skin and fingers pause at my pulse point.

"His pulse is strong," a voice says—a nurse maybe? Because I'm not in the park; I'm in a hospital. "It's uneven, but that's to be expected. It's better than it was before we sedated him."

I feel something cool poke at my chest, gauging my heart.

It thumps against my chest, and it feels bigger than it should be, more powerful, stronger.

Thump.

Thump.

Thump.

I never realized how much I took that for granted before. That one lump of muscle, pounding in my chest, beating day in and day out every day of my life, tirelessly.

I never had to think of it before.

But now, it's all I can hear.

Thump.

Thump.

Thump.

Keep beating, I think to it. I focus all of my energy on that one thing.

The nurse leaves and someone picks up my hand again. I can tell from the perfume that it's Elin.

"Did you say he thought you were an angel?" she asks.

When did that happen? When did I think my mom was an angel?

I focus on that, trying to pull all of my fragments of thought together, and then . . . I remember.

An Angel.

Angel!

Where is she?

She should be here. She would be here, if she could.

Are they keeping her out? Did they ask her to leave?

I can imagine what she would look like to them—a druggie. They wouldn't want her here, but God. I need her. She kept me alive when I didn't care about life at all.

She would never leave me. Not of her own accord.

Oddly, when I think about her, I get a panicky feeling in my gut. I'm afraid for her, and I don't know why.

That can't be good.

I WOKE UP WITH someone watching me.

My vision was a foggy product of coming down from a high. I shook my head, but it didn't help. I shook it again anyway.

I was alone when I'd passed out, but I definitely wasn't now.

Something rustled around in the dark, and then, and then, a dirty white Converse poked into the moonlight.

"Hello?" someone said. A female voice. A girl. Maybe my age. Maybe a little older, or maybe a little younger. It was hard to say.

"What are you doing here?" I asked the shape.

"What are *you* doing here?" she answered.

A question with a question. I fucking hated that.

"I was here first," I said, stating the obvious.

She laughed and stepped into the shadowy light.

"So?"

I examined her. She was small, tightly compact, skinny, and I knew she was a user. I could see it on her, I could sense it, I could smell it. Her hair was short, dirty blond but also just flat-out dirty. Her shirt was tight and there was a hole near the collar. Just a tiny one, but it was there. The red hem was frayed. I could see all of this in the dark by the light of the dim streetlights shining in through broken windows.

Her eyes were large and I thought they might be blue.

"You got anything?" she asked. Her mouth was pink, although her lips were dry.

"Maybe."

She stared at me.

"I'm not going to fuck you for it."

"No?" That was unusual. She must not be as addicted as I thought. Or she had stronger principles than most. That made me laugh. An addict with principles.

"No. I only fuck someone I like, and I don't know you."

She sat down in the middle of the room, cross-legged, and waited.

What the fuck was she waiting for?

I waited for her to tell me, but she didn't. She just pushed her elbows down onto her knees, like she was stretching her legs, and her fingers were bony.

I pulled out my Bic and my spoon. Her blue eyes darted over my hands.

My thumb shoved down the handle, and the flint ignited. I warmed the spoon with the flame. The girl watched me, her eyes hungry, her mouth set.

I reached for my syringe and her pupils dilated in reaction.

"I'll blow you, though," she said quickly. "If you share."

"I don't even know your name," I answered, and I didn't know why I said that. It didn't matter.

"I don't have one," she said as she got up and came to me.

"You're lying."

"Yes." She didn't even bother to deny it.

"What can I call you?" I asked instead. She thought on that.

"Angel," she said. I eyed her.

"Are you? An angel?"

She laughed bitterly.

"I wish. What do I call *you*?"

"King," I said immediately out of habit. They had called me King once, back when throwing a football the length of a field was all that mattered.

"Well, my King," she said. "Unzip and let's do this."

I thought about it, and about the other times that girls said that to me—*Let's do this, King*—and they were cheerleaders and student council leaders, but I never wanted any of that, because I wasn't a cheater. Now, I'm technically free, but I still don't want it.

All I wanted was to plunge that needle into my vein and empty that fucking syringe so hard.

"Maybe later," I told her.

I took the hit. *Fuck, yeah*. I felt the release of reality flow away, like the ebb and flow of the ocean. It was going, going, gone. My fingers tingled and nothing mattered anymore. I focused enough to look at Angel. "You got a needle?"

Her hand thrust into her pocket and emerged with it. It was old, the barrel dirty. But that was her business. All that mattered was that I was still with it enough to know not to share mine.

I handed her the spoon and the one crystal that sat in its belly.

I closed my eyes as she was closing her own, as she pulled in a shuddering breath of ecstasy, as H took her pain.

Fuck, yeah.

We slumped together, shoulder to shoulder. My eyes were slits and I saw the needle still hanging out of her arm, but her mouth was slack and she was out of it now. So was I.

I closed my eyes.

I thought her hand curled around mine.

I didn't know.

But it didn't matter.

twenty-one

NATALIE

WHEN MY PHONE BUZZED WITH A MESSAGE, THEN TWO, then three, I shook my head thinking it was my sister. I finished folding shirts for the kids, fresh out of the dryer, then poured a glass of ice water before I heard one last text come through, so I picked up my phone.

When I did, I instantly started to shake.

Mom, I miss you.

I'm so sorry for everything. You deserve better than me.

I hope Annabelle and Devin turn out better. Forget about me.

The fourth one was several minutes later, and it was different. The tone, the words. If I had to guess, he had gotten high then texted me again.

Mommy, I hate it here. I hate myself. I want to die.

My heart exploded, and I dialed his number as quickly as I could with fumbling fingers. It rang and rang, then went to voice mail. I tried again, then again. No answer.

I texted him instead.

Beck, you don't want to die. You're high. You can't trust your thoughts,

*baby. Please, come home. I'll help you. We'll fix everything. I love you.
Everyone misses you. You are worthy of help. Please, let me help.*

Please.

God. My head dropped to the kitchen table, my skin against the
wood, and I stared at the grain. If only I had known when he was still
home how bad it was. If only I had paid attention and allowed myself
to believe.

If only.

If only.

But *if*s didn't matter now.

They were useless.

The only thing that mattered was when.

When he came home.

If he came home.

I cringed. I had to get rid of *if* from my vocabulary. It didn't help
anything.

Fuck *if*.

twenty-two

BECK

ANGEL CREPT BACK INTO THE WAREHOUSE THROUGH THE morning light slanted across the dirty floor.

When she saw my eyes open, she stopped short.

"Oh," she said. "I didn't mean to wake you."

She had something in her hands and offered it to me.

"Breakfast." She was apologetic. "It's all I could get."

I took the crust of the McMuffin and the partially eaten sausage patty.

"I'm not really hungry," I said truthfully.

"Eat it anyway," she answered. "You'll get too skinny if you don't."

"You're bossy."

"Yeah."

I couldn't deny the truth in her logic—I *would* get too skinny if I didn't eat. I ate the few mouthfuls, not thinking about (and not caring) whose mouth had been on the sandwich before it was discarded. I didn't even ask if it came from a trash can.

"Where are you from?" I asked Angel when I finished.

She glanced at me, then looked away. "Nowhere."

"You're not really a talker, are you?"

She smiled ever so slightly.

"I am. Just not about myself."

I examined her again. Her hair was short, really short, and sort of jagged and spiky.

"Did you cut your hair yourself?"

"Nah. I went to a spa yesterday and had it done, along with a mani and pedi."

"Sarcasm is lazy," I told her, which was something my mother always told me. "It means you don't want to go to the trouble of forming a good response."

Angel threw her head back and laughed, a barky noise in the cold, empty warehouse.

"I like you," she decided, cocking her head. In that position, with her short hair and her skinny arms, she reminded me of a bird with scraggly wings.

"Thank you?"

She rolled her eyes.

"So, how did you start using?"

"I borrowed my mom's Xanax. I was stressed out, and it helped."

She nodded, like she totally got it. "Ah, yes. Good ol' Xanax. It takes the edge off without making you feel like a user. I personally started with Percocet."

"Okay." I didn't know why any of this mattered, but I didn't ask.

"Do you ever regret it?" she asked in a small voice. "Starting, I mean?"

I glanced at her. "Yeah."

She nodded because she understood in a way most people wouldn't. Then she shook her head, like she was shaking all the bad stuff away.

"We should go get a shower. You smell."

I grabbed my bag, a tattered purple velveteen Crown Royal backpack. I'd picked it up outside of a liquor store a few weeks ago, and now it held everything important, everything I have. My ID, my pipe, my spoon, the lucky marble that Devin gave me. I'd never let it out of my sight. It was dumb to keep it, but it was home.

Together, we stepped over the broken boarded-up side door of the warehouse and made our way down the street to the YMCA. We paused in the parking lot, watching the people go in and out.

Contrary to popular opinion, the Y didn't just allow people to come in and use their facilities. You had to be a member, and of course, we weren't.

So we waited, our breath puffing in the air like smoke.

When a particularly large group of people went inside, we slipped in behind them, inconspicuously weaving our way down the yellowed hallway to the locker rooms. I ducked into the men's while Angel disappeared into the women's.

Once inside, I acted like I belonged. I strode toward the showers, grabbing a pool towel on my way. No one even looked twice at me, and I stepped unnoticed inside the tiled stall, hanging my Crown bag on the faucet handle. It might get damp, but at least it wouldn't get stolen.

I showered as quickly as I could, although I did allow myself to revel in the hot water for a scant minute, as it thawed my skin and my flesh and my bones. I let the heat go bone-deep, my head bowed, the water beading off my skin and running down my neck.

God, that felt good.

It's amazing the little things that I once took for granted that are really such a pleasure in life. I never would've thought of a hot shower as a luxury before. I was low now, and because of that, my emotions swung heavy and hard, razor sharp from the absence of heroin. A wave of sadness swept over me, sadness that I couldn't control.

I missed my home. I missed my mom. I missed my life.

I grabbed my phone, even here under the water, and texted my mom. She deserved to know.

When I had sent the message, I finished washing off the best I could without soap, scrubbing at my hair and my face with my hands. Plain water was better than no water at all.

After five minutes or so, I turned off the water and toweled off. I needed to get out before I was detected.

I put my dirty clothes back on because I didn't have a choice, but at least my body was clean. I was melancholy and sad, and that's when I saw it.

My saving grace.

Down the bench, just a little ways away, someone had left a duffel bag unattended while he was in the shower. I could see him through the flimsy shower curtain, so I acted fast and didn't allow myself to feel guilty.

I rifled through the bag, quickly and efficiently.

There was a brown wallet at the bottom.

I pulled it open and found three twenties and two ones.

I took a twenty and walked away, because Jesus, I couldn't not.

When I stepped out into the hall, Angel was already there.

"God, princess," she said. "Took you long enough."

Her hair was still wet and was plastered to her forehead. It made her look even smaller. Sort of like a drowned rat, but a pretty one.

She *was* pretty, in a user kind of way. She would definitely be pretty if she were clean and her cheeks weren't so hollow.

I decided I liked her, though. She was like me. She did what she had to do, and she understood the need we both had. I didn't have to worry about hurting her feelings, or misrepresenting myself. She already knew what my priorities were, because she shared them.

Commonality was a great thing.

When we were a block away, I pulled the twenty out of my bag.

"Look what I got!"

"Someone left their stuff unattended?"

"Yeah."

"Dumbass."

"Yeah."

I used to feel guilty about this shit. I really did. But now . . . it was like I didn't have feelings anymore. Or at least, they weren't vibrant and real like they used to be. They were muted now, dull and cloudy, and in many ways, that was a very good thing.

"Do you want to eat, or . . ." Her voice trailed off and I knew what she meant, and I knew that it really wasn't even a question.

"Or," I confirmed. "Definitely *or*."

She nodded in satisfaction and we headed to the bridge, to the dirty underpass where the dregs of society lived, where they met, where they dealt.

We waited on the edge, our feet sinking into the cold mud, until we saw someone who looked like a dealer.

When he looked over at us, I nodded, and he approached us.

"Whatchoo got?" he asked, his eyes flitting around the perimeter.

"Twenty," Angel told him.

I wasn't even nervous anymore. I used to be. I used to be terrified of getting caught. Now it didn't matter. It was like a broken record, an endless cycle. Get high, crash, get high, crash. Everything in between was meaningless. It was almost funny how fast that happened.

The dealer mumbled something I didn't understand, took the money, then shoved something into Angel's hand. The plastic crinkled when she grasped it. The mere sound made my blood pulse in trained response. She shoved it into her pocket and we left without another word.

"See you soon," he called after us.

We knew.

twenty-three

I AM NUMB NOW.

I sit with my feet on the cold floor, my hand intertwined in Beck's. His IV line is draped over his arm, and I'm careful not to pull on it. He's got a plastic thing on his finger, a *pulse oximeter*. The nurses call it a pulse ox. It monitors the amount of oxygen in his bloodstream. I watch the results on the screen, a tiny blinking heart.

The beeps, though. They're enough to drive a person insane. Constant and unrelenting.

The ventilator on the other hand . . . it's soothing. A rhythmic whooooooosh. In . . . then out . . . One breath in, then out. Another in, then out. It keeps my son alive, bit by bit. I listen to it gratefully. As long as it's going, my son breathes.

It's just me and Elin in here now.

Sam and Kit are pacing outside, nagging the nurses, harping on the doctors. I'm not going to waste my time with that. My time is better spent in here, with my son. Time is so precious now. I check my watch. It's been about nine hours since Beck collapsed on my porch.

The doctors said the first twenty-four hours are the most critical. If he's going to make it, we'll know at the end of that period.

I have fifteen left.

But then I start to worry . . . Are they really going to bring him out in the middle of the night? What if he's not ready?

My heart starts to race, and I can't think like that.

We have fifteen hours left.

That's what I focus on.

"His fingers are cold," Elin says, and she rubs his hand to warm it. I nod because I'd noticed it too. And he's so very pale but for the dark blue smudges beneath his eyes. "His knuckles are so beat-up. I hope he didn't damage his hands. I mean, for football next year."

I look at her, startled, and find that she's in denial. She's so young and innocent, and she wants to focus on what Beck was going to do, not on what's in front of us now.

I don't tell her that there's no way my son will be eligible to play now. Not after this. And I certainly don't tell her that football is the fucking least of Beck's worries.

Once upon a time, yes. Matt and I both worried about where Beck would go to college, where he would play. But now . . .

It's such an odd feeling. When you're a parent, you're always thinking about your kid's future. Plotting it, planning it. But now, in a blink of an eye, I only want one thing.

For him to live.

Later, maybe he can reapply to Notre Dame. Maybe he can even get a scholarship. But first, he has to survive tonight. The door opens and Elin and I both look up from our vigil. Sam is there, her face grim.

"How's he doing?" she asks, and her voice seems loud in this silent room.

"Hanging in there," I say, and she positions herself by my shoulder.

"Natalie," she says, and her voice. It's so grim.

I'm afraid to answer, afraid to even look at her, but she continues.

"I was just speaking with Dr. Grant."

She pauses and I wait, silently terrified.

"Do you want to wait for Dr. Grant to come speak to you, or would you like me to explain what's happening?" she asks softly.

I can't wait.

"Please tell me," I manage.

"Beck is experiencing organ failure," she says bluntly. "They say they expected it with the massive amounts of drugs that were in his system. His kidneys aren't working. So Dr. Grant is ordering hemodialysis to cleanse his blood for him in the interim."

I exhale.

Elin begins crying, her shoulders shaking gently, her hand over her mouth.

"What does that mean?" I finally ask. "I mean, what is going to happen? What exactly did they say?"

Sam is quiet, and she grasps my shoulder in a gesture meant to comfort me.

It doesn't.

"It's up to Beck," she says finally, her voice gentle. "The doctors are doing everything medically possible. Beck will be the one who has to overcome this."

Or not.

I don't say it, and neither does she.

"We should keep talking to him," Sam says aloud. "I know the doctors say that patients can't hear when they're in a coma, but maybe the sound of our voices . . . I think it'll get through to him."

Elin nods and whispers words that I can't understand into Beck's ear.

I lift my eyes to my sister's face and find that hers are wet.

"I'm sorry you're going through this," she tells me sincerely.

I nod, my throat full of emotion.

"I'm sorry I got angry with you," I answer. "When you tried to tell me to watch for Beck's behavior. I was so angry with you . . . and you were right all along."

She straightens, all business now.

"Well, I wish I hadn't been right," she says simply. "But none of that matters now. All that matters is Beck and you and this. Dr. Grant is going to stay. He's not leaving until it's time to bring Beck out from under the sedatives."

"That's nice of him," I acknowledge, because it really is.

"Everyone is pulling for him," Sam says. "The entire ICU staff." She stands up. "I'm going to the chapel to say a prayer for Beck. It can't hurt, right?"

"No, it can't," I whisper.

He needs all the help he can get.

I've already failed him. But surely God won't.

———

"HOW IS THE LAWSUIT going?" Sam asked me as she reached for the chips and salsa over the restaurant table. I was surprised because she'd never asked about that. We all tried to pretend that life was normal, at least as much as we could.

I think she saw the confusion on my face, because she paused.

"I only ask because I know you hate shit like that," she explained. "It must be stressing you out."

"It would be," I agreed, "if Kit weren't handling most of it. I had to meet with the attorneys once or twice, but Kit is taking care of the paperwork and things. He says I have enough on my plate."

Sam lifted an eyebrow.

"That's very thoughtful of him," she answered. "How do you feel about that? About him chipping in to help with things?"

"I'm grateful," I said immediately. Everything seemed so overwhelming, so when Kit offered to help, I was totally fine with it.

"What is the main basis of the suit?" Sam asked.

"Matt's seat belt and airbag were faulty. He always wore his seat belt without fail, and that night I have a picture with him wearing it. They'd . . ." My voice trails off, and I square my shoulders. "They'd taken a selfie when they left South Bend to come home, and Matt was buckled in. The mechanics said the sensors must've gone bad, since it unlatched upon impact. But that doesn't make sense since the car was only two years old."

"So Matt was thrown from the car?" Sam asked hesitantly. She'd never wanted the details, and I'd never wanted to give them.

"Yeah. When Beck woke up from the crash, he was alone in the car. He was disoriented and stumbling around, but he found Matt in the ditch."

"Jesus," Sam breathed, and her hand shook. I nodded.

"Like you know, Beck called me when he found him. He tried CPR, I tried to talk him through it, but Matt was . . . he was not responding. Beck did CPR, and the EMTs did CPR, but at the hospital they called it."

Matt's injuries were insurmountable.

"Attorneys contacted us afterward," I continued. "I didn't return any of their phone calls, but after I started getting all the hospital bills, I decided to call one of them back. The car company should pay for that. The car malfunctioned. It shouldn't have."

Sam glanced at me. "Do you feel badly about filing suit? You sound like you feel guilty."

I shrugged. "Maybe. I hate lawsuits. I think America has become too trigger-happy with them."

"But sometimes they are warranted," she said, looking at me thoughtfully. "You are right in this, Nat. When Matt died, you lost his income, his health benefits. Beck has suffered incredible emotional harm."

"Well, you're right about one thing," I said. "Beck's suffered. I worry all the time that he'll never recover. That he'll always hide from the pain and he'll never really learn to handle it."

Sam nodded and grabbed my hand. "We'll face this together. You're not alone."

She paused for a minute.

"I think Beck feels guilty," Sam continued, and she was hesitant. I stared at her.

"Of course he does. Anyone would."

"I know. But I think . . . I think he feels guilty for *living*," Sam answered. "He doesn't understand why his airbag deployed and Matt's didn't."

"That's not logical," I answered. "That wasn't his fault. And God. If something worse had happened to Beck, I don't know what I would've done." My voice broke from the sheer thought.

"I know that, and you know that, but grief can do strange things to a person's logic," she answered. "Beck is struggling."

The waitress came with our check, and I opened my wallet. It was empty.

I stared at it for a minute because I specifically remembered getting cash from an ATM yesterday.

"What is it?" Sam asked.

"I thought I had money." I was uncertain.

Sam eyed me again, almost knowingly, and I didn't like the look on her face. "Maybe Beck took it."

My head snapped back, and I stared at her, not following.

"Beck would never steal from me," I said, surprised. "He's so honest. All of my kids are. Why would he do that? If he needs money, he'd just ask me."

"He wouldn't if he wants money for something you wouldn't approve of," Sam answered, and she seemed so knowing now. I wasn't following.

I stared at her, trying to comprehend.

"Something to help him cope," she continued. "Have you noticed any other strange behavior? Mood changes, or has he gotten into trouble?"

"You know dang well that he got caught drinking at prom, but they all did. That's normal," I told her slowly, as her words sunk in. "What are you insinuating?"

The lunch bustle of the restaurant faded into a soft buzz around me as I waited for my sister to explain. She couldn't possible mean what I think she meant.

"He could be self-medicating, Nat," Sam finally said bluntly. "Weed. Maybe worse."

I was already shaking my head. "Are you crazy? He would never. He's got a football scholarship to worry about. He wouldn't jeopardize that."

"Nat, I've seen his eyes bloodshot. I've seen him 'out of it.' I know you don't want to think about it, but—"

"Stop it," I snapped at her. "How could you even say that? You know him, Sam. You know him better than anyone, other than me. You should know he'd never do that!"

My sister remained calm, her voice steady. "Nat, he's been through so much. We don't know what exactly he might do to cope."

I practically roared at her, loud enough that the couple at the next table stopped eating and stared at me. "He wouldn't do that. He wouldn't do it to me, and it just isn't him. If you loved him at all, you'd know that."

I grabbed my purse and stood up while my sister watched. "Nat, I *do* love him. I'm just saying maybe we should keep an eye out."

"Fuck you, Sam," I spit. "You're believing the worst of a kid who has only ever tried to do everything right. You don't know how much he's been doing around the house to make up for my slack. If you did, you'd never accuse him like this. You're crazy."

Sam remained unfazed. "You've told me that you're going through your Xanax much faster than you realized, that you don't remember taking so much. You've been missing money from your wallet. Those two things are enough to make us keep an eye on him. Natalie, sit back down. I'll pay for lunch today."

She's annoyed, but so am I. How dare she.

"I told you those things because I was concerned about myself," I hissed at her. "Because I'm losing snippets of time, and that's scary. Beck hasn't done anything wrong. *I'm* the one losing my mind. Don't you dare say something like this about my son again. Not ever. He has enough to deal with without his aunt thinking he's on drugs."

I stormed out and stomped to my car, and Sam didn't follow.

twenty-four

BECK
Mercy Hospital
10:03 A.M.

SOMETHING NAGS AT ME, SOMETHING I CAN'T PLACE RIGHT now. I know something. Something about Angel. I focus, but the memory doesn't come.

I strain to listen to the conversation around me, hoping to put the pieces together.

"How do you think he survived?" Aunt Sam asks out of nowhere. "You said his bank account was empty."

"Yeah," my mom tells her. "I have no idea what he did for money after he emptied his account the night he left."

My mom sniffs like she's crying.

"I should've tried harder to find him. I should've done something. Somehow he transitioned from weed to heroin, and now the doctor says he was using meth. How does this happen? A good mother would've known. A good mother would've stopped it."

"You *are* a good mother," Elin says, speaking up, and I wish I could hug her for that. "I've always told Beck he's lucky to have you. He knows that, Mrs. K. He knows he's lucky. He loves you."

"But he hid so much from me," Mom says limply, and I want to tell her that it wasn't personal. I hid things from everyone. I had to.

"Addicts lie," Aunt Sam says stoutly. "I was talking to his nurse in the hall earlier, and she was telling me about how the chemicals in hard drugs literally alter a user's brain. Finding another high becomes all that is important. They'll lie, steal, do anything to get high. It's just the way it is. Nothing about it is your fault."

"Beck didn't steal," my mom answers, and she sounds so sure of herself, yet so uncertain. "He didn't."

I die a little on the inside. She has no idea what I've done.

———

"I HATE DOING THIS," Angel complained. "People look at me like I'm a bug they want to squash."

Our cardboard sign read: HOMELESS. ANYTHING WILL HELP. THANK YOU.

"I know." I never thought I'd do something like this. Ever. But I was doing it now and what was more, I didn't care. I was far from my house, far from anyone who knew me.

"We aren't lying," she pointed out. "We *are* homeless."

Three cars passed because the light was green. It was when it turned red that we might get something. People found it uncomfortable to sit next to us without giving, especially if we made eye contact.

"Where do your parents live?" I asked. "I know you don't like to talk about it, but . . ."

Angel stared at me with hard eyes. "But what? I don't like to talk about it."

"But maybe I should know. Just in case."

She laughed, one quick, sharp sound. "In case of what? Something happens to me? Trust me, no one back home will care. They'd probably laugh and I don't want to give them that satisfaction."

"They wouldn't laugh," I protested, but clearly I didn't really know. I didn't know anything about her.

"They would," she assured me. "They're pathetic excuses for human life."

"They brought you into the world," I pointed out. "So they did at least one good thing."

She shrugged, and clearly she didn't agree. Her hand shook against her leg, needing another hit after not having one since last night. "If I ever overdose, or get hit by a car or something," she said, "don't call the cops. Just carry me to the lake and let me float away. Will you do that for me, King?"

I stared at her. "I don't know."

The light turned red and I held up the sign again. A Lexus sat at the front and the elderly woman behind the wheel glanced at me, then studied her phone, purposely avoiding eye contact.

Behind her, a Ford pickup with an old farmer at the wheel didn't offer anything either. He studied us both with a glinting stare, a cowboy hat on his head and gnarled hands on the wheel.

But behind him, a hand reached out of the window of a beat-up Toyota Camry waving a five-dollar bill. Angel hopped over to get it, and the man told her to have a good day.

"It's always the poor people who help," she pointed out as she pocketed the money and stood back beside me.

"Usually," I agreed. "But not always. I think they know what it's like to have nothing. And the rich people always think they're getting taken advantage of."

I didn't have to state the obvious. Today, we *were* taking advantage. We weren't collecting money for food and we knew it. But we didn't lie on the sign. All we said was that we were homeless, and that was true.

It was cold out and you'd think people would have more pity. Some did. We collected a handful more dollars, and after a few hours, we had fourteen.

Not a lot.

But more than we had before.

The cold wind bit our faces, but we didn't have coats. I'd had one, but I didn't know what had happened to it. It was probably in an alley somewhere.

Things are a blur sometimes. Images and fragments, mostly.

Angel shivered and I wondered how cold it was.

Thirty? Thirty-five? The snow wasn't melting, so it must be under thirty-two.

"We're going to get frostbite," I mentioned. My fingers were purplish blue.

Angel just grunted. "We should go back to the warehouse," she suggested. "We can find something to build a fire."

There was a lot of trash to choose from there. We could pile it all together and light it.

"I know where we can get some coats," I told her instead. "Come on."

We went to Ogilvie station and I bought a ticket for each of us. For both, it was seven bucks.

"Dude," Angel protested. "We've got to get back somehow."

"Don't worry," I assured her. "It'll be fine."

We settled into a car in the back, and huddled together. The train was dingy and smelled a little like lemon air freshener and a lot like body odor. I stared out the window as the scenery passed, the snowy landscapes, the frozen trees.

It was an hour before we reached Ravinia Park, and I'd had to wake Angel. She was crashing, so she was sluggish.

"Where are we?" she mumbled as we got off the train. Her steps were shaky and unsure.

"Close to my home," I answered. "We've got to stay out of sight." I didn't want my mom to see us. This wasn't her neighborhood, but it was close enough.

We hiked the rest of the way, and it was so cold that my bones ached. By the time we reached Kit's house, I couldn't feel my face.

"*This* is your home?" Angel asked as we stood on the sidewalk looking at Kit's Cape Cod home. "Swanky."

It's not overly fancy, so the fact that she thinks so tells me a little more about her. I store that away in my head for a time when I can put the pieces all together.

"No, it's a family friend's."

The lights are off, as I figured they would be. Kit works late usually, since he doesn't have a family to get home to.

I knew what the door code was, and I punched it into the garage keypad. The door opened, creaking mechanically, and we stepped into the garage.

We walked through, past his motorcycle that was covered up, waiting for warmer days. I opened the kitchen door, and the warmth was instantaneous. It flooded us, and I exhaled in relief. I didn't necessarily care about dying, but freezing to death seemed like a painful way to go.

"Is he out of town?" Angel asked hopefully. I knew what she was thinking. That we could stay here if he was gone.

"Nah. He's at work. He has a construction company. He works long hours."

I opened his fridge.

It was empty but for beer, water, and ketchup. Kit lived on takeout.

I took a bottle of water and offered one to Angel. She shook her head.

"My hands are still too cold."

I led her to the couch and offered her a blanket.

"You can wait here and get warm."

She didn't ask questions. She leaned her head back and closed her eyes, giving in to the crash. She'd sleep for days if I let her.

I found the coats in the closet in Kit's extra bedroom, along with a backpack. I knew he wouldn't mind, or at least that's what I told myself, so I chose two older, warm winter parkas and a blanket. I rolled it up and shoved it in the backpack next to two pairs of work gloves.

I felt a twinge of guilt. Kit used to be my friend, a true friend. Honestly, I knew he'd give me these things if I asked. But at the same time, after what he did, it almost seemed like poetic justice to steal them.

Fuck him.

On my way back to the living room, I stopped in the dining room. In the buffet by the table, I knew there were rolled-up quarters in the top drawer. Kit tossed all of his change in a big jar, and then when he got bored, he rolled them up while he watched TV. He'd done it as long as I'd known him.

I was right. There were about ten rolls of quarters. I took four.

Forty dollars.

I woke Angel and handed her one of the coats. It was Kit's and he was giant, so it drowned Angel, the hem falling past her knees. But that was okay. That meant that her legs were protected from the cold. The gloves swallowed up her hands, but again, they'd keep her warm.

I folded the blanket and tried to put everything back exactly as we had found it, leaving no trace that we'd ever been here at all.

Outside, our footsteps in the snow were the only evidence of our existence. Hopefully, new snowfall would cover even those, and Kit would never know.

"Thanks for the coat," Angel told me, her voice gruff. She didn't like to show emotion. I added that to the list of things I knew about her.

"You're welcome," I told her. "I knew Kit would have something."

"What kind of name is Kit?" She raised an eyebrow.

"I think his real name is Christopher," I answered. "But he's always gone by Kit. He's practically my uncle."

I was pissed at him, but that didn't change what he used to be to me.

Angel's attention was drawn away from me, though, by a whimper nearby.

A little dog, a mangy little thing, shaggy and small, sat in the snow a few feet away, his eyes sad.

Angel sucked in a breath and darted toward it, scooping it up in her arms.

"Oh my gosh, little guy. You're so cold." She shoved it inside her coat until I could only see its eyes peering out. Long eyebrows shagged down over them. "You poor thing. Did someone abandon you?"

I recognized the look in Angel's eye, and I was already shaking my head.

"We can't keep him, Angel. We can't afford to feed him."

Her head snapped up. "Does he look like he's getting fed as it is?" she demanded, and she had a point. He was ragged and skinny. "I'm keeping him."

Her arms tightened protectively and I knew that dog was coming with us.

"Okay."

"Damn straight."

We trudged through the snow and she cuddled the dog and at the next McDonald's we came to, we bought it a hamburger. She fed the dog inside her coat. I could see him licking her fingers.

"What are you going to name it?" I asked as we made our way toward the station.

She shrugged. "I don't know. He'll tell me what his name is sooner or later."

"The dog will tell you?"

She nodded. "Yeah."

"Okay."

twenty-five

BECK

SOMETHING WASN'T RIGHT.

Usually H gave you a warm tranquil high, a feeling of euphoria so engulfing that it felt like you were wrapped in a soft blanket, lying in front of a crackling fire while it was snowing outside.

Tonight we'd smoked it instead of injecting, and something wasn't right.

I felt like a caged tiger, ready to climb out of my skin, and I paced paced paced through the warehouse, one step two steps three. My veins throbbed and I felt all of them and I had millions of them and they were intertwined and they all itched.

"Where did you get this shit?" I muttered to Angel. She sat by our little bonfire, and her eyes were glassy. She was scratching at her arms, her long fingernails leaving red streaks, but she didn't stop. The dog was sitting at her feet and she scratched at it too.

"From the guy," Angel answered, and her voice was thick. "The guy."

Her vague answer annoyed me. In fact it sent rage coursing through my veins, and that wasn't right it wasn't right it wasn't right. I didn't usually get mad like this. But I was furious now, I was a raging bull, and I wanted to tear someone's head off.

I saw red. Every shade of it, every hue. Everything was tinted with it, and I wanted to burn the world down.

"Fuck you, Angel," I growled, and I banged out the door, hitting my shoulder on the board, but I didn't care and I didn't feel it. I knew enough to get away, because I wanted to hurt her, but I knew that I really didn't.

The winter air hit me in the face and took my breath away, but it still felt good. It felt like it was cleaning my lungs out and was filling them up and I was a balloon and I might float away.

But I shouldn't.

So I tied myself to the ground.

I bobbed in the wind, and I was lost I was lost. The stars twirled together and they were in my eyes and the light was bright.

The reds were endless, tinting everything, outlining the world.

I collapsed onto a park bench in a place I didn't know. I looked around and there were trees and a merry-go-round and it was rusty and red because of course it was red. Everything was.

My head fell back and thunked against the metal bench and I stared at the night, my eyes wide open, because I could see now, I could finally see.

Everything made sense.

Everything was clear.

I was all alone in this world. Everything else was an illusion.

My knuckles clenched and they hurt but they were insignificant.

I pulled out my phone because I understood life, I understood everything, and I had to share that. I had to share it before I forgot it or I slipped away.

I dialed at numbers, memorized numbers, and my mom answered on the second ring, and she knew me immediately because of course she did.

"Honey," she blurted. "Where are you? Are you okay?"

"I understand everything," I told her. My voice was slurred, but she'd know what I was saying. She knew me. "I get it. Nothing matters.

That's the point. None of us matter. You don't, I don't. It's all a sham. It's a fucking scheme."

I was agitated, getting more so by the minute, and she was confused.

"I don't understand," she said slowly. "Just come home. We'll talk about it when you get here."

I laughed because she was trying to trick me because everyone was trying to trick me because the world was a scam. Did they think I didn't know that?

"Nice try," I told her. "I'm never coming home. Don't you understand? I'm going to be a fucking star in the sky. And you can't find me. No one can."

"You're not a star," she said, and she sounded scared. "You're a man. We've got to get you some help. Please."

"That's a lie," I insisted, and I was shouting. "That's a fucking lie. I'm not an addict; I just know the truth. You need to find the truth, Mom."

From the corner of my eye, I saw people standing in the shadows, and they moved and reached for me with long pointy fingers, and I startled, glaring at them.

"Get away," I shouted at them.

"Beck, what's wrong?" my mom asked quickly. "Who is with you?"

"They're trying to get me, but they can't," I told her. The people backed up now, until they were just black blurs swirled into circles where their faces should be.

"Beck," she said, pleading now. "Please. Tell me where you are."

"You just want to put me away," I told her. "I know that now. You don't want me around because I'm a problem. I'm difficult. Well, guess what? I won't bother you again. You won't ever see me again. Forget that I exist. I'm going to forget about *you*."

She cried out but I hung up. And I threw my phone into the trash can so hard it shattered into a billion pieces.

"Fuck you," I told it. I was telling the world.

I didn't have a phone now. I couldn't be tracked; I couldn't be caught. I'd be a star. Or I'd be the moon.

I awoke on the bench, and Angel sat on the other end, watching me. She had the shattered remains of my phone in her lap.

It was daylight now, and my hands were curled into my lap. They throbbed, both of them, and they were covered in scrapes and blood. What happened to them?

"How did I get here?"

My voice tasted like rust and I cleared my throat.

Angel shrugged. "I think our stuff was laced with meth."

That woke me up. "Meth? How do you know?"

"Because when I came down, I puked my guts out, and I always do that with meth. Plus, you were pissed as fuck, dude. That's what dope does."

"I've never done meth," I told her honestly. "And I don't remember much, but I don't think I liked how I felt last night. I don't want to do it again."

"You don't right now," she amended. "But you will."

I ignored that. I didn't need another addiction.

"You were shouting at shadow people," she added. "That's what meth does. It makes you paranoid. It makes you see people who aren't there."

I did remember that.

"I thought they were here to get me," I told her.

She nodded. "Yeah. I know."

There was a whimper and the dog's head poked out of her coat. "This is Winston Churchill," she told me.

"You named the dog after an old prime minister?"

She glared. "You got a problem with that?"

"No, no problem. Nice to meet you, Winston."

She was satisfied, and the dog whimpered some more, and my head pounded.

I was crashing now, and so was Angel, so we went back to the warehouse and slept for what felt like days.

Maybe it was.

twenty-six

NATALIE
MERCY HOSPITAL
11:16 A.M.

"THERE'S A HUGE GROUP OF FOOTBALL PLAYERS IN THE waiting room," Sam tells me as she comes back in the room. She'd washed her face and called to check on the kids. "There must be thirty of them. I can't believe they're here. Beck was gone for two months."

I glance at my sister. "They treat each other like they're brothers. I'm not surprised. So many of them called me to check on him when he was . . . gone. They've been worried."

"Not Tray, though," Sam says grimly.

"No. It'd be a bit hard for him, since he's in jail." From what I'd heard, the court had been lenient since it was his first drug dealing charge . . . only given him a few months.

"Do you hear that, Beck?" Elin whispers to Beck. "Your friends are here. Your *real* friends. They want you to get better."

"Elin, honey." I turn to her. "Would you go give them an update? Let them know that it's going to be hours until we know anything more. Tell them we appreciate that they came, but that they can go home. They don't have to sit here."

She nods and leaves. I look at the clock.

In thirteen hours, we will reach the twenty-four-hour mark since Beck collapsed on my porch. Thirteen hours is so short, so few, so little.

I swallow hard.

Sam stares at the door where Elin had just walked out.

"What if he wakes up and doesn't want her here?" Sam asks hesitantly.

I think about all of the pictures I have at home of Beck and Elin, Elin and Beck, and that's just not possible.

"I know my kid," I finally answer. "He loves her. He wants her here. I'd bet my life on it."

Sam lets that go, and we sit in silence again.

"I hate hospitals," she says. "Ever since Matt . . ."

Her voice drifts off, and she shakes her head.

"So if it's bad for me, it must be a nightmare for you," she decides. "What can I do?"

"You're doing it," I tell her. "You're here. I'm not alone."

She has no idea how much that means to me.

"You've never been alone," she answers. "You might've felt like it, but you weren't. I'm always here for you, Nat."

"I know."

And I do. She's been with me the entire time. She's who held me up at the funeral, the blackest of all my black days. She'd held my hand tightly as they'd lowered my husband into the ground.

"It smells the same in here. Jesus." Sam stands up abruptly and sprays a couple spritzes of her perfume. "What the fuck is that, anyway? Sterility? Misery?"

I have to crack a stiff smile at that. I've been thinking the same thing for hours.

"Iodine and fear, I think."

She rolls her eyes. "I wish I could open a window. Beck could use some fresh air."

I look at my son, and he's so unchanged. So still, so pale. I bend and hug him, pulling him against me.

"Fight," I instruct him. "Just fight, Beck."

I release him, and he falls limply back to the bed.

I squeeze my eyes closed because it's hard to see. He's an empty shell.

"Everyone wanted to be you and Matt," Sam tells me, and I know she's trying to distract me. I look over at her, and she's got a faraway look on her face, a dreamy gaze. "Back in college. Always, actually."

"Well, I'm sure they don't now." My answer is bitter and jaded, and Sam flinches. "I'm sorry," I add. "I didn't mean that."

But I did. Life sucks sometimes.

"Look, you didn't deserve this. Matt didn't either. He was in the prime of his life, and he'd worked so hard at the firm."

"Yeah. He was so focused on making partner," I say, and when I think about it, all of the hours and hours wasted at work, working toward a goal that would be meaningless in the end, it makes me sad. And pissed. Does nothing matter in the long run?

"He was a role model for everyone who knew him," Sam reminds me. "He came from nothing, from a terrible family, and he had no money, and he worked hard to make himself who he became. He was an inspiration."

God, that hurts my heart.

The word *was*. It's so much different than *is*.

"Yeah."

I yank my purse off the floor and root through it and finally come up with my prize. The bottle of Matt's cologne. I take off the lid and sniff at it, closing my eyes as memories overtake me.

Matt holding me. Matt laughing with me. Matt teasing me.

Matt.

"You're still carrying that around?" Sam lifts an eyebrow and there's the faintest hint of disapproval in her voice. She thinks I'm making things harder on myself by clinging to these things. I ignore her. She has no idea.

"Don't judge. You can just go home to smell Vinny. I can't."

Properly chastised, my sister looks away. "Well, he stinks half the time, so I don't want to."

But she knows what I mean, and she lets it go.

"Does Vinny need any suits?" I ask her, and she looks at me before she laughs.

"At the restaurant? Whatever for?"

I shrug. "I don't know. Matt's are still in the closet and they're expensive. I don't want to just throw them away. Vinny could have them altered, if he wanted. For weddings, or . . . funerals."

I don't think the unthinkable.

That he might need one for Beck's.

Jesus.

A tear slips down my cheek and it's hot and wet.

Sam reaches over to wipe it away and then pulls me to her chest, holding me tight.

I STARED LISTLESSLY OUT the kitchen windows, a cup of coffee in my hands.

Through the glass, blades of grass pushed through patches of snow in stubborn indignation, desperately trying to linger in a life that had moved beyond it.

I couldn't help but see a metaphor there, even if it did make my heart stutter.

"It's time, Nat," I said aloud, and I wasn't talking about waking for the day. I was talking about reawakening for life. At times, it felt like my husband had been gone two years or ten years, and at times, it felt like two minutes. But it was time for me to stop clinging to a life that no longer contained Matt. The sadness, the grief, the trying to hold on . . . it had cost me my son. He left because I couldn't handle it.

I had to handle it.

After I took the kids out to the bus, I came inside with purpose, my shoulders back.

With an empty box in my arms, I took several deep breaths before I gathered the nerve to go in.

One, one thousand. Two, one thousand. Three.

I stepped inside my master bath.

Matt's bathrobe hung on a hook by the shower. It was waiting for him to use it, to drape it over his damp body. I closed my eyes and envisioned him wearing it, as he had so many other times. The white terry cloth skimmed his muscular shoulders, and I felt woozy at the thought. He'd never wear it again.

I slowly took it off the hook, folded it neatly, and put it in the box.

I gathered Matt's soap and bath gel and tossed them into the box too. My fingers slid along the cool glass bottle of his cologne, and I sprayed it once into the air, sniffing at it. I'd never liked this particular scent, but Matt did. It was oceanic, salty and brisk, and he'd loved it. And now I loved it too because it smelled like him, and this bottle was all I had left.

I gulped at the air and put it in the box.

Matt had to go in the box.

All of him.

Because it was time and I was holding on to a past that would never come back. Looking at these things on a daily basis only served to make me sad. They weren't comforting anymore; they were just a reminder of what I'd lost.

Within an hour, I'd emptied Matt's things out of the bathroom. I'd cleaned his sink, his whiskers from the porcelain. I ran my fingers around the edge. I used to get so mad at him for leaving toothpaste spatters or tiny hairs after he shaved. Now it was clean, and it would stay clean, and I'd never been so sad.

And angry. All of a sudden, anger bubbled up in me.

"How could you leave me?" I asked the empty air, but the question was directed at Matt. "How?" I whirled around, and the emptiness, the aloneness . . . it was infuriating. He should be here.

I kicked the box and watched his belongings roll across the floor.

"Fuck you!" I said, and then I screamed it. "Fuck you, Matt! How dare you do this to me. I wasn't ready!"

I paused, trying to sense his presence around me. Could he see me? Could he hear me?

"I was supposed to have decades left with you!" I snapped, as though he were right next to me. "I was supposed to nag you for years. I was supposed to be able to hug you and talk to you and cry with you for years, Matthew Kingsley. You fucking left. You abandoned me. And I'm left with the pieces of this life, and I don't want this. Do you hear me? I don't want it!"

He'd been the one to want a third baby. I was too tired, too over-worked to consider it. I'd protested, and he'd talked me into it.

And here I was now, alone. With three kids who counted on me, and I was falling apart.

"I hate you for this," I whispered. The words burned me as I real-ized that I felt them. A part of me hated him for leaving me. I felt be-trayed. I felt abandoned. I felt empty. The weight of that was too heavy to bear. I collapsed into a heap by the dirty-clothes hamper. I hadn't used it since Matt had died. Which meant his clothes were still inside, exactly as he had left them.

I reached up and pulled out the T-shirt on top, the light blue Super-man shirt the kids had given him for Father's Day two years ago. With another gulp, I buried my face in it, and through the slight smell of mustiness, I smelled my husband.

His skin, his scent, his sweat.

A wall inside of me broke, tumbling piece by piece into my bones. He was mine. *Was.* He was gone.

I wept.

Tears fell and fell, streaking from my cheeks onto my shirt. My hands grew wet, and my nose grew snotty. I sucked in air, and I couldn't lift my face from the shirt.

"Please come back," I whimpered. "God, I miss you. Please, please . . . don't be gone."

I didn't know how long I cried, but when I was exhausted and shaking, I thought about my rage and the traitorous thoughts that had just overwhelmed me.

Had I really begrudged Annabelle's life?

Oh God. I was a terrible mother. I loved her. I did. No matter that Matt had been the one to push for the third baby. I loved her now, more than life.

If anyone ever knew what I had just been thinking . . .

I swallowed hard.

They wouldn't. I was safe here. I was alone. I'd broken down, but that was to be expected, wasn't it? Shouldn't everyone be allowed to break down in my situation?

On shaky legs, I stood. I gripped the edge of the marble counter and felt the cool of the stone beneath my hand as I balanced myself. It grounded me, held me in place, reminded me that I existed.

I was still here, even if he was gone.

For the first time in a year, I felt in control. Like I was running this shit show of grief. By allowing my feelings to erupt, I felt like I purged them, that I could harness them now. At least for a minute.

The box was heavy, and the flaps almost tore as I picked it up.

I lugged it to the curb and got another cup of coffee. I sat on the porch steps, sipping my coffee, my sweater wrapped tightly around me, until the truck came rumbling down the street. The diesel engine pierced the silence.

It stopped at my house, and the garbage man lifted the box onto the rack, and the panic set in. I jumped up and ran.

"Wait," I called out, skidding to a halt in front of the startled man. "Wait."

I stood on my tiptoes and peered into the box, digging through it and pulling out the cologne bottle.

Not yet.

"You can take everything else."

"Sure, lady," he said in confusion. "You sure you want the rest of this to go?"

No.

But I nodded firmly and the box moved again, dumping into the truck bed. All of Matt's things tumbled out into the trash, into the used Kleenexes and rotting potato skins, and I felt numb.

But I did it.

I did it.

I tightened my grip on the glass bottle in my hand.

Almost.

I went back inside and put the cologne bottle in my purse for safe-keeping. I could keep this one thing. I wasn't Superwoman, for God's sake.

twenty-seven

BECK
MERCY HOSPITAL
12:54 P.M.

BIRDS, BLACK ONES, AS BLACK AS NIGHT, AS BLACK AS INK, FLY at my face and I try to get away from them. I swat at them, and I hear the flutter and rustle of their wings and then then then . . .

I wake up.

Only I still can't open my eyes.

Son of a bitch.

On the inside, it feels like I'm heaving, that I'm blowing, that I can't breathe, but on the outside, I'm still and quiet. The ventilator still whooshes as it breathes for me, as it fills my lungs up.

As I think on that, I realize that blackbirds must be in my mind for a reason—they were too vivid not to mean something.

I see them, flying at me, claws outstretched, beaks sharp, eyes beady.

What the hell?

What do they mean?

Is my brain telling me that I'm going to die?

Shouldn't I be more afraid?

I'm actually a little worried because I don't feel anything. My legs, my arms, my hands. They're numb. They feel washed-out, like any second I might fade from the page like old ink.

That can't be good.

———

ANGEL AND I WALKED along the block, our glances flitting in and around the corners, waiting, watching. It was then that Angel saw the shoes, high above us, tossed over the electric line.

Ahhhh. The universal signal of a dealer.

I felt a rush of relief.

We stood under them until someone showed his face. He was jittery, nervous. He looked this way and that before he stepped out of the shadows.

"Whaddya want?" he asked quickly.

"H," I answered. "We've got eight bucks."

"I need ten," he said firmly.

"We don't have it," Angel answered. "But we can bring it back later. I promise." Winston stuck his head out of her coat.

"Nope. Now or never. Your word means nothing to me," the dealer answered. He appraised her. "But we can trade." He eyed her up and down.

"No," I said firmly. "Not gonna happen."

"Suit yourself," the dealer said, shrugging, and turned to leave. Angel's face went desperate. My veins were already pumping in anticipation, and I'm sure hers were too.

"I won't fuck you," she told him. "But I'll blow you."

"Angel, no," I argued, but she pulled away.

"King, I need it." Her eyes were hollow and dead, and she was already detaching herself from what she was about to do.

I needed it too. She thrust Winston into my arms, and I said nothing as she disappeared into the shadows with the dealer.

I'd never felt so low.

I'd never felt so subhuman.

But even still, I waited for them to return, because I needed what they had more than I needed pride. More than I even needed to breathe.

twenty-eight

NATALIE
MERCY HOSPITAL
1:35 P.M.

ECK'S FOOT TWITCHES, AND FOR A SPLIT SECOND I THINK he's going to wake up. It's ridiculous, but I can't help it. His pulse is quickening, racing, and I'm confused.

"What's wrong, baby?" I whisper, trying to soothe him by stroking his hand. Is he fighting for his life in there? "Please fight," I add.

"He is, Natalie," my sister assures me. "Go take a break. Please. You look horrible."

"Um, thanks?" I grimace. She shakes her head.

"No, you look like you're going to fall over. You can't help him if you're passed out."

She's right. I'm not even doing *this* right.

Feeling like an utter failure, I walk down the hall to get ice chips. As my heavy feet drag me one step farther away from my son, a giant shadow appears behind me. I know who it is before I even look.

"I'm trying to give you space," Kit tells me, taking the pink plastic cup from my hand, and scooping ice into it. "But if you need me, just say the word. I'm here for you, Nat. I'm here for all of you."

"You're a good friend," I tell him. And I mean it. He always has been. He hands the ice cup to me.

"Beck's teammates are still here in the waiting room," he tells me. "I'm gonna run down the street and pick them up some hamburgers."

I'm grateful, and he knows. "You're okay," he whispers to me, then grabs my hand, squeezing it. "You're strong."

I nod, even though I feel weak.

"Thank you."

He's turning to go when nurses rush past him toward Beck's room. I freeze, and then a doctor comes through, and then a cart. They push and the door opens and then closes, and I'm suddenly able to move.

I run past Kit, burst through the door, and everyone is surrounding my son. Sam and Elin stand against the wall, horrified and helpless.

"Get me some Betapace," the doctor snaps, and a nurse fills a syringe and hands it to him quickly.

Beck is limp in the bed, although the monitors are shrieking. His heart rate is spiking over and over on the screen.

"What is happening?" I cry out, and no one takes the time to look at me.

"His heart . . ." Sam says, and then her words trail off. Obviously, I can see it's his heart. Jesus.

The noises and images blur together as my own heart pounds. Is this it? Is this where I lose him?

I can't take it.

I can't.

The doctor says something else that I can't understand, because I'm hearing everything through a roar in my ears now. He and the nurses move and speak, and I stand and wait.

I'm a statue.

It seems like hours pass before they finally step away.

The doctor comes straight to me, and he's got sweat on his brow.

"He's on very fragile ground," he tells me. I'm actually thankful for his direct approach. "His heart is arrhythmic, meaning it's got a very erratic and tachycardic beat. It's too fast. I've given him further medication to ease the workload of the heart. All we can do now is continue to wait."

He walks out and I rush to Beck, grabbing his hand. It's cold and clammy, and he doesn't feel alive.

"You've got to live," I insist, and I hear Elin crying. "You've got to, Beck. You cannot leave me. You cannot."

Tears burst through the dam of my determination and shock, and instead of falling apart at his bedside, I rush out blindly. The ugly fluorescent lights are a blur above my head, and the tiles race past beneath my feet. Nurses step out of the way, and I don't care who stares at me.

I cry as I run, but I don't stop until I am standing in front of the wooden chapel doors, breathing heavily.

I push them open and step inside.

I'm the only one here.

I don't hesitate.

I rush to the front and kneel in front of the altar.

"Please, God," I beg, and I stare above me at the stained glass. "Please. Save him. Take me instead. I'll do anything you want me to do. I'll give you anything. Just strengthen his heart. Give him the will to live. Save my son."

God doesn't answer.

The chapel remains quiet.

I pray and pray, aloud and silently.

When I finally stand and turn, a man is watching me from a pew. I didn't even hear the door open.

"I'm a chaplain," he tells me. "And I want you to know, God hears your prayers."

"But what will He do about them?" I ask. "Will He answer them?"

The chaplain can't answer that, and I know it.

The only One who can stares down silently from the cross on the wall.

———

I SAT IN A pew at the back and stared at the stained glass.

I was such a stranger in this church that no one approached me. I didn't belong here, and they seemed to know it, but I didn't know where else to go. I couldn't go to the police station for help; Beck's friends were no help. There was nothing left for me to do but beg a higher power.

I folded my hands, my chin resting on my fingertips as I squeezed my eyes closed.

"Please, God. Make Beck come home. Protect him from harm, shield him from danger. Be there when I can't. Please, make him come home. Bring him home."

I slipped out the same way I came in, quietly, without drawing attention to myself. On the way home, I scanned the ditches, the sidewalks, the corners.

No Beck.

When I got home, I found my sister waiting for me on the porch, her jacket drawn around her shoulders.

"Hey," Sam said, greeting me. But she had that *I want something from you* voice, and I cringed.

"What?" I demanded.

"Whatever do you mean?" she asked innocently.

"Uh-huh. Just tell me what you want."

"I don't want to now," she sniffed.

"Because I know what you're up to?"

"No. Because I was going to do something nice for you and now you've ruined it."

I sighed. "What is it?"

"Well, Vince has a company thing on Friday night. It's a formal thing, very la-di-da, and I thought maybe you'd like to go. It'd give you a chance to dress up and get out of the house."

I was confused. "Why can't you go with him?"

My sister paused. "Um. You wouldn't be going with Vince. You'd be going with one of his coworkers, Ezra."

I was stunned silent, and my heart pounded.

"Nat?"

"You're trying to set me up on a . . . date," I said slowly, and the mere words made my hands clammy. "I can't," I told her. "I can't."

"Why?" she asked simply, and is she really that obtuse?

"Can you really be asking me that?" I demanded. "It's too soon!"

"It's been a year," she said quietly. "I know no one can replace him, Nat. You don't have to marry this guy, for God's sake. I just want you to get out of the house. Get a change of pace. Rejoin the land of the living. Matt would want that."

"The land of the living?" I was incredulous now. "Are you freaking kidding me? You get to sleep in bed with your husband every night. I visit mine in a cemetery. You don't get to tell me what is best for me. You don't have the first clue!"

I was pissed, and she knew it.

"Okay, that wasn't the right way to say it," she said, backtracking quickly. "You know I loved Matt. And I love you. And I just want you to move forward. Just a little bit. Can you do that, Nat? For me?"

She meant well.

But I . . . I just couldn't.

"I *am* moving forward. In other ways." My answer was firm. "I'm not ready to go on a date."

"Fine," Sam said, accepting without argument. "This time."

"Any time!" I snapped back. "Until I choose otherwise. This is my decision. Not yours. And you know what? I can't leave the house that long. What if Beck comes home? Did you even think about that?"

Sometimes I got so frustrated because it was like I was the only person who felt his absence so profoundly. The only one who thought I needed to bleed or to sacrifice for him to come home.

Sam stared at me.

"Do you think I don't care about Beck?" she asked slowly. I didn't know what to say, and her lips twisted into a scowl.

"Are you freaking kidding me? I love that kid like my own," she snapped.

"I know," I tried to interrupt, but she continued.

"You think you're the only one who is affected," she went on. "But you're not. We all are. I watch for him everywhere. Vinny and I . . . we go out and hunt. We've posted pictures of him on streetlights. Did you even know that?"

No. I shook my head slowly. "You know I'm doing that already," I told her. "Right? I've made progress. I spend all of the time I used to spend going to the cemetery on going out and hunting for Beck. I knock on doors, I talk to people."

Sam eyed me. "Nat, Vinny and I aren't looking in this area. If he's using, he's not in all the upper-class places that you've been looking. He's on the South Side. He's on State Street or Archer Heights or somewhere."

That reality slammed into me hard and fast, and I stared at her.

"I didn't think of that," I admitted, and I hated that thought. It was too vile, too scary.

"And I didn't want to say anything because I knew it would upset you even more," she said, and her eyes were so kind.

My shoulders slumped, and Sam wrapped her arms around them. "Let's go in," she urged. "I'll make you some hot chocolate while we wait for the bus."

I allowed her to guide me into the kitchen and push me gently into a chair.

"I love you, you know," she said, less stern now. "I know you're hurting, sis. I know."

I nodded, and she made hot chocolate, and I tried to focus on the present. Because I wasn't in control of anything but this.

twenty-nine

BECK
MERCY HOSPITAL
2:47 P.M.

"Hi, Jessica," my mom says, greeting someone. Hands poke at me again in that medical way.

Her voice is soothing and low, her gloved hands cool on my warm skin.

"I'm just checking his vitals," Jessica assures my mom.

My mom grasps my hand now, and I know it's her because she's not wearing gloves. The touch is comforting. It makes me feel human.

"How does his heart sound?" Mom asks anxiously.

"It sounds good," Jessica assures her. "It sounds steady."

The machines are still beeping and whooshing, so I know I'm okay. For a minute, I wasn't sure. Everything sped up, and there were lots of voices and hands, and then everything went dark. When I came to, it was quiet again.

"Everyone is pulling for him," Jessica says. "So just know that you have a lot of support. I'm here until eleven tonight. But I might stay late . . . if necessary. If you need anything, let me know."

If necessary?

Oh, right.

They're going to take me off the machines.

Will I be ready?

I don't know.

And I'm not afraid, for some reason.

That, in itself, is a weird feeling because for the last three or four months, I'd been filled with so much anger. From grief and from using. The combination of Xanax, marijuana, heroin . . . all of it. It made my mood volatile.

It's nice to get some peace from that.

Is that what dying is like?

A descent into peacefulness?

I can't say that that would be a bad thing.

———

ANGEL LEFT HOURS AGO to refill our stash. She should've been back by now.

I wondered for a second if she stopped somewhere and used it all herself.

But that wouldn't be like her. She shared her stuff. She played well with others.

I moved around the warehouse and tried to make it feel like home. I piled empty boxes in different places to form makeshift walls for little living spaces. Our bedroom was smaller than the rest so that hopefully, between the two of us, we could generate some heat. It got cold at night.

I thought about my room at home, with the big soft bed, the flat-screen television, the privacy. I'd taken it all for granted. But at least I had freedom here. Freedom from the condemning glances and the pity and living under a microscope.

Freedom from always having to make excuses.

Here it might be dirty, it might be empty, it might be cold, but I was free.

I waited more, and I was antsy and my hands were shaking. I needed a hit. I needed it. My nerves were shot; my pulse was thready. My body was craving the toxin that was poisoning me. It was ironic, but I didn't care.

I tapped my finger against my leg as I waited and I didn't know exactly how long it'd been. Time was immeasurable without a watch.

I got up to pace, and I sat down to twitch, then I got up to pace again. That's when I saw her.

Through a dirty window, she was slumped into herself, her shoulders curled inward, and she was holding her stomach with one hand and Winston with the other. Her face was bloody.

I don't know how I got to her—all I know is the next moment I was by her side, holding her elbow and trying to help.

"What happened?" I asked, and I saw her eyelid was swollen closed. "Who did this to you?"

She couldn't answer that since her lip was puffy and bleeding. All she did was limply hand me the dog. "Is Winston all right?" she asked hoarsely, like she had gravel in her throat. That's when I noticed the red marks around her trachea. Fingerprints.

"What the fuck?" I screamed, reaching out to touch them. "Who did this?"

"Don't yell. That doesn't matter. Winston can't breathe. Check on him."

I looked at the dog, and she was right. He was breathing in tiny labored pants, and I took him inside and put him on the ground. I felt around his little body with my hands, and he whimpered when I touched his ribs. I could feel sharp spikes beneath my fingers.

"I think his ribs are broken," I said, looking up at Angel. Her eyes were fire, and her tongue was pink.

"Fuck that asshole," she spit out and lowered herself carefully to the ground next to Winston. "Poor little baby," she crooned to the dog. "Poor baby."

She didn't dare pull him into her lap.

"We have to get him help," she said wildly, but we didn't have the money and she knew that.

I was helpless in this moment, and so was she as we stared down at the little dog.

Winston whimpered now, a little yelp, and he stared up at me, begging me for help with his coal-black eyes.

"Who did this?" I asked one last time. Angel glanced at me.

"The fucking dealer. He kicked Winston for no reason and then he beat the shit out of me when I tried to stop him."

"I'll be back," I said, and I leapt to my feet. I ignored Angel's cries of protest, and I headed for the bridge.

Fuck that guy.

Who the fuck did he think he was?

I saw him from across the street before he saw me. I headed straight for him, taking long steps, and I didn't hesitate.

I grabbed him by the throat, in the same way he must've grabbed Angel.

"Whoa, whoa, whoa," he tried to say, and he struggled, but I was furious, so I was stronger. "What the fuck?"

"You left a mark on my friend and my dog," I said, and the words were like venom between my teeth. "You're a fucking prick."

I slammed his head against the bridge, his skull a ripe watermelon against the stone. Addicts looked up from their trash can fires and makeshift beds, but no one came to his aid. They were all interested, but not concerned.

"You fucking prick," I said again. I pounded my knuckles into his nose and I didn't feel it as my fists said more than my words ever could. My rage was red, my vision was blurred, and I didn't know how long I beat him. I only knew that when I was done, he was limp and he was bloody, and my knuckles were mush.

"Fuck you, dude," I told him again, and I kicked him hard in the ribs, once, twice, three times. "That's for Winston."

Winston.

He needed help.

I knelt and took everything I could from this asshole's pockets. A wad of cash and tiny baggies full of drugs. His eyes glazed over and he struggled just a bit more.

"Don't be dumb," he cautioned me.

"Fuck you."

"My name is Pete. Remember that," he said as the blood filled up his teeth.

I paused. "I won't."

"Yes," he gurgled. "You will."

I strode away and no one tried to stop me. But they'd all seen my face, and I could never go back to that bridge.

I hurried back to the warehouse, and when I arrived, I was almost afraid to go inside. If Winston had died, Angel would be inconsolable. But I pushed through the door, and she looked up at me, her eyes red.

I lifted my eyebrows, and she nodded.

"He's still alive."

I picked him up and went outside. Angel limped behind me.

"What are we doing?" she asked, and her eyes grazed over my knuckles. "What did you do?"

"We're finding a vet," I said simply. I walked straight to the nearest convenience store and asked the clerk for a phone book. My hands were bloody, but she gave it to me anyway, and I rested Winston on the counter as I looked. He whined but didn't lift his head.

"Three blocks away," I told Angel. "Can you make it?"

She nodded and I carried Winston and we looked pathetic as we walked the three longest blocks of our lives.

The lady behind the counter looked up when we came in, then she stood, her eyes on our dog.

"What happened?" she asked, coming around from the back. She stretched her arms out for Winston and I handed him over. He didn't open his eyes.

"He got kicked," I told her.

"A lot," Angel added. "Hard."

"Can you help?" I asked, and produced a fistful of cash. "We can pay."

Angel's eyes got wide, but she didn't say anything and the woman didn't even look.

"I'll take him straight back. You can wait out here."

She disappeared with Winston, and Angel and I sat in the empty waiting room where it smelled like dog food.

I was unable to sit still. I felt ants on me, only there weren't any. It was my imagination, and I scratched at my arm. It was the effects of coming down, of craving hard, of wanting what I couldn't have right now, of knowing that I had what I needed in my pocket.

"Are you okay?" I asked Angel, and her face was more swollen than ever.

She shook her head. "It doesn't matter. I'll be fine."

"We should get you some ice," I told her, and the woman was coming back around the corner so I asked for some.

"Of course," she said, and disappeared again. She came back a minute later with an ice pack.

"Here, honey." She pressed it to Angel's face. "Use this. Can you come with me into the back and we can clean you up?"

Angel had dried blood all over her face, and she tried to say no but I urged her to go. Finally, she nodded.

"Thank you."

When they were gone, I was alone. I waited, and I tapped my foot on the floor, taptaptap. And when they didn't emerge, I went into the bathroom. It was right off the waiting room, and I assumed it was for customers.

I was a customer.

Once in there, behind the locked door, I took out the baggies and found pills among the rocks and lumps. I didn't know what they were, but anything would help. I took several and the room started to waver in and out, the shapes outlined by brighter lights than normal. I saw spots and lines where there shouldn't be, but the shaking in my hands stopped. The ants stopped crawling up my legs.

I sighed a breath of relief and stuffed the baggies back into my pocket.

I went back out and sat down, and I leaned my head back.

I closed my eyes and I waited.

They came out eventually, and Angel was cleaned up now, and she had a beatific smile on her face.

"He's going to be okay," she told me happily. "Winston. He's okay."

I looked at the lady, and she nodded. "The vet is taping him up now. His ribs are broken, but they aren't penetrating any organs or his lungs. He'll need to be sedated and kept still, but he's fine."

I breathed a sigh of relief, although I didn't know why. He was Angel's dog, not mine. But he was small and he was sort of under my protection, so I was glad he was okay.

"Thank you so much," she told the lady. "Thank you. He means the world to me."

The lady dug in her purse and handed us a bottle of ibuprofen. "Take that," she told Angel. "Since you can't go to the doctor. It'll help."

"Thank you."

I got up to pay and she only charged me fifty dollars.

"Are you sure?" I asked, because I thought it would be more.

"Absolutely. I'm going to get the bottle of sedatives for Winston, and then he'll be out shortly."

She left again, and I counted the rest of the money. There was $185 in my hand. Angel's eyes narrowed.

"Where did you get that?" She was suspicious, and she eyed my knuckles again. "Did you go see the dealer?"

"His name is Pete," I told her in answer. "And we can't go to the bridge anymore."

"Did he pay for what he did to Winston?" Angel asked, and there was hope gleaming in her eyes.

I nodded. "And for what he did to you."

Angel laid her head on my shoulder and her hand slipped into mine. We waited and waited, and finally the lady came back out with Winston.

She put him, all taped up, in my arms.

"Here are the sedatives," she said. "Make sure to give them to him, per the instructions on the bottle."

"Thank you," Angel said, and her eyes welled up, and the lady hugged her, carefully.

"Take care of yourself," she said, and her eyes were kind. "Oh, and one more thing."

We waited.

"Those aren't for human consumption," she said. "The pills."

Angel's cheeks flared red, and the lady was uncomfortable.

I nodded and we left.

Angel didn't say a word as we walked, even though her hands were clenched into fists. It was humiliating; it was degrading.

But the lady wasn't rude. She was matter-of-fact. Medical.

We were users, and it was obvious, and there was nothing else to say about that.

We walked slowly back down the three long city blocks, waiting at each pedestrian light. The cold licked at our faces, and Angel's nose turned red.

"Is it safe to go back to the warehouse?" she asked, and even through her swollen cheeks, I could see the circles under her eyes.

"I think so," I said. "They don't know where we live."

"Okay." She trusted me. If I said something, she took it as the truth, and after months of having my mom doubt me, that was a good feeling.

When Winston was laid down on the floor in front of a small trash can fire, Angel turned to me.

"Is money the only thing you got from him?"

I knew what she was asking. I shook my head and pulled out the baggies.

Angel's eyes widened again, because it was a lot.

I kept out a rock of heroin and put the rest of it in my purple bag.

We sat on the dirty floor and shot up the H, and in a few minutes, it took all of our pain. We floated on a sea of tranquility and darkness, and nothing mattered but this.

thirty

BECK
MERCY HOSPITAL
4:28 P.M.

THE BIRDS ARE SITTING ON THE WINDOWSILL NOW, WATCHING me. One cocks its head, another caws, and then they all fly off in a mass flutter of wings.

I startle awake at the beeping of my machines.

Fuck.

I'd been asleep again, and the birds were back.

What the hell is the deal with those birds?

I'm quickly distracted, though, because someone is stroking my hand, and the perfume is Elin's.

"Beck," she murmurs. "Come back to me. Please."

I want to tell her to run away from me, that I'm messed up and not worth her time. But I know she'd roll her eyes and tell me I'm worth everything, that she loves me no matter what.

She used to be the only thing I thought of. She was the first thing on my mind in the morning and the last thing on it at night. But that was then.

Now I have a tube down my throat, pinching the sides of my mouth, and she's in the chair next to me, whispering words she doesn't think I can hear.

I don't deserve her.

I wish she'd just realize it.

—————

ANGEL SAT IN THE wintry sun, waiting for me to wake. I knew this was true because she was the first thing I saw when I opened my eyes, once the blurriness faded and I could focus.

"How long have I been sleeping?" I mumbled. It was daylight, so it was hard to say.

"A day, I think," she answered. Winston was in her lap and he stared at me soulfully. "Maybe two. I don't really know."

"How are you feeling?" I asked as I sat up. Her face was heavily bruised and still swollen, and she looked like a bus had smashed into her.

"Eh," she said, waving off my concern. "I've had worse."

"Yeah?" Someone had beat her worse than this?

She shrugged. "Don't be a drama queen."

"Where are you from?" I asked, and I tried to be casual as I rubbed my eyes.

"Not here," she answered, and she was evasive and it was annoying.

"Angel, seriously. I want to know about you."

She groaned. "Fine. Here's something. I'm an only child, thank God," she said. "So I'm the only opportunity they had to fuck up."

"That's good, I guess."

"But I'm not *that* fucked up," she argued in defense, and I nodded at that too.

"No, you're not."

"Well, which is it?" she demanded. "Am I fucked up or not?"

"I don't know," I told her honestly. "Sometimes it seems like it, and sometimes it doesn't."

"Well, you're not perfect either," she said pluckily, and I wondered how I managed to insult her when all I was trying to do was agree.

"I know," I said, nodding. "Far from it, actually."

"That's probably why we get along."

Maybe, although I doubt she'd done anything wrong. Her name might be Angel, and she might not be one, but from what I'd seen, she was a pretty damn good person. Only good people rescued dogs.

"My parents aren't in my life," she said eventually. "My father left when I was a baby. My mom kicked me out last year. Her boyfriend hated me."

She fidgeted now, twirling the hair on Winston's chin, and it seemed like she was waiting for me to judge her on something that wasn't her fault.

"She chose him over you?"

"Yes."

I was appalled and didn't even know what to say. Angel shook her head and waved her hand.

"It's okay, King. It makes my life easier. All I have to worry about is myself and Winston now. And you."

"You don't have to worry about me," I said, rolling my eyes. "I can take care of myself."

"I like taking care of you," she admitted like it was a deep, dark secret. But it made me feel a little sick, down in the pit of my belly.

"Don't," I told her. "Don't get attached to me. Trust me, I'm not good for anyone."

"Yes, you are," she argued, but I held up my hand.

"I'm not. End of conversation."

"Whatever, King."

"Have you finished high school?" I asked, and I knew I was pressing my luck now.

"No. I'm close, though. I could finish in a semester."

"You should," I told her. "You need to."

"I will," she agreed. "One of these days."

I eyed her, and her eyes were glassy and haunted. I reached out and cupped her hand, and she closed her eyes, shutting it all away.

"Fuck them, King," she said softly, and her fingers tightened around mine. "Fuck them all."

She wet her lips and they were dry, really chapped. I hadn't noticed before.

"We have to get dog food for Winston," she added. "He's really hungry."

"Okay."

We stepped over the broken boards in the back window and slunk down the alleyway toward the closest convenience store. Trash blew against the brick buildings, and there was a painted penis on the fence, which was charming, but soon the 7-Eleven loomed ahead.

When we entered, the cashier watched us.

"Hello," I said politely.

"Hello," he answered suspiciously. "Can I help you?"

"We just need a few things."

He didn't answer, just watched my every move. I hadn't showered in a while, and my clothes were dirty. I knew what we looked like to him, and I couldn't say that I blamed him, but it still pissed me off. I had money, goddamn it. I wasn't going to steal anything. Today.

While Angel got the dog food, I found the lip balm and grabbed a tube, making sure I kept it in plain sight of the cashier.

We plunked our stuff down, and the cashier rang us up.

"Sixteen forty-two," he said, and I think he was waiting for me to say I didn't have it. He was annoyed with me already and I hadn't done anything wrong.

I handed him a twenty.

He was surprised, but he counted out my change.

"Have a nice day," he said as he handed it to me. I glanced at it, at the $4.58, then handed him back a dollar.

"You gave me too much," I said stiltedly. I didn't say anything else and he didn't thank me for being honest.

"We should've gotten something to eat," Angel said as we walked into the cold. "We haven't eaten in a while."

She was right. I didn't remember the last time we had eaten. Was it days ago?

Up the road, there was a shady little sports bar.

"Keep Winston in your coat," I told Angel as I guided her inside.

They brought us chips but I didn't eat them. I shoved the basket toward Angel and she nibbled on a chip while she pushed another into her coat for Winston.

"Have you ever had a car?" she asked, quite randomly, and she was staring out at the parking lot. Rows of cars gleamed there in the sun, nice ones, crappy ones, old ones, new. I nodded.

"Yeah."

She looked at me, her eyes large over her water glass.

"What happened to it?"

I looked away. "I don't remember."

But I did.

I gave it to someone in exchange for a week's worth of hero. "It's too bad you don't still have it," she said simply. "We could sleep in it."

The waiter eyed us suspiciously as he brought out our food and, with a little distaste, asked if we wanted anything else.

I was sick of being treated like this.

Once upon a time, I tipped very well. My dad taught me that. He also taught me to be very kind to waiters. But this one was being a dick.

"That'll be all for now," I said, dismissing him, and he left, but he didn't like it. I'm pretty sure he was afraid we'd steal the flatware. That hadn't occurred to me, but it would make eating out of cans easier, so I slipped a fork in my pocket and then grabbed a new one from the next table.

"When you're finished, take yours too," I advised Angel. She nodded.

"Good idea. And maybe a napkin. I can use it for Winston's whiskers. They're cloth."

I nodded and we ate and it tasted like cardboard to me because heroin shuts down the olfactory sense. I didn't smell the food and I didn't want the food, but my body needed it, so I chewed and swallowed, chewed and swallowed.

It was while I was chewing that I noticed a girl sitting across the room.

Her back was to me, but it was Elin.

I recognized the long blond hair and the dainty way her shoulders moved while she talked.

I sucked in a breath, and this couldn't be happening, because I couldn't see her. Not like this.

Especially not when she was here with another guy.

He was tall and muscular and I didn't know him. But he was clean and he was handsome and he wasn't me.

They laughed and talked, and her hand fluttered in her hair—that was what she did when she was nervous. They were on a date, I realized, and my heart sank because I loved her more than I cared to admit, and now she was sitting with someone else.

I didn't pay attention to the fact that I was too, because it was different.

So different.

Elin was on a pedestal in my mind, and there in that safe place, she'd always be mine, always waiting for me to get better, to return.

But here she was, and she wasn't waiting.

I couldn't stop staring and Angel noticed.

She looked over her shoulder and then turned to me, questioningly. "What?"

I shook my head. "Nothing."

But I couldn't shake it and we had to walk past their table after we'd paid and were leaving.

The guy leaned over and grabbed her hand, and how could she have moved on so fast?

I was stunned, and even though I needed to walk out the door, I needed to see her face even more. I was driven by a need I couldn't control, so I stopped by her table.

I wanted her to see that I'd seen her, that I knew. That I knew she'd moved on, and *how could she?*

She looked up and I was shocked speechless because she wasn't Elin.

She wasn't Elin at all.

Her eyes were brown and her nose was too big, and her boyfriend was annoyed.

"Can we help you?" he asked, and he looked down his nose at us.

"No, my mistake," I muttered, but the relief flooding through me was ridiculous as I pulled Angel toward the door. We almost plowed over a father and son coming in.

"What was that about?" she demanded as we hit the pavement, and I shook my head.

"Nothing," I told her. But she knew.

"Was that the girl you dream about?" she asked, and I was astounded.

"I dream about her?"

"You say her name sometimes," Angel answered. "Was that her?"

I shook my head again.

"No."

"But you thought it was?"

I couldn't answer.

Because I was staring through the window of the sports bar at the little boy who was now sitting there with his father. They were both watching the football game on television. Notre Dame was playing Navy, and the blood . . . it pulsed through my veins over and over and over, and throbbed in my ears.

That would never be me again. I'd never sit with my dad, and he'd never be proud of me again. I'd never see him laugh; he'd never see me smile.

It was over.

"King, are you listening?" Angel demanded, and I had no idea how long she'd been talking. "You love her. Clearly you love her. Why don't you just make it work with her? What happened?"

I was frozen to the pavement as the father dipped his French fry in his son's ketchup, and the little boy glared at him for taking his precious condiment.

"I can't," I finally was able to say, and God, it felt like I might die.

"That's ridiculous," Angel said wearily. "Why not?"

"Because I killed my father."

thirty-one

NATALIE
MERCY HOSPITAL
5:57 P.M.

BECK'S HEART MONITOR STARTS BEEPING FASTER AND I GLANCE at the screen to find it's at 112 beats a minute. It was only 75 a few minutes ago.

I'm scared, but I try to stay calm. The breathing tube looks like it's pinching the edge of Beck's lip, so I wiggle it around a little bit to loosen its grip. It's keeping him alive, so I can't move it too much.

"You're okay," I tell him softly. "You're okay."

"What if he's not, though?" Elin asks, and she's terrified. "Even if he wakes up, he'll never get over the accident, Mrs. K."

"Don't say that," I tell her firmly, probably harsher than I needed to be. "He's strong. He can move past it."

"You know he blames himself," she says shakily. "Because he was driving."

"It wasn't his fault," I tell her. "Matt shouldn't have let him. It was too late, and they were too tired. It wasn't his fault." I say that last bit more firmly than the rest, like I'm trying to convince myself. Because the horrible truth of the matter is, deep down, I do sometimes blame him.

I blame my son for taking my husband.

And it's not fair. It's not right. But it's the truth.

"He has nightmares a lot," Elin says, and she rubs her finger on Beck's cheek, stroking his cheekbone. "Did you know that?"

I look down because no, I didn't. He hadn't told me.

"He dreams about the accident. He sees the tangled-up wreck, the red car, his dad . . ." Elin's voice trails off, and she doesn't know how far to go, how much to tell me. "He used to text me in the middle of the night when he couldn't sleep. Before he left."

"Go on," I encourage her.

"He tortures himself," she says, and her eyes fill with pain. "I wanted to help. I really did. But nothing I did mattered. He just . . . he was drowning in it."

"I know," I whisper.

"He's a good person," Elin tells me, and that's not necessary because of course I know that. He's my kid. I brought him into the world and I raised him to be good. "I feel like everyone here will judge him now. Because of this."

She sweeps her arm over the bed, motioning toward the tubes and tape, and I flinch.

"What they think doesn't matter."

I know she's right, though. They'll look at Beck like the boy he is right now. They don't know who he was before.

He was such a good boy, from the very beginning. Even as a baby, he'd rarely cried and always smiled. He'd always been a people pleaser, someone who wanted to make everyone around him happy.

I would've never in a thousand years guessed that we'd end up here, in this sterile room.

I suddenly wish with all my being that I could reach into time and just change it, that I could strangle it into submission.

It's not fair that things happen and we don't know that they will be the last time. The last time I'd kissed Matt goodbye. The last time I'd tucked Beck into bed without worrying about him. The last time I'd gotten into my car and fastened my seat belt without wondering if it would malfunction and I'd die.

Time is a bitch.

If only I'd known ahead of time, I would've changed things.

I would've warned them.

————

I SAT WITH ANNABELLE and Devin and watched the brand-new shiny black Honda Civic slowly circle the high school parking lot. It was such a beautiful day with a blue sky and cotton candy clouds that when Matt had come out of the bedroom and announced that Beck was going to learn to drive today, we'd decided to make it a picnic.

We'd made sandwiches and brought a lawn blanket, and it had been perfect so far.

Beck had been nervous, though he'd tried to hide it. He was far too cool to experience jitters. At least, that's what he wanted us to think. But I'd noticed how he was dragging out his lunch, eating his sandwich so slowly and nursing his chocolate milk.

"You'll be fine," I'd whispered to him. "Don't worry."

"I'm not," he said, winking at me, and I'd only seen the uncertainty in his eyes for a second.

Beck was behind the wheel now, a hundred feet away from us, and he studied the pavement so studiously that we all three giggled. We'd never seen him concentrate on anything so hard before. Of course, next to him Matt was solemn too.

Teaching his firstborn to drive was serious business.

Annabelle slurped at her Capri Sun and pointed.

"Daddy looks mad," she chirped.

"He's not mad, honey," I assured her. "He's just focused."

By focused, I meant terrified.

I chuckled again. His hand was curled tightly enough around the oh-shit bar that his knuckles were white.

I was glad it was him and not me.

He'd set up all the cones in perfect configurations, and Beck had only hit two. Of course, Beck was only going eleven miles an hour.

He was having issues changing gears. But that was one thing Matt was insistent about.

"All of the kids will learn on a stick," he'd told me. "That way, they can drive anything."

I'd agreed because it had made sense.

But now, watching the car lurch around the lot and Matt's face turn green, I had to wonder if he was reconsidering.

He stuck it out, though. I helped Dev and Annabelle with their homework on the blanket under the tree, and Beck and Matt went round and round the pavement.

Within an hour, Beck was whipping in and out of the cones like a pro, and both father and son were beaming when they finally parked the car and rejoined us under the tree.

"I'm an excellent driver," Beck announced as they sat down and he gulped a soda.

"He can only dream he'll be as good as me," Matt told me, smacking Beck on the back in the way that men did.

This was such an interesting age for a boy. Beck was starting to become a man, and he questioned Matt's knowledge every now and again, but today . . . today had been perfect. He'd accepted Matt's guidance without a word, and the sun shone down on our shoulders.

It was the stuff that all good memories were made of.

Later that night, in the privacy and darkness of our bedroom, Matt turned to me.

"I know you're nervous about him driving. But you don't have to worry about him," he told me confidently. "He's going to be a great driver. He's too cautious to be anything else."

I had to laugh at that. "Beck? Cautious?"

"You know he doesn't like to make mistakes," Matt said introspectively. "He likes to toe the line, and he likes to do it perfectly. If he puts his mind to something, he does it."

That was certainly true.

If Beck did something, he did it all the way and he did it right the first time.

thirty-two

"WE'RE GOING TO BRING HIM OUT AROUND ELEVEN," THE
doctor tells my mother. I feel a jolt at that, adrenaline
pumping into my fingers and toes. What time is it now? How long do
I have to wait to know whether I will live or die?

"Why?" my mother asks, her voice forced and thin. "What about
his kidneys? Why not just wait until morning? Why not give him a little
more time?"

"The swelling in his brain has shown signs of reducing," the doctor
answers. "His kidneys are stable for the moment, enough so that we're
discontinuing the dialysis. Recovery from this type of thing isn't linear,
because the medication we use builds up in his system. The longer he's
on it, the longer he might take to come out. Because of that, I want to
stop the use of Versed as quickly as I can."

"But will he be ready?" my aunt whispers.

The doctor is silent.

"I hope so," he finally says. There is a rustling of paper and then the
door opens and closes, and I think he's gone.

"We have less than four hours," my mom says, and she's in shock.

She grasps my hand and pushes the hair back from my forehead.

I don't know why she's so kind to me. I killed Dad and she knows it. She tries not to talk about it, and she probably tries not to think about it, but the fact is I deserve to be in this bed.

If I could die and trade places with my dad so that he was alive again, I'd do it in a second.

Unfortunately, it doesn't work that way.

If only it did.

I try to remember the accident. How exactly did it happen? Why are parts of my brain simply not working? Why am I even thinking at all? Aren't I supposed to be comatose?

I'm a prisoner in my own body.

Maybe that's my own karma. My own penance for killing my father. It's only right that I should suffer.

I focus on that day again. I remember getting up, and I remember driving to South Bend with my dad. We were visiting the Notre Dame campus. I thought it was a day like any other.

But it wasn't.

————

"VISITORS, FOLLOW ME," OUR tour guide said, and he was such a nerd. My dad rolled his eyes because the kid's voice actually squeaked.

"Don't worry," Dad said. "You won't turn into that guy. Lots of amazing people went here. Joe Montana, Knute Rockne, Condoleezza Rice, Tim Brown . . ."

"You forgot *you*," I mentioned.

"Well, yeah. That goes without saying. This is a great school, kid."

"I know," I said. "I've never said it wasn't. I just kinda wanted to go farther away from home."

We walked out from the locker room, under the legendary PLAY LIKE A CHAMPION TODAY sign, and onto the football field. On the far end, Touchdown Jesus stood tall and golden in the night. We stay in the legendary stadium for a few minutes.

"We're going to tour the basilica now, so follow me," the kid said. While everyone else followed him across campus, we stayed in place, breathing the crisp air.

"It's far enough away that it's not right next door," Dad pointed out. "An hour and a half—that's pretty far. But it's still close enough that if you need us, we're here. You know?"

"I get what you're saying," I said as I followed him into a nearby inlet. It was made from rock, and candles were lit everywhere around us in the night. "It's just that I don't want you to have to bail me out. I want to sink or swim, Dad."

My dad laughed, a loud guffaw that echoed against the rock.

"Lord, you remind me of me," he said, and I took that as a compliment. "But trust me. It took me at least twenty years to figure out that taking help when you need it isn't anything to be ashamed of."

I didn't answer; instead, I turned my attention to whatever it was we were standing in.

"What the heck is this?" I asked.

My dad turned slowly in a circle, taking it in.

"This is the grotto," he said with reverence. "It's a replica of Our Lady of Lourdes in France. People come here to pray and for quiet moments."

I stared at the flickering candles and realized that each of them had been lit during a prayer.

"We're not Catholic," I reminded my father. "In fact, we're not even religious. I'd be so out of place here, Dad."

"Nah," he answered. "I wasn't Catholic either. Lots of kids aren't, and they come here anyway."

"Yeah, but most of them probably go to church at least," I argued. "We never have. I don't know the first thing about religion."

My dad studied me.

"You know, I've wondered before if your mom and I failed you kids in that area," he said slowly. "I don't personally like organized religion, but I do believe in God. I think there's something bigger than us, smarter than us. And I think there's a grand plan."

He waited and I realized he wanted me to speak.

"Well, me too," I told him. "It'd be dumb otherwise. There has to be something pulling us all together. A reason for everything. Otherwise, it would be kinda pointless."

"Right," my dad said. "And I don't want to live like that. I want to live in a place where I think things happen for a reason, where they have a point."

He bent down and picked up a lighter. With one stroke, he lit a nearby candle, then put his arm around my shoulders.

"God, if you're there, and I know you are, please guide my son. Let him choose the right path for himself. He doesn't have to come to Notre Dame, even though I did and it's the best school in the country." I gave him side-eye and he chuckled. "Let him know that he'll be okay no matter where he goes or what he does, even when his mom and I aren't there. Let him know that he's going to shine. Thank you."

I couldn't deny that the beauty in this grotto was incredible as the light lapped at the rocks, the shadows of the flames flickering into the night.

"Thanks, Dad," I told him, even though he was being pretty corny. He meant well, and I knew that. He only wanted me to come here because he thought it was best. But he wouldn't try to strong-arm me. He just wasn't like that.

"I'm tired," he said. "You want to skip the last part of the tour and go home? It's a long drive."

I rolled my eyes now because he emphasized that it was a *long drive* to make me think that Notre Dame was far enough away, and he laughed because he knew that I knew.

We found his car easily and when we reached it, Dad turned to me.

"Do you want to drive?"

I was startled. "Really?"

He nodded. "Yeah. I think you can do it."

"Sweet!"

We got in, buckled up, and hit the road.

Once we were sailing toward Chicago, Dad started digging in the console. "I forgot," he told me. "I made something for you a while back. You've been getting up so early to work out in the mornings, and I know some days it must be hard."

He produced a CD and I laughed, keeping both hands on the wheel. "Dad, no one uses CDs anymore."

"Well, I didn't know how else to record myself. I'm a dinosaur."

He slipped the CD in the player, and his voice came on, loud and firm.

> *I know you want to sleep in, Beck. But before you reach for the snooze button, remember this:*
>
> *You want to be the best, and the other players do too. They won't press snooze. The best players are already up, and they're already running, their feet on the floor.*
>
> *I want you to get out of bed and remember that you are the best of the best. You breathe in challenges, and you spit out wins. You do not accept failure, and you fight for what is yours.*

I looked at my dad. "Seriously?"

He laughed and pushed the eject button, interrupting whatever he was saying on the CD, and put it back in the console.

"Fine. Laugh at it now. But if you download it to your phone, or whatever you kids do, and set it as your alarm, it might help you get out of bed and get to the weight room on the challenging mornings—the mornings when you're feeling too tired to go. There's some good stuff on there, kid."

"I bet," I said, and there probably was, because my dad always knew just how to motivate me. But not tonight. Tonight, I needed music.

I turned up the volume and Dad settled into the seat next to me, reclining just a bit.

He yawned. "If I fall asleep and you need me, just holler. But it's an easy drive from here."

"I know," I told him. "I'm fine, Dad."

He nodded. "Wake me up when we hit the second rest stop. I'll have to pee by then. I've got the bladder of an old man now."

He was only thirty-eight.

He closed his eyes and I absorbed the music, letting the stress of the day fade away. I'd choose my college another day. For now, I'd revel in the rare treat of driving my dad's sports car on the highway at night. Normally he said it was too much car for me, which was so annoying. I'd been driving for a year already. I could handle it.

The road noise was soothing and hummed us toward Chicago, and my dad started snoring within twenty minutes. Maybe he was old, after all. I laughed to myself.

Whenever I stepped on the accelerator, the V-8 engine roared in response and that was so fucking cool. I got a surge of adrenaline each time. I kept finding myself speeding, and each time, I'd purposely slow down.

But if Dad woke up and I was doing ninety, he'd make me pull over and switch places with him.

I watched the scenery blurring past, and the city got closer and closer. We roared past the first rest stop, and I sang along with the radio. My dad was sleeping so hard that it didn't seem to bother him a bit.

As we approached the second rest stop, I looked over at him. His mouth was open ever so slightly and he was dead asleep. Home was only another twenty minutes or so from here, so he probably wouldn't actually need to stop. I was contemplating what to do, when my phone rang.

I could hear it, but it was under the seat belt, tucked into my pocket. It rang again, and I dug under the belt to get it.

Then I dropped it between the console and the seat.

"Damn it," I cursed, reaching to get it. The car swerved over the line, and I yanked it back. "Son of a bitch."

My fingers grasped the rubbery corner of my phone case, fishing it up and out of the crevice. When it was firmly in my hand, I glanced down to push the Accept button.

thirty-three

I LOOK OVER AT ELIN AND SHE IS SO WORN OUT. HER FACE IS pale from exhaustion, and she has barely left Beck's side.

"Sweetheart, you should really at least go splash some water on your face, or get some juice," I tell her. "You're going to collapse on your feet in a second."

She sighs, a long exhale. "I don't want to leave you alone," she answers. "You shouldn't be alone."

"I'm not," I argue. "Beck is here. And my sister and Kit are right outside. It'll be fine. Really. I want you to take care of yourself too."

Elin smiles tremulously. "You're so good to me," she says. "I've missed you so much these past few months. You're like my second mom and I feel like this whole part of my life has been snatched away from me."

She cries now, and I rub her back and I don't really know what to say, because what *can* I say? Beck broke her heart, and nothing can heal that except time. It's something I know all too well.

"Beck will wake up, and he'll remember how much he loves you," I reassure her.

I don't know if any of that is true, and Elin knows it. She nods through her tears.

"The worst part is that we should never have broken up. If we hadn't . . . if we hadn't, maybe he wouldn't be here right now. Maybe I could've talked him out of going down this road, and he wouldn't be in this bed."

"Don't do the 'what if' thing. You couldn't have stopped him, Elin. He made his own choices. None of this is your fault."

"If only that were true," she sniffs again, and she cries and I should be comforting her, but something about the way she said that gives me pause, and then she says something under her breath, something that sounds like *it was all my fault.*

"What do you mean?" I ask her slowly. "How in the world could any of this be your fault?"

Elin looks at me, and her gaze is pointed like a spear and it pins my heart. Heavy unease hangs between us, and I feel something with gravity getting ready to emerge.

"Beck didn't tell you?" Her words are slow and deliberate. She is shocked, and this can't be good.

"Tell me what?" I fight to remain calm, because we're just having a conversation.

"About the phone call?"

Her voice is empty now, but sad, and it's hiding something awful. I feel it, and I'm afraid of it.

"What phone call, honey?"

My hands shake and my intuition knows. It knows.

"I called him the night of the accident," she says simply. "Every-thing *is* my fault."

The world crashes down in this moment.

I had built castles in the air around me, a fortress to protect my heart and it was invisible, but now I know it's coming down and the walls will crush me with the weight of the stones.

"You called," I say slowly, to clarify. "That night."

She nods and it's painful and everything is in slow motion.

"I didn't know he was driving," she whispers. "I swear. When he picked up, all I could hear was noise. Then metal crunching." Her eyes squeeze closed. "He was screaming . . ."

She'd called that night.

Beck had answered, and then he'd crashed into an oncoming car.

"I thought he'd dozed off," I say, my words like sharp razors on my tongue.

"That's what he said," Elin says, nodding. "I don't know why. Maybe he didn't want everyone to hate me. Maybe *he* didn't want to hate me. But now he does. He says it's our fault and he can't get past it. He was hunting for his phone, Mrs. K. That's why he crashed."

"Because you called," I say, and *I'm not blaming her—I'm not.*

She nods again, and the reason my whole world ended is sitting here in front of me.

I can't quite catch my breath, and everything makes sense now, all of it.

"Beck broke up with you because he can't forgive himself . . . or you," I murmur.

She nods.

"Because you called, and he answered."

She nods again.

"I . . . I need a minute."

I walk out of the room, and I go out into the hallway, and I still can't breathe. I lean against the wall and I try to inhale, but the breath won't come and my husband is dead and my heart is pounding and Elin called and Beck answered and Matt is dead.

My thoughts swirl and blend, and I can't stay in here. I rush down the halls and burst outside into the ambulance bay. The cool air hits my face but it doesn't help. I still can't focus and I still can't breathe.

I realize with a start that my Xanax is back in the room.

Far from me.

My heart pounds.

There are sirens in the distance, but I don't know where they are. Lights flash against the wall, against my skin, red and blue, then blue and red, and back again. People rush past, and no one notices me, and no one cares.

No one cares my world is crashing.

I picture that night. I picture Beck and Matt driving along. I picture Matt dozing off, and he never knew what hit him and Elin called.

She called and Beck answered and his attention was away from the road for one second.

One.

Second.

And now Matt is dead, and this is why Beck feels guilty. This is why he used drugs. To get away from this.

Beck killed Matt.

He's been carrying this on his back, and it forced him to the breaking point. And I hadn't even noticed. In fact, all I'd done was blame him too. To myself mostly, but that one time . . . that one time, I'd told him that if he hadn't gone to the campus with his dad, Matt would still be alive.

How could I have done that? It had been a faulty seat belt that killed Matt. Not Beck. Not Elin. And I hadn't done a good enough job making sure that Beck knew it.

Jesus God.

I open my mouth and I'm like a fish on pavement. I can't suck in air, and why can't I breathe?

I pull my phone out of my pocket because that is my only lifeline.

I send a text.

Help.

My eyes close.

My hand falls to the side.

Images of the crash, of how I've always imagined it, are replaced with new ones. Did Matt open his eyes when the phone rang? Did he hear? Did he see? Did he know he was going to die?

Did it hurt?

Tears spill wildly and I can't breathe, and then I'm drifting away and I never want to come up for air.

thirty-four

BECK
MERCY HOSPITAL
9:12 P.M.

"NATALIE'S HAVING AN ISSUE," KIT SAYS, AND I THINK HE'S standing now. "I'll go get her. Be right back."

"What kind of issue?" Sam demands, but Kit is already gone.

What's wrong with my mom?

There's nothing for me to do but wait to find out.

The whoosh of the ventilator is an odd feeling. It pulls the air in, and my lungs are just along for the ride. Years of innate response make them exhale the carbon dioxide. I feel a little proud that at least I can do that part on my own.

I feel ashamed that I'm here.

How did I let it get this far?

My mom is a wreck because of Dad, and now she has to deal with this, and God, I've been a shit to her.

She didn't deserve this.

Elin didn't deserve this.

No one deserved this.

And where the fuck is Angel?

For a second, I worry that something happened to her. She was okay on her own before she met me, and I'm sure she's fine now.

A flickering of a memory comes to me. Something . . . *something* is there. I grab at it and try to hold on.

And *there it is.*

She wanted to get clean.

Maybe she's clean now. Maybe that's why she's not here. She wanted to get clean, and I didn't. Is that what happened?

I curse at my faulty brain and try harder to remember but all I can see is blackness now.

It's frustrating as hell, but my theory makes the most sense.

She must've gotten clean.

Maybe she's even in rehab. Maybe my mom paid for the rehab. That'd be something my mom might do. And maybe Mom isn't talking about that because she doesn't want to upset me.

What she doesn't understand is that it wouldn't upset me.

Angel deserves to be clean.

She's had a hard life, and she's one of the best people I know.

I relax a bit at the mere thought that she's in a safe place, surrounded by people trained to help her.

Thank you, God.

ANGEL AND I WERE high again.

It was no surprise, of course, but what was startling was that our supply was getting low faster than I'd thought. We needed to find a new dealer, which wasn't impossible, just annoying.

I couldn't feel my arms or legs, and Angel's eyes were glassy. I put down the pipe and she leaned against me, and her back rested against my chest.

"How did you kill your dad?" she asked, her voice thick from heroin. "Did he hurt you? Was it self-defense?"

"God, no," I said quickly, or as quickly as I could with a tongue made from wood. "He was the best father ever."

"Then why did you kill him?" Angel turned her big eyes up to me and I think they were bigger now than they used to be.

"It was an accident," I mumbled. Even as high as I was right now, it still hurt it hurt it hurt.

"What kind of accident?" she asked, and her foot was tapping, slower, then slower as the hero worked itself into her heart.

"A car accident." I choked on the words and Angel's hand tightened on my fingers.

"Hey, it's okay," she crooned.

"It's not," I told her, and I could see that night flash in front of my eyes. It was dark and the radio was on, and that song will be in my memory always. My dad was sleeping, and he trusted me, and I answered my goddamned phone.

"My phone rang," I said, and my voice was just fragmented pieces of guilt. "It was in my pocket and then I dropped it. I only looked down for a second."

Just for a second.

"There were car lights when I looked up," I admitted, and I'd never said this out loud before. "In my eyes. I think I was screaming, and it happened so fast. We hit head-on and my dad died. I couldn't help him. I couldn't help. The other driver died too, but they were impaired, so I didn't get charged with anything. I could've been charged with involuntary manslaughter, and I probably should've been."

I was crying now, and my heart was splayed open and my rib cage was scooping out the feelings, scraping them out of my heart like a scalpel, and I didn't want to feel this. I didn't want to feel this.

"I couldn't take it," I told her. "It was too much. I slipped and slipped. My friend gave me heroin pills. I wasn't going to take them. Seriously. But everything spiraled, and all I wanted to do was escape."

"I understand," Angel told me softly. "I do."

"I fucked everything up," I practically whimpered.

Angel held me tight, pulling me onto her lap, and she stroked my hair and sang.

It was a tune I'd heard before, but never the words until now.

Day is gone. Gone the sun. From the lakes, from the hills, from the sky. All is well, safely rest, God is nigh.

"Isn't that taps?" I asked finally, and my eyes were wet. I didn't look up.

"My mom used to sing it to me when I couldn't sleep. It was the only lullaby she knew," Angel said defensively.

"I'm not attacking your mother," I told her.

"I know."

"Why did your mother send you away?" I asked, because Angel's song was so sad, and her voice was so broken. "She must've loved you."

She shrugged and held me tight, her fingers afraid to let go of me.

"She said I was better off going back to foster care. That she couldn't afford to live on her own, and her boyfriend hated me. She said she wanted me to have a shot at life, and she couldn't give that to me."

"I'm sorry." I patted her back with my free hand. It was a mindless motion and it didn't help, but I tried. "How long were you in foster care?"

"Awhile," she answered. "The state thought I was better taken care of there. I lost my virginity to a foster father. I don't have a sweet story like yours and Elin's."

Her voice was bitter now and she was so hurt and she was so used.

I wanted to pick her up and shield her from the world.

I told her that.

She laughed, a hard sound. "Too late, King," she said.

"It's never too late," I argued.

She was thoughtful now.

"So why did you leave your home?" she asked. "If it's never too late, maybe you should go back."

"It's complicated," I answered. "I can't go back."

"But why? Your mom is a good mom, right?"

I paused. "Yeah. She is. But she's got her own shit going on. There's a lot to deal with, you know. When someone dies."

"Yeah, I bet," she answered. "But she probably misses you."

I shrugged. "It's hard to say."

The silence swallowed us up, and we wallowed in it, stretching our legs and swimming in it.

"I was thinking that when this is done," and she gestured toward my Crown Royal bag that held our stash, "we should give it up."

That hit me in the face and I stared at her.

"Give it up?"

The idea was ludicrous, because without H, I'd feel everything. I wouldn't be able to escape and there was nothing I wanted less than to do that. But Angel was nodding and she was serious.

"I think we should," she said finally. "Look what it did to my mother. She gave up her own kid. You left a good life behind. For what? For this?" She swept her arm around, gesturing to the rickety walls of the warehouse. "We've got to make good on ourselves, King."

I eyed her.

"What's your real name?" I asked, trying to change the subject. She scowled.

"Don't do that. This is serious."

"So is your name," I answered.

"My name is Angel now," she answered. "And I want us to get clean. We'll have to do it together so we can help each other. We'll get each other through it, King."

I stared at her hard, and she was so solemn, so determined.

"You can't be serious," I said, and I was shaky just thinking about it.

"I am," she said, nodding. "You don't know it because you haven't seen it, but when I'm sober, I can do anything, King. We could get a little house and be roommates. Winston can have his own little bed. You can go to college and I'll get a GED, and we'll have a life, King. A *real* life."

I thought on that for a second.

A real life.

I studied the track marks in my arm, and I knew what I'd have to give up.

"I don't know if I can," I said truthfully. "I don't know if I'm strong enough."

"Of course you are," Angel said firmly. "You just don't know that right now. But I do, King."

"My name isn't really King," I told her. She smiled and in this moment, she was pretty, even with her jagged extra-short hair.

"I know," she answered. "I'm not stupid. But you're *my* King, and I like it that way."

"Do you want to know my real name?" I gave her the choice, but she squeezed my hand.

"No. That was then, and this is now. You're King and I'm Angel."

She fell asleep, so I was left awake alone.

I held her tight because she was all I had, and her breathing was soft and quick. It was still chilly enough in here to see her breaths in the air, but I kept her warm with my body.

She was Angel and I was King.

I thought about that.

Then I thought about a time when I was still Beck.

I was another person, with the world on a string, and all the promises it had to offer sat on my lap.

Potential was a shiny thing and I'd been full of it then, so much so that I couldn't see past the bright promises.

But with those promises came curses. If I hadn't gone to Notre Dame that day, if we'd chosen an earlier tour, then it wouldn't have been so late when we drove home. If Elin hadn't called, and if I hadn't answered. My dad wouldn't be dead.

My life would still be shiny and bright.

I would still be at home and my mom would be making me banana pancakes on Saturdays.

I was sure she was still making them now for Dev and Annabelle. Thoughts of them hurt my heart and I missed them. I hadn't allowed that for weeks and weeks, but it was true.

I missed them.

Looking down at Angel's face, I wondered what they'd think of her. But I already knew.

They'd take one look and know she's an addict too, and I'd be just another disappointment. One of many.

No matter how much I missed my life, that was then. This was now.

Angel stirred and moaned a little, and I soothed her quietly, my hand on her shoulder.

"Shhh," I said into her ear. "It's going to be all right."

"King, promise me we'll quit," she said, half-asleep. "Promise me."

I didn't want to. I wanted to. I didn't want to.

"Okay," I finally said. "Okay."

She smiled and her lips were curved and pink in the night. *She was happy now*, I realized with a start.

"Sing to me," she said. "Make me feel safe."

I sang her mother's lullaby and she closed her eyes to sleep.

thirty-five

NATALIE
MERCY HOSPITAL
9:33 P.M.

"JESUS, NAT, YOU SCARED THE SHIT OUT OF ME." SAM flutters about like a bird, trying to get me into a chair and hand me water and give me an aspirin all at once.

"Calm down," Kit tells her, and he is calm like he's always calm. Sam glances up at him, annoyed with his calmness. "It was a panic attack. It wasn't her first one. And she's going to be fine."

"It wasn't your first one?" Sam practically screeches now, and Elin flinches.

"It doesn't matter," I tell her tiredly. "Not now. Beck is all that matters."

I look at my son, and Sam hushes because she knows. She knows that is true.

She sits down in an extra chair in the corner and she's still flustered. But she's silent now. For a minute.

"I just wish you'd have told me," she blurts out a few minutes later. "I could've helped. Damn it, Nat. You didn't have to suffer through it alone."

She's offended but she's wrong.

I hadn't been alone.

I tell her that, and her eyes widen, and she looks at Kit.

Her mouth forms an O as she gets it, as the pieces finally click into place for her.

"*Oh.*"

"Yeah. Oh." My shoulders slump and I'm not proud. But it happened and I can't change that. I don't know if I want to. I don't know if I *don't* want to. I don't know anything anymore.

———

I WAS WASHING DISHES when my phone rang. I wiped them off on a towel, expecting it to be Sam, since the kids were on their way over to go camping for the weekend. Beck was driving them over at this very moment.

But the name on the phone wasn't hers.

It was my lawyer.

I answered hesitantly.

"Natalie, they want to settle," Ed said, and I could tell from his voice he was happy about this.

"Really?" This could all be over? The stress? The waiting?

"They're offering you twenty-one million."

I paused, and my hand clenched on the phone.

"Twenty-one million dollars." It seemed surreal.

"They took into consideration the lost salary that Matt would've made over the course of his lifetime, and added a cushion for your emotional suffering. And for Beck's."

"What about the seat belt?" I asked, because that was the important thing. "Are they going to recall their cars to fix it?"

Ed is silent.

"They feel it was an isolated case, and one of likely user error," he answered finally.

"They're saying it was Matt's fault."

My stomach dropped into my shoes, because it wasn't. I knew that. Matt was meticulous about safety.

"That doesn't matter, Natalie," Ed said fervently. "That's their official stance on it. But obviously, they know it's not true or they wouldn't be settling. The important thing is that you and the kids will be taken care of. Their college tuitions, your retirement, everything. You won't have to worry."

"But it could happen to someone else," I said limply. "Someone else could have their whole life torn apart just like me."

Ed was silent again, unsure of how to handle me.

I felt the familiar rush of adrenaline swelling up, filling my chest cavity, making my heart pound. *Fight or flight*, my brain whispered. *Fight or flight?*

"I've got to go," I told him numbly. "I'll think about it." I hung up before he could say anything.

The room started to swirl as my breathing got shallower and shallower until I was panting. My hand gripped the granite counter, and the stone was cool under my fingers. But not cool enough to jolt me back into the present.

I slid to the floor, the panic overtaking me, and I was there for what seemed like forever before I heard a voice calling to me from the front door.

Kit is here.

I didn't know why, but I was so glad.

He would help. He knew me.

He found me quickly and his voice was deep.

I was picked up and my feet were dangling and he was strong. He was solid. He had me.

He had me.

I thought I was dying but Kit had me.

Then I was on something soft and I opened my eyes, and I was lying on top of my bed. Kit was next to me, his eyes troubled.

"Can you hear me?" he asked, and that seemed silly now. Of course I could.

"Yes," I told him. I could breathe now. "Did I pass out?"

"It seems that way," he said. "I'll be right back, okay? Don't go anywhere."

I shook my head because of course I wouldn't. My legs were jelly, and I'd stay right here.

It was a little while before he came back, but when he did, he brought the scent of fresh air with him, and he was holding a bottle of water.

"Take this," he told me, giving me a pill. "I found it in your purse."

It was Xanax—I should've been embarrassed, but I wasn't. I took the pill.

"What happened?" he asked after I'd drunk it down.

"I . . . I . . . I've got some anxiety," I said, and he rolled his eyes.

"I can see that," he answered drily. "And it's understandable. But I'm really asking what happened today? What triggered this *today*?"

I swallowed hard because the truth of it was impossible to bear.

"The insurance company wants to settle. It's a lot of money, but they won't fix the seat belt problem. They're saying it was Matt's fault. But . . . they put a price on him, Kit. They say he's worth twenty-one million dollars. He was a person. *Not a price tag.* Twenty-one million dollars doesn't change the fact that my kids' father is never coming home, or that my bed is empty at night. Or that I'm so, so alone."

I was limp and illogical and totally spent.

Kit patted my back awkwardly. "You're not alone, Natalie. You're never alone."

He squeezed my hand, and his eyes were troubled. Tortured, actually.

"Sam loves you. The kids love you. Vinny loves you." He paused. "*I* love you."

"I know." And I knew they all loved me, but it didn't help the hole in my heart, which was so big, too big.

There was tension now, though, in the air between us. Some sort of . . . something. The words *I love you* held such weight. He loved us all. It wasn't a big thing, but yet, in this moment, it was.

And in this moment, for some reason, it was what I needed.

I needed to not be alone. Just for one goddamned minute.

He started to get up, to move from beside me, and I grabbed his hand. "Stay," I urged him. "Stay."

"Always," he said evenly.

He looked at me and I looked at him, and then everything happened at once.

I reached for him, and he folded me to him against his chest.

I lifted my face and his lips met mine, and they were not Matt's, and that was okay. In this moment, that was okay.

His hands stroked my back and soothed me in a way that no one else's could. His touch spread fire along my skin, tiny flames that lapped at me, at my nerves and my cells, and he could extinguish them.

Kit.

I was breathless and he started to pull away.

"No," I told him and I was dizzy. He paused.

"I don't want you to do something you'll regret," he said quietly.

"I could never regret you," I told him, and it was true and he crushed me to him again with a groan, and then everything happened fast.

So fast.

I kissed him hard, with need and pent-up frustration. He met my desperation and lifted me up onto him, and I was cradled on his lap, and he was hard against my hips.

He was hard for me.

This was Kit.

I was in wonderment now, wonderment that I wanted this, that I needed this. That this was Kit and me. It was wrong, but it felt right. In this moment, it felt right.

"Are you sure?" he asked against my lips, and I nodded, unable to speak.

His hands were in my hair, and my legs lifted, and he slid into me and it was like breathing.

Easy, normal, familiar, safe.

He was my safe haven.

He was strong and he made me strong.

He slid into me, and his breath was on my neck, and he murmured words that I couldn't understand because I was in a hazy fog.

When we finished, we were limp and the room was no longer spinning.

Reality was back and with it came the guilt.

How could I have done this?

There was a sheen of sweat on Kit's forehead, and he was looking down at me. It was almost like he knew I was starting to spiral.

"Are you okay?" he asked, his hand on my hip, and that wasn't right.

Matt should have been doing that. Not Kit.

"I don't know," I answered honestly.

"Nat, hey, you're okay," he told me.

But he was lying in the place where Matt used to sleep, where he rested his head, where he came to me every night, without fail.

He was in Matt's spot.

I cleared my throat and tried to figure out something to say, something that wouldn't hurt Kit. Because I never wanted to hurt Kit.

I couldn't think of the words, though. My heart pounded.

Fight or flight?

I got up and pulled on a robe. "I need a drink. Do you?"

"It's only four in the afternoon," he said, but then he looked at my face. "I could always use a drink."

We went downstairs and I grabbed a bottle of wine, taking it to the living room. I sat in the chair, not the couch. I needed to be alone, without the heat of Kit's body next to mine. I needed to think clearly. I opened the wine and poured us glasses, filled to the brim.

"You've had a rough day," Kit said, taking a gulp. "I'm sorry."

"It's not your fault," I told him. "You came to my rescue."

And then he'd slept with me.

My belly tightened. I had slept with someone other than Matt. I was a traitor.

I took another drink and so did Kit, and then he spoke.

"Have you ever wondered about roads?" Kit asked, and I was confused by the change of subject.

"Roads?"

"Yeah. The roads that lead us to where we're meant to be. You were on your road with Matt, minding your own business. I had a road too. We all had a path and we were walking on it, and then he died. I thought the world ended, but my path continued and it led me to you, only you were always with me. Always there. Was I always meant to be with you in the end?"

I was frozen because this wasn't what I wanted.

I wanted comfort. I wasn't ready for *this*.

I sat up a little, and the wine in my glass was hit by the sunlight, making it gleam purple, and then there was a voice speaking, only it wasn't Kit.

"That's an excellent question, Mom," Beck said from the doorway. "Maybe Dad had to die so that you could fuck his best friend."

I could feel the blood drain from my face.

My son is here.

And the look on Beck's face . . . He was so angry, so hateful. I'd never seen that expression before, and then he was gone, and I was scrambling to follow him.

"What are you doing here?" I asked, and he glared at me over his shoulder.

"You forgot to send Devin's backpack. I came to get it."

He threw open the front door and headed for his car.

I clamored down the steps. He dropped into the driver's seat of his car, slamming the door. I pled with him through the window but he was shoveling pills into his mouth, blue flat pills that I'd never seen before.

"What the hell is that?" I asked him, and he was sneering at me, an ugly expression for an ugly emotion.

He locked the door and let his head rest against the seat. His eyes were growing glassy, and I was frantic.

I pounded on the glass because he was picking up a baggie and pulling out more pills.

"Beck!" I shrieked. "Oh my God. Oh my God. Don't!"

This couldn't be happening and Kit broke the glass. He snaked his big arm in to unlock the door and then he was yanking Beck out.

"What the hell are you doing, Beck?"

Beck's eyes flashed angrily, his pupils huge, and he shoved Kit away.

"Leave me alone," he snapped. "Leave me alone. You're both traitors . . . to my dad. To me. You wanted me to think that you loved me, that you understood. But you don't. You only wanted to do what you wanted to do. *Each other.*"

"That's enough," Kit barked, and he grabbed the baggie out of Beck's hand. He tossed it to the ground next to me and grabbed Beck, holding him tight against his chest. My son dangled there furiously.

"We've got to get him to the hospital or something," I said to Kit. "Put him down. I think he needs his stomach pumped."

"It's in my system by now, Mom," Beck said, and his mouth was a line. "It won't help."

"How long have you been doing this?" I demanded. This couldn't be happening. "*Why* would you do this?"

Beck laughed sharply.

"Well, you can start by looking in the mirror," he said, and he was derisive and ugly.

The implications of what he was saying slammed into me and I felt wobbly and weak.

"You can't blame this on your mother," Kit told him, his voice raised and firm. Beck squirmed out of his grasp.

"You don't know anything," Beck snapped back at him. "You don't know what she's been like. She's been living on Xanax and wine, barely wanting to get out of bed. She can barely take care of herself, much less us, and now *this.* I gave up college so that my mom could fuck my father's best friend? *I can't deal with this shit.*"

"Beck, I'm sorry. You can still go to college. We'll fix everything."

But he got back into his car and slammed the door, the remnants of the window falling onto the ground like shattered diamonds in the light.

"Beck. Just get out of the car. We'll get you some help."

"It can't be fixed," he said, and his words were fading now, his voice weak. "You need the help. Not me. Leave me alone. Forget I exist. Because to you, I don't. From now on."

His engine roared to life and his tires squealed because he couldn't get away from me fast enough.

He was gone and he was high and there was nothing I could do.

"I'll track his phone," I said. "I'll call the police. I'll . . ."

I collapsed into Kit's chest and he held me as I cried.

"What do I do?" I asked him helplessly. "I don't know what to do."

"You love him," Kit finally answered. "No matter what. That's what we do."

"But he's gone." I raised my head and my eyes were wet and Kit wiped my tears away.

"He'll come back," he assured me. "This is his home."

"When?" I asked, and my voice was crazed. Kit held me tight.

"I don't know," he said, and he was confident. "But he will."

thirty-six

BECK
MERCY HOSPITAL
10:03 P.M.

" S o . . . YOU TWO WERE A THING," MY AUNT SAM IS SAYING, and I listen intently.

"It wasn't like that," my mom insists, and she's embarrassed. What are they talking about?

But then Kit speaks with his deep voice and I can't even hear his words because all of a sudden, I *know*.

Kit and my mom.

"It sounds like that," Sam says uncertainly. And I have to say I agree— after all, I was there. He'd basically said all roads had come together; he thought my dad was meant to die so that he could be with my mom.

That's fucked up.

Anger pulses through me, rich and hot. I want to jump up, to shout at him, to scream. But I can't move. Not even a muscle.

This is fucked up.

"Look," my mom tells Sam. "Kit has been close to me for a very long time. He's been our best friend—mine *and* Matt's. We didn't do anything wrong. He was comforting me, and it was nothing . . . ." Her voice trails off.

Kit's silent now, and if I were him, *I'd* be hurt.

Did my mom mean to do that? Surely not.

The room is quiet, and I can hear restless sounds of pacing and of shoes on the floor. It's awkward and uncomfortable. And for just a minute I'm grateful that my eyes aren't open and I don't have to deal with this situation.

My coma had come in handy for something.

Funny. But not funny.

"Can I have a minute alone with Beck?" Kit asks finally, and that was unexpected. I don't want it, but of course I don't have a choice.

"I guess," my mom finally answers. "But don't take long. It's already after ten."

We all know what that means.

Less than an hour until it's time to get up.

Fuck. I don't feel ready.

Mom brushes my hair out of my face like she always does, and then I'm alone with Kit.

I sense it in the silence.

Kit's hand is on my arm and it's rough with calluses.

"Hey, kid," he says, greeting me, even though he's been here all night. "I know you're mad at me."

He pauses and I don't know if he thinks he can get a rise out of me, but it's not working.

"I want you to know your mom is a good person. She's worked so hard to keep it together. She's suffered such a great loss, and while all you saw was what you thought were her failings, she kept you all afloat."

I feel a twinge of guilt.

I *had* been hard on her. I know that now. I was so lost in my own pain I wasn't able to see hers.

"And what you saw that day . . . what you heard. I've loved your mom for a long time. Even before your dad died, if you want the truth. But I would have never acted on it. Your father was my best friend, and I consider you guys my family. Matt was like my brother."

I'm struggling now. Struggling with having to stay silent. There is so much I'd like to say. But even as I think of the words, I also think of memories.

Of Kit coming to our BBQs. Of Kit and my dad laughing over a beer. Of Kit and my dad tinkering on a car or screaming at a football game on TV. If I'm honest, I have to admit that Kit never did one inappropriate thing when my dad was alive.

He was simply a good friend to both of them.

And then after . . . well. As much as I didn't like it at the time, he helped my mom.

He picked up my mom's pieces after my bomb went off.

I feel my anger ebbing, slipping away into the dark.

How can I be mad at them when I handled things so much worse myself?

Kit's voice is filled with pain and guilt, and I actually wish I could speak up and tell him.

That I don't blame him anymore.

I'm stunned that I don't.

But it's the truth.

"So, don't be mad at her," Kit says, talking again. "She loves you so much, and one thing I've learned from all of this is to not take for granted the people who love you. Sometimes they're gone in an instant. It sucks that we don't know what we'll miss the most until it's gone. It's a travesty of life."

He pauses for one beat and then continues.

"I miss the way your dad called me Kitten when he was teasing me," he admits, and the thought of that is funny. My dad calling this big guy Kitten. But then Kit's voice cracks and he breaks down and cries. I hear the tears, I hear the wetness in his voice, and it's actually terrifying because he's always so unflinching, so strong. If he's weeping . . . Jesus. This must be bad.

"Just wake up, son," he urges me. "Don't be afraid. Just come back to us. Everything will be okay."

But it isn't always.

I know that, and so does he.

———

I COULDN'T HELP BUT think about the differences between Angel and me as I sat against the blocks of the building, smoking and blowing puffs toward the sun.

"Your mother left you, and I left my mother," I told Angel. She was next to me, blowing smoke rings.

"Yeah," she agreed.

"I was a dick to my mom," I said. "She didn't really deserve it. She was doing the best she could."

"Then what happened?"

Angel snapped her fingers at Winston because he was getting too far away, but he bounded back to us and she smiled at his flopping ears.

I shook my head. "Everything. I was a mess. I was using. Pot and Xanax, H. I couldn't take reality anymore, you know? It was all closing in on me."

She nodded because she knew.

I watched the dog chase his tail and the sun was so very cold, which wasn't as it should have been.

"Have you ever felt yourself do things, things you know you wouldn't normally do, but you do them anyway?" I asked her. "It's like someone is moving your arms and legs, and you let them."

She stared at me, but she wasn't getting it.

"I was out of control. I was so pissed. At everyone, everything. I think I was grieving, but I *know* I was pissed. Then my mom started seeing my father's best friend and I fucking snapped."

"Jesus," Angel breathed. "That's messed up, dude."

"I know. But I don't think I should've been such a dick."

"They'll forgive you," she said, and she was so sure of herself for someone who didn't even know them.

"I don't know. I told her I never wanted to see her again and then I left. I went and got high in a crack house and didn't come down for two weeks. When I came down, I'd lost my car and my wallet."

"Well, thank goodness your driver's license was in your purple bag," she mentioned, because she liked to see the bright side.

"Yeah. I still had that."

"Don't beat yourself up too much, King," she said, matter-of-factly. "Doing drugs is easy. Doing *life* is hard. And sometimes, we have to hide from it in the best ways we can."

"I hurt everyone I love," I told her. "That's why I don't want to get close to you. I'm not good for anyone."

She laughed, and I saw her humor in the air in a mist of gray and white.

"It's too late for that bullshit, King. You are close to me. And I'm close to you. We're all we have, or have you not noticed? King, I had this foster home once. The dad was nice enough, but the mom wasn't. She wasn't a nice person, but she was religious, if you know what I mean."

I instantly pictured a pinch-mouthed Bible-thumper. Angel smiled when I told her that.

"Sort of," she admitted. "She went to church a lot and Bible study. But anyways, something she said stuck with me. She was talking about carrying crosses."

I lifted an eyebrow because I had no idea what she was talking about.

She sighed. "People like to carry their burdens with them," she said. "We feel like if we punish ourselves long enough for everything that has gone wrong in life, we'll somehow make it right again by our own sheer misery."

She messed with the frayed hem of her jeans and didn't make eye contact with me. Her voice was very solemn, and I know she meant every word.

"I was upset about my mother, and that's the pep talk that this woman gave me." Angel shrugged now. "It made sense at the time. And

I think it makes sense now. She said people create their own crosses and become their own martyrs. We feel like if we punish ourselves enough, we'll cleanse our own sins."

I stared at her, speechless. It made sense but I didn't think it applied to me.

"What happened *was* my fault," I told her slowly. "If I don't punish myself for it, who will?"

Angel's eyes were so very soft as she looked at me, and she picked up my hand and stroked my fingers.

"Things just happen sometimes," she said simply. "We'll never know how or why. They just do. You've been punishing yourself for something that *just happened*. It's time to lay your cross down, King. It's not yours to carry."

My breath was coming steady now, but I wasn't sure why, because my heart was thump thump thumping while I considered this revelation. It couldn't be so simple as to just lay something down. It wasn't a book or a bag. It was a burden, and it was heavy and it was mine.

"Don't overthink it," Angel said. "Just don't. You're a good person, King. You don't deserve this pain."

She laid her head against my shoulder and watched the clouds. Time passed and I was jittery but I also didn't want to move. It felt good here with Angel, and I liked allowing her words to sink in.

"I want to get a job," Angel told me after a while. "Maybe work at the counter in a card store. Everyone is happy when they're buying greeting cards."

"I can see you doing that," I told her. "You'd have to be nice to everyone, though."

"I'm a nice person, King," she growled, and I laughed.

"Obviously."

"I am," she insisted, and I assured her that it was true.

My hands were growing shaky now and I needed to use. I peered into the bag. "We've only got one hit left," I told her. "Are you sure you want to go through with this? We can just go buy some more."

That thought brought me comfort. Going without made me panicky. But she was resolute.

"I'm sure, King. We need this—you know that."

"It's just . . . what if I'm not ready?" I asked. "They say you have to be ready to get clean. What if I haven't hit rock bottom?"

She looked around, an exaggerated response. "We're living in a warehouse and we're peeing in the bushes," she pointed out. "How much further down can we go?"

"I know," I agreed. "But still. How am I supposed to know if I'm ready?"

She changed the subject and we tried to ignore the elephant in the room for the rest of the day as we nibbled on our stale bread crusts, as we breathed in and out.

We didn't have much to do to pass the time today except for the endless task of trying to stay warm. We gathered trash from the bins outside and lit a fire with old papers, expired magazines, even a dog-eared oven mitt. We hovered around it and tried to pretend that we weren't consumed by the craving, by the want.

By nighttime, my hands were shaking so badly I couldn't stand it. My eyes felt like they were popping out of my head as I stared at Angel.

"I wanna use it," I told her. She did too. I could see it in her hollowed-out eyes and her hands that shook as she stroked Winston's head.

"But," she reminded me, "after this, *no more*. It's going to suck. But we'll be done. Do you promise, King?"

I didn't want to. I wanted to. I didn't want to. I wanted to.

We had to.

I nodded. "Yeah."

The mere thought, though . . . shit. It pounded my heart into my ribs because this stuff *was* life and what would I do without it?

I was careful not to drop the baggie as I reached for the last pebble. It was more precious than silver or gold in this moment, more precious than life.

"Give it to me," Angel urged, holding out her hand. She had a hole in one of her glove fingers. Her hands were shaking more than mine and she might have dropped it. I shook my head.

"I've got it."

She pursed her lips but didn't argue, and she was patient, more patient than me. She watched and waited as I heated the spoon. When it was ready and it's belly was blackened, Angel held out her arm, and I think her teeth were chattering, but I couldn't focus on that.

I had to focus on this.

On hitting a vein, on giving Angel release from this life for one last time. After this, we'd be better. We'd be good. We'd be strong. But reality was hard, and I didn't look forward to it. It was the sea pounding into cliffs, and it was hard and it was vicious.

Angel's eyes fluttered closed when it hit, and she dropped her head back in relief, like someone had lifted a great weight from her shoulders, and Winston rested his head against her chest.

She floated to her heels, like gauze in a fancy dress made from layers and layers of lace. She floated to the ground like a skirt, and she rested there, waiting for me to join her. I hurried.

I found a vein easily, quickly. I injected and withdrew.

The warmth took my everything, and I exhaled shakily, not wanting to move. I didn't want to tempt fate. I didn't want this last high to end.

I was suddenly next to Angel, though, and I didn't know how I got there, but she was pulling on my arm, and then lying in my lap, and my hands were on her thighs, steadying her, resting. My hands were too much to support, they were blocks of cement or stone.

"It's like we're in a canyon," she said in wonderment, although we'd been here before. "And we're never going to climb out, King."

"We will," I told her, and I was confident now, invincible. "This is our last time here."

"Mmm-hmm," she agreed, and her eyes were closed and her hand was hot and clammy. She stroked my face with it over and over, like my skin was a piece of velvet or the satin edge of a beloved blanket.

"I'm a hollow reed," she said in her singsong voice. "And you're blowing through me, bending me, King. You've bent me."

"Is that a good thing?" I asked. Her words were like a poem I didn't understand.

"It's a very good thing," she answered. "I thought I couldn't be moved. I thought I was a stone or a tree, but I was a reed all along."

I was lost and she knew it, and she turned my face to her with her grubby thumbs.

"You've made me feel again," she said. "And that's *something*, King. That's something."

She made me feel something too, something warm, something soft. Something I hadn't felt in a long time. She made me feel accepted, and her acceptance wasn't laced with condemnation or judgment, and that was the purest thing in the world. I told her that.

"But do you love me?" she asked simply, and in this moment, I'd never seen anything so beautiful as Angel. I found myself nodding, and her smile was the sun.

"I do," I said out loud.

"Good," she decided, and deflated into my arms. "Real love should be reciprocal. It's sad when it's not."

She was troubled now and I knew she was thinking about her mother, but I wanted to distract her from that. She was worth more than her mother gave her credit for.

"Some people don't recognize true value," I told her, and when did I become so wise? "And they never will because it cannot be taught. It just is. Your mom . . . she just didn't know how to love you."

Angel nodded, her eyes closed. "I know."

She was so peaceful now, and I wondered if she'd finally accepted that. Her mother was missing something inside of her, an important piece. It wasn't Angel's fault. It never was.

I started to point it out, but I was interrupted by something wrong. Something very, very wrong.

Angel began to shake. Hard and vigorous and violent.

Even in my stupor I saw it. Her head snapped back and her chest arched up and she was convulsing and I didn't know what to do.

"Angel," I tried to say, to snap her out of it, but she couldn't answer because there was foam in her mouth and her nose. Flecks of it flew as her head shook, and her eyes rolled back in her head until all I could see were the bloodshot whites.

"King," she managed to say, and her teeth slammed together like prison doors. "Something's wrong."

"I know." I grabbed at her, trying to soothe her, but whatever was wrong was wrong inside of her, and there was nothing I could do. "I think it's bad heroin."

I was starting to shake now too, just a little, and it was taking longer to work into my system because I was bigger and she'd gone first.

"Hold on," I told her. "Just hold on. I'll get you to the doctor."

But she was crying now, and her snot was mixed with the foam, and Winston was running around and whimpering because he knew something was wrong. Angel tried to say something, but her jaw was clenched tight, like it was stuck. She tried again and grabbed my arm, her fingers sharp as talons.

"Sa . . . rah . . ." she managed to say, and there was blood on her lip. "My . . . name."

I was stunned and I stared, because she didn't want me to know that, because that was her past life and this was her new one. And Sarah didn't fit her at all.

"Greene," her teeth chattered, and her arm flopped on the cement. I grabbed her up and buried my head in her shirt, and it was wet with foam and blood. *Sarah Greene.*

"Angel," I begged. "Stay here with me. It's okay. You're my Angel. You're okay."

But she wasn't and I knew it.

She was convulsing now and her head was lashing from side to side and she couldn't talk or breathe.

"I love you," I told her, and I was desperate. "Stay with me. Stay."

Time stopped and her eyes said a million things, some good, some bad, some terrified. I wanted her to say she loved me too, but a tear slipped from the corner of her eye onto the bridge of her nose, and time started again, and things moved so fast, too fast.

"Stop!" I shouted, and I begged God to help her but He didn't. He wasn't even listening.

I knew this because she died.

It happened suddenly, like someone turned off a light and closed the door behind them.

Her body seemed to deflate, the birds that were sitting in the broken windowsill fluttered into the night in a flurry of black rasping wings. The sound filled my ears. *Whir whir whir.*

Angel's arms were limp and her eyes were open. But she was so very, very still. The tear on her nose dripped down down down and fell onto the ground.

Then there was nothing else.

I was shaky and hot and flushed and it was happening to me too, but I tried to press on her chest to pump her heart, and it wouldn't work.

She wouldn't breathe and her heart wouldn't beat because she was dead.

"No," I yelled, my teeth starting to slam together, and it was coming for me. I lay down next to Angel and I draped her arm over me like we slept, and her body was still warm and this is how I would go. Next to someone I loved, next to someone who loved me.

The end doesn't hurt, I decided.

"It's like falling asleep," my teeth chattered to Winston, and Angel would kill me for leaving him.

But I rested my head next to Angel's and Winston lay down next to me, and for a minute, just a minute, I was ready.

I was ready for this to end.

For it all to be over, this struggle, this fear, this addiction, this *life*.

But then . . . but then . . . I heard Angel's voice. From somewhere and from nowhere.

"Get up, King. Get help."

I opened my eyes and they stung and twitched, and the bad heroin was pulsing through me, deeper and deeper, and I felt it penetrate my heart, into the tissues and valves, and Angel was gone, but her voice was so loud in my head.

Get up.

Get help.

I'd do anything for her and she knew it.

"I'm Beck," I whispered into her ear, even though she couldn't hear me. Her eyes were open, and I could hear her voice in my head. *Get help.* "My name is Beck."

She deserved to know that.

I staggered to my feet and my vision was tunneling, darkening, and it was hard to see but I managed to stagger out of the alley and the few blocks to the L. I pushed my way on and dropped into a seat, and I was convulsing but no one noticed or no one cared.

I don't know if I can make it, I thought to Angel.

You can, she assured me. *You will.*

But I didn't think so.

The light was fading away, and no one was around me, but everyone was, and I knew that. I could hear their voices and they all blended into each other like notes in a song and I was so fucking high, so messed up, and I couldn't feel my hands. I couldn't feel my feet. Was this real?

The orange flecks on my sleeves from Angel's mouth told me it was.

I clenched my fingers together to try to stop the shaking and I thought they might snap like old wood, and the train squealed to a stop and I somehow got to my feet. I didn't know how.

But I did.

I stepped one two three four five steps before I ran into a wall and someone said *Dude, you okay?*

But I couldn't answer, and they didn't ask again.

They were gone and the light was gone and everything was dark, and I walked as much as I could and my feet found their way. They had a memory and they knew where they were going. They knew where home was. It wasn't far. I had traveled this path many times home from practice.

I fell going up the steps, but I saw the porch and I fell again.

I hit hard—my cheek slammed into the brick—but I didn't feel it. The porch light turned on, and it was in my eyes and I shook hard hard harder and then the foam came.

It came out of my nose and throat, and into my mouth and onto my shirt, and I heard my mother.

"Beck," she cried out, and I was in her arms.

I'd made it.

I tried to tell her about Angel, to ask for help for Angel, but my lips wouldn't work. They weren't connected to my body anymore, and the muscles were fading and my tongue had fallen away. I tried again, and I might've gotten it out. I felt a hand on my head, and then there were lights, red and blue, and I couldn't stay awake anymore and everything was gone and it was just like falling asleep.

thirty-seven

NATALIE
MERCY HOSPITAL
10:39 P.M.

I'M WATCHING THE TIME TICK BY ON THE CLOCK. SECOND BY second, it pushes forward toward eleven p.m.

"It's almost time," Elin tells Beck, and she's nervous. She's been here almost the entire time, and she hasn't wavered. I'll never question her love for him again.

Over the intercom in the hall, the "Rock-a-Bye Baby" chime plays and a baby has been born while my baby lies still in this hospital bed. I try not to think about that, or wonder again if the universe has to balance life with death.

The door opens, and I look up to find Vinny standing there, hesitant. He finds Sammy with his eyes.

"We're here," he says simply, and my mouth opens.

"We?"

"I told him to bring the kids," Sam answers. "Nat, they need to see Beck. They should have the opportunity."

I want to argue, to say that they'll have plenty of time for that, but I look at my son and he's so pale and tired. Devin and Annabelle didn't get the chance to see Matt. But they can have it with Beck.

I nod, and Sam is relieved.

Vinny pushes the door open wider and Dev and Annabelle come in, timidly, nervously.

"Mama," Annabelle cries, and she runs to me, her eyes on Beck. Devin is more reserved, but that's just who he is. Elin makes room on her side, and Devin joins her, his small face pale behind his glasses.

"Is he going to die?" he asks seriously, and he lays his freckled hand down on Beck's. His fingers are small and Beck's are long. My throat tightens up and I can't lie.

"We hope not," I tell him. "Your brother is strong. He's a fighter, Dev."

"So was Daddy," Annabelle pipes up. I think we all flinch. Matt *was* a fighter, but his injuries were *insurmountable*. No one could've survived them.

Annabelle gets up and sits next to Beck, and she's so careful not to bump her big brother.

"Becky, don't forget your promise," she reminds him, and loops her pinkie through his. "You can't break a pinkie promise."

She's so serious, and I don't know what she's talking about.

"What pinkie promise, sweetie?" I ask, my voice low.

She glances up, her hand still entwined with her brother's.

"He promised me he wouldn't die," she answers simply.

Oh God.

Sam sucks in an audible breath, and my throat is so tight now I can't breathe. Annabelle's face is grave.

I'm getting ready to comfort her, to give them both a hug, when the monotonous beep from Beck's machines changes. It turns from a staccato beep into one long wail, and the green line on the screen turns flat and straight.

I'm shocked, and I can't move, and the medical staff rushes in, surrounding Beck in a swarm.

"Code blue, room two twelve," the intercom shrieks. "Code blue, room two twelve."

I'm paralyzed with fear because *we're in room two twelve.*

thirty-eight

BECK

THERE IS CANDLELIGHT EVERYWHERE AND I FEEL SO LIGHT. All of the weight from my shoulders has lifted and there is no pain at all.

How can that be? Where am I?

I look around, surprised to see I'm surrounded by stones and candles and an immense sense of peace.

It seems familiar here. I'm warm and safe, and I realize suddenly that I'm in the grotto on the Notre Dame campus.

How did I get here?

"Isn't this a nice place to sit and think?" my father asks, stepping from the shadows. He's wearing khakis and a tucked-in polo shirt, just the same as he was the last time we were here.

"Dad?" I'm standing, no longer confined to a hospital bed. He smiles at me, and suddenly he's next to me, giving me a warm hug. I hadn't seen him move, but his arms are strong, his body is warm. I'm enveloped by a sense of safety, the safety that only comes from being with my father.

"Were you expecting someone else?" he asks, and he's so flippant, like always.

"I don't know," I admit, and I feel a little stupid. "I don't know what I was expecting."

"Well, that's life," he says, shrugging, and it's not even important. I sense that very little of my former life is important now. I feel it in my bones.

"I've missed you, Dad," I tell him. "So much."

"I've missed you too," he answers, and his eyes are solemn. "You don't know how much."

"Am I dead?" I ask, and I'm hesitant.

"Do you want to be?" My father isn't worried, and *he* isn't hesitant. He's matter-of-fact. He's calm.

Do I want to be?

"I don't know," I admit because it's the truth. "It's nice here."

Serenity seeps into my bones and everything feels right, like I'm meant to be here. Like I was *always* meant to be here.

"You'd miss your mom," Dad tells me knowingly. "I know I do."

"Then why'd you leave?"

"I didn't have a choice," Dad says.

"I'm so sorry," I tell him, and my mood darkens and the weight threatens to return. "I'm so sorry. It was my fault."

My dad stares at me with that level stare that he often gets, and he almost laughs.

"Why are you sorry?" he asks. "I'm the one who let you drive. It was nighttime and you were tired. You were a new driver. I shouldn't have done that. I'm the one who's sorry, Beck. I don't want you to carry guilt. It wasn't your fault. It was mine."

Not long ago I wouldn't have believed him. But tonight his words seem to have so much weight. It's as though once he spoke them, they became fact in my heart. Why didn't I think of that point of view before?

"Do you really believe that?" I ask him. "Do you really think that's true?"

"Of course," my dad says, nodding. "It is absolutely the truth."

"I've been a bad person," I say doubtfully. "I've made mistakes."

"Who hasn't?" Dad asks. "No one is perfect."

"Mom was with Kit," I tell him, and I don't know if I should have. "It turns out that Kit has loved her for a long time."

"I know that," Dad tells me, rolling his eyes. "Do you think he could hide anything from me? He's the worst at secrets."

"Don't you care?"

Dad stares at me. "Kit would never have done anything inappropriate," he says sternly. "You should know that. You *know* him, Beckitt."

"So you're not upset?"

"I think I'm incapable of being upset now," Dad says thoughtfully. "All I feel is peace. I love your mom but I want her to be happy. I want you to be happy too."

"I'd like to be happy," I say quietly. "I just don't know how."

"Well, the first thing I would suggest is waking up," he says, and he's staring at me again. "I love you, but your mom needs you. You can come here some other time."

"But do you think I will?" I ask, and I'm worried now. "What if I can't come back?"

Dad smiles and I feel the love coming from his teeth, shining upon me like a light. "Of course you can, son. Just wait for a few years. Maybe seventy."

He laughs, and is this happening?

"Am I dreaming?" I ask, because I've grown used to the line of reality and fantasy being blurred.

"Does it matter?" my father asks. "I mean, *truly* matter?"

I think on that, and I guess it doesn't.

"Did you ever listen to that CD I gave you?" Dad asks.

I shake my head. "No. It was too hard. Your voice. And you gave it to me that night . . ."

My voice trails off and Dad shakes his head. "You should. There's some good stuff on there. I'm a pretty bright guy."

"And modest," I point out. He smiles.

"You're just like your mother."

"Thank you."

"It's time to wake up, son," he urges me. "You can do it. Just open your eyes and it will be done."

I try, but nothing happens. I'm still here in the grotto and the candles flicker in the night.

"I don't know if I can," I say. "It's harder than you think."

"You can do it," he tells me confidently. "That's one thing about you, Beck. You can do anything you put your mind to. I love you, son."

"I love you too, Dad," I answer.

He smiles at me, and it lifts me up and buoys me, and suddenly I'm free.

thirty-nine

NATALIE
MERCY HOSPITAL
10:41 P.M.

I'M IN THE CORNER OF THE HOSPITAL ROOM. EVERYONE ELSE was shoved out, but I stayed and they didn't order me out.

Beck's hand once again dangles on the side of the bed as they try their best to resuscitate my son, to restart his heart and breathe life into his lungs.

"Please, God," I whisper. "Please. Take me instead. Let him live. Please. Let him live."

One of the nurses turns and it's Jessica. She starts to say something to me, to tell me to leave, but she changes her mind, her eyes kind. She motions to me to stay where I am, and I do. I'll stay out of the way and they'll save my son.

I watch and hold my breath and chant prayers, hoping God will hear my uttered words.

I've never been so afraid. I've never been so desperate and out of control. My son, my beautiful, beautiful son isn't breathing. And his heart isn't beating.

I'd listened to that heartbeat when he was still in my womb. I'd listened to him take his first breath, and God, I don't want to listen to him take his last.

I stare at the bed and the boy in it, but I can't really see him now. Only his fingertips dangling in the air, and his hand moves as they pump at his heart, but it moves with their efforts.

I see him when he was a baby . . . the first time he smiled at me. It was bright and wide, like the sun.

I see him when he walked for the first time, his steps so shaky and new, toddling toward me with outstretched arms as he trusted me to catch him.

I see him on his first day of kindergarten, as he waited outside the school with his backpack that was bigger than he was and his hair carefully combed.

I see him when he got his driver's license and he came in the door waving it above his head like a trophy.

I see him as he left for prom, wearing his tuxedo and shiny shoes, trying to hide from me that his heart was broken over Elin.

I swallow hard, because that was then. Now my heart pounds and only a minute has passed but it's been the longest minute of my life.

Please, please, please.

On the intercom, the "Rock-a-Bye Baby" charm sounds again, and there's another life in the hospital.

Please, God, don't take Beck to balance it out.

Please, please, please.

The nurses and doctors work fast and furiously, and their words blend together. They work like an oiled machine, efficiently and quickly, and I know they've done this before.

But this time, it's my son, and they can't fail.

They've been working and working, and they're getting discouraged. I can tell and I'm terrified.

Jessica looks over her shoulder and her forehead is sweaty, and her eyes give her away.

She's scared.

They're failing.

"Please," I whisper, and she sees.

She turns away, her hands on Beck's chest, and she keeps pumping.

"Clear," someone calls again, and everyone steps back. Beck's chest lurches upward again, then again.

The monitors are silent, the green line still flat.

A tear streaks down my cheek, onto my lip.

"Please," I whimper, closing my eyes.

And then.

Then.

As my eyes flutter closed, there's a beep. Short and loud in the room, above the chaos.

Then another.

The medical team cheers and I open my eyes, and Beck has a pulse.

It's 10:44 p.m.

forty

BECK

M Y EYELIDS ARE CONCRETE CURTAINS, AND I CAN'T LIFT them.

But I'm in the hospital bed again. Of that, I'm sure. I don't know how long I've been asleep this time.

My mom and Sam and Kit are murmuring again, but I can't understand the words.

And then I see light.

Bright light.

My eyes are open.

I'd done it and hadn't even realized.

"Ow," I mutter out loud when I move my hand, and I look down to find a needle embedded in my skin, and a tube taped to my arm. Everything hurts now. I'm no longer numb. I'm dizzy and my head feels like it weighs a thousand pounds, and my vision is just a little bit blurry, and the lights are just a little too bright.

My mom is next to the bed. Elin is on the other side, and they both see my eyes open at the same time.

Everything happens at once—they all leap toward me, grabbing at my hands and exclaiming my name. My mom is the closest, the most insistent.

"Beck, oh my God," she cries. "I didn't know if you'd . . . oh my God, you're awake."

Her shoulders shake and my eyes are dry and I am not in my right mind. My thoughts are fuzzy and I know they're giving me something.

"Mom," I manage to say.

My tongue is wood, but I try to wet it, to limber it up.

Elin hugs me gently, her arms around my neck. My eyes meet hers and she is so warm and sincere.

"I'm . . ." I tell her. It's hard to speak. My tongue is uncooperative.

"Stop," my mom says. "Don't. We know. We're just thankful you're here. Aren't we, Elin?"

She nods and I'm grateful too. But I'm also scared. Why is that?

I think on that, and think on that, and then I remember.

Angel.

"Mom," I stutter. "Angel."

Mom pulls back and wipes her eyes and looks at me. "Do you really think you saw an angel, baby?"

That's when I know; I see it in her eyes. She thinks I was hallucinating when I was high. I shake my head and it hurts.

"No. There's a girl," I tell her, my words slow and thick. "Her name . . . Angel. She . . . overdosed. We . . . find . . . her."

My mother's head snaps up and she's terrified. I see it in her eyes, because she's scared for a girl she doesn't even know.

"Where was she?" she asks quickly, and though it takes me a minute, I manage to tell her where the warehouse is. Then she's talking to Kit and he calls the police and they are all going to look.

It happens so fast, but I'm satisfied that they're listening to me.

I close my eyes, just for a minute, to wait.

forty-one

NATALIE

BECK DOESN'T STAY CONSCIOUS VERY LONG, BUT IT WAS LONG enough.

He woke up.

I'm limp as I wrap my head around that, as I thank God for that.

I'm limp as I relay the information about the girl named Angel to Kit, and he speaks to the police.

I'm limp as I wait, as Elin and I continue to stand vigil.

"Angel was a girl?" she asks, and I can hear that she is afraid. Afraid Beck had found someone else.

"Don't worry about it right now," I advise her, still clutching my son's hand. "The police are going to find her. I'm sure it's not what you're thinking."

I squeeze Beck's fingers, tracing them with my own, memorizing the way they lay between mine.

"Do you think he was living there? In a warehouse?" Elin asks, and her voice is razor thin. "Do you think he was living with a girl?"

"I don't know, honey." I'm honest with her. "I have no idea."

The *not knowing* is actually the worst. Every minute of Beck's life, it has been my job to know. And now I don't know anything.

Kit comes back into the room. "The police are headed down there to look," he tells me. "I think I'll go too."

"Thank you," I murmur, and my eyes meet his. There is something there, for a second. He's hesitant. Tender. Sweet. He doesn't know how to act around me, and I certainly don't know how to act around him.

When he leaves, he does so in a slight breeze of Old Spice.

"Don't hurt him, Nat," Sam tells me. "I don't really know what all's gone on, but I know you, and I know you don't want to hurt him."

"I don't know what I want," I tell her simply. "But no. I never want to hurt Kit."

How can I explain to my sister what it feels like—to feel guilty for even looking at another man? To not want to, yet to want to?

I hope she never knows what it's like . . . this agony of conflicting emotion, of guilt and of need. It's a perfect storm for losing one's mind.

A doctor comes in and pokes around at Beck.

"He's a lucky man," he tells me, and it takes me a second to realize he's talking about my boy. As a man. I swallow hard at that. "The swelling has gone down, and the effects from his stroke seem to be minimal. I believe he should make a full recovery."

He scribbles on a chart and then turns to me.

"I have some recommendations for a rehab facility, if you'd like."

My fingers are shaky as I reach out to take the pamphlets from his hand. "It's imperative that he seek treatment when he's ready," the doctor tells me. "He was lucky this time. He might not be so lucky the next."

"There won't be a next time," Sam answers for me, and she's so sure in that conviction.

I'm not. I'm terrified. I've seen it spiral out of control before. If it happened once, it could happen again.

The doctor leaves and we sit in silence.

Beck no longer has a ventilator breathing for him in that rhythmic whoosh, so it's eerily quiet but for our breathing and the metallic scrape whenever someone moves their chair over the floor.

When Kit finally returns, the odd look on his face says everything.

"There wasn't a girl," he says quietly. "We looked everywhere. There was no sign of another person at all. No blood, no clothing, nothing."

"Im . . . possible," Beck says, and I turn to see his eyes open. They're hollow still, dark, and filled with pain. "She was . . . there. She over . . . dosed."

"Is it possible that someone moved her, or took her to another hospital?" I ask. Kit shakes his head.

"It's unlikely. The police called the hospitals. There's been no one admitted, and they don't have any reports of an overdose like hers."

Beck closes his eyes.

The weight of this new reality crushes each of us in the room.

There was never a girl. Beck had been so high, he'd imagined her all along.

forty-two

BECK

WHEN I WAKE THE NEXT MORNING, MY MOTHER AND ELIN are still with me, although Elin has changed her clothes.

My first thought is that my brain is less sluggish now, and also of Angel.

Angel.

My chest tightens with the story they told me . . . that she'd never been.

That seems impossible. Even for me, when half of the time I couldn't decide what was real and what wasn't. Among all of that, Angel had always been the realest thing. She'd grounded me to the earth and held me there.

Only . . . it turns out . . . she hadn't. Was I actually Angel all along? The things that Angel had to do—and I cringe at the thought—was that me?

No. It can't be true. I know what I know.

"Beck," Elin exclaims, and her hand almost crushes mine. "How do you feel?"

I examine that.

I feel sad. Empty. Discouraged. Crushed. Confused.

"Okay," I tell her, and the word rolls more easily off my tongue than before. The muscle is more cooperative, more willing to speak.

"You do?" my mom asks, and her eyebrow is raised.

"Okay enough," I amend. "I still don't understand about Angel."

Their faces are both blank, carefully controlled. They don't know what to say about Angel.

"So . . . tell me about her," Elin finally says, and I think she can tell I want to talk about it. "She was a girl, obviously."

Her face is worried, which is odd, since they've already decided she wasn't real.

"It wasn't like that," I tell her. "Angel is a friend."

They wait for me to say more, and Elin looks oddly relieved that I didn't have an imaginary romantic relationship.

"Angel is a girl," I insist, and stare out the window. "She has short hair that's jagged because she cut it herself, but she kept me alive. And I know you say she wasn't real, but she was the best person I've ever met."

My voice trails off because my heart knows she's dead. I didn't imagine it. I watched her die. Winston and I watched her die. *Oh my God—Winston.* "Mom, there was a dog, my dog, our dog."

My mother squeezes my hand and she doesn't know what to say, because what is there?

Kit bursts into the room and I can tell he's tense as his eyes meet mine. His are cautious, worried.

"Did you find a dog?" my mother asks him.

Kit nods. "Yeah. There was a scraggly little dog there. He's in my truck—I couldn't bring him into the hospital. I'm bringing him to the shelter but wanted to see Beck first."

"I want to see him," I say, and I'm adamant. "Sneak him in. Please. I have to make sure he's okay."

Angel will kill me if he's not.

"Beck, it's against the rules," my mom starts to say but I'm panicking and she grabs my hand. "Okay, it's okay," she says. "We'll sneak him in for a minute."

She gazes at Kit and he nods. "I'll be right back."

He's true to his word. He comes back within minutes with Winston hidden in his coat.

My mother stands watch at the door as Kit bends to put him in my lap. I struggle to sit and Winston laps at my face and he's wagging his whole body and I grab him into a hug.

I bury my face in his dirty fur and I've never been so happy to see anything in my life.

I'm crying and didn't realize it.

Kit hands me a tissue and I shove it around my nose.

"I need to keep this dog," I tell my mother. "Please."

"Of course," she agrees immediately, even though she doesn't like dogs.

"Thank you," I whisper. She nods.

I stroke Winston's head and I think I smell Angel on his fur, although I guess I'm imagining it, because they say she wasn't real.

I turn my head and squeeze my eyes shut, and Kit takes Winston.

"I'll take him with me," he promises. "No shelter. I'll keep him safe until you come home."

I nod because I trust him, because Kit never lies.

He leaves and my mother stays.

"I'm here now," she croons to me, and I'm wrapped inside her arms. "I'm with you now."

Something inside of me lets go, of my past hurts and my past anger. It's irrelevant now. All that matters is now and this moment and trying to forget the pain of losing Angel. Because whether they say she was real or not, she was real *to me*. I watched her die. I feel her loss.

I've got to swallow it down. I can't deal with it.

But then again, I decide, as I stare at my mom's shaking hand, forgetting about pain, burying it deep, hasn't done me any favors. That path led to this hospital bed.

I'll have to figure out a different way to handle things, and I'll need everyone's help for that.

I clutch my mom's hand and close my eyes.

forty-three

NATALIE

B ECK STAYS IN THE HOSPITAL FOR TWO MORE WEEKS.
He's undernourished and weak, and they have to build him back
up. They have him on medication to help the withdrawal, but it's still
a struggle for him.

Beck is the one who has to do the heavy lifting. He's the one who
lives with the constant need to use. All I can do is be there for him.

I sit with him when he sweats and shakes, and I sit with him when
he's dark and low.

"It's never going to get better," he tells me today, and his face is dark
and his eyes are hollow. "What's the point of being sober if I feel like this?"

"It *will* get better," I assure him, even though I don't know when.
"Just give it time. Just some time."

He tells me about Angel, about the warehouse, about how she rescued Winston. He speaks of her with such reverence that even though I
know she was a product of Beck's drug use, I think she really may have
been an angel. I tell him that.

He smiles. "She'd hate that," he confides. "She was very self-
deprecating."

"What would she say about you going to rehab?" I ask curiously. He immediately nods.

"She'd be all for it. The last time we used . . . it was supposed to be the last time. We weren't going to buy any more. It was her idea. She wanted to move away, get a new start, get clean. She had a hard life. And it never got better."

That breaks my heart a little, that Beck would imagine someone so troubled. It's a good insight into where he really was, where he had been.

"I have to go home and shower," I tell him. "Is there anything you need when I come back?"

He shakes his head. "No. I'm fine, Mom."

His hair is damp around his forehead, and I hate to leave him. But I can't stay every waking minute. I have to bathe sometimes too.

When I get home, Winston greets me at the door.

He's been groomed and his fur isn't in his eyes anymore and they stare up at me, big and soulful and brown.

"What kind is he?" Dev asks, because he's coming in the door from the bus.

"The vet says he's a Yorkie mix of some sort."

"I'm glad we're keeping him," Dev says, bending to scratch his chin. "How's Beck today?"

"He's good. Stronger every day."

At first, I'd tried to hide Beck's issues from the kids, but that wasn't smart. Kids are intuitive, and they know more than we think.

"Good," he says. He scoops up Winston and heads upstairs. "I've got spelling words." Of course he does. He's competing in the county spelling bee next month. Matt would burst with pride if he were here.

I'm sitting in Beck's room when Kit finds me.

"What time is it?" I ask when he sits next to me on the bed.

"Five. What do you want to do for dinner?"

Kit has been here every day, day in and day out. I'm not sure where we'll go from here, or even what I want, but his presence gives me comfort. But I do know that Kit will always be in my life, in one form or another.

"Let's get takeout for Beck," I suggest, and Kit grabs my hand.

"Did you find out when they're transferring him to rehab?" he asks quietly. He knows that when they do, I won't be able to see him for a week. It's rehab policy.

"Tomorrow," I reply. "It's a good thing."

"Yes, it is. He's strong enough, Nat. He can do this."

I nod and Kit pulls me into a hug, and I rest there against his chest. His heart beats and it soothes me into calm.

"He can do this," I repeat finally.

Kit smiles. "Yes."

I hear the commotion before I see it, but I hear Dev and Annabelle shriek and clamor about, and I hear Beck.

My head perks up, and Kit and I scramble down the stairs to find him in the kitchen with the kids.

"What are you . . . what are you doing here?" I stammer.

He looks so much healthier now already—I can't help but notice because he's backlit by the evening light from the window.

He stares me in the eye.

"I need to take care of Angel."

I'm confused and I don't know what he's saying, because we've already told him that she wasn't real. Doesn't he understand?

"How did you get here?" I ask.

"An Uber."

I nod because I don't know what else to do.

"I have to do something," he tells me. "I signed myself out of the hospital, but I'll go to rehab tomorrow. Do you trust me?"

No.

I can't.

He's shown me that. He ran away and got high and didn't come home.

But he's here now.

As I stare into his serious face, I see the little boy he once was, and he's sincere.

"Okay," I say. "What are we doing?"

"I have to go somewhere," he says simply. "Will you take me?"

I nod. Again, I don't know what else to do. I can't imagine what he needs to do, but he's going into rehab tomorrow. So whatever he needs, I'll do it.

Kit stays with the kids while I get into the car with my son.

Beck directs me to a neighborhood downtown, and a little bit later, we pull in front of a vet's office.

I'm confused, but I don't say anything. I just follow Beck inside, past the beat-up door, into the dingy lobby.

There's a woman behind the counter, and she has kind eyes. She looks at Beck and I see the flicker of recognition. She knows him.

"Do you remember me?" Beck asks her. She nods.

"Of course. How is Winston?"

"He's fine," I answer for my son. "We're getting him fattened up."

"That's good." She looks at me, probably wondering who I am and why we are here.

I wonder that last part myself.

"Was there a girl with me when I was here?" Beck asks her now, hesitantly. He's uncertain, and he feels uncomfortable. That's clear.

The woman cocks her head. "A girl?" She shakes her head. "No. Just Winston. But you were talking to yourself a lot. You were . . . pretty out of it. Pretty banged up. I thought about you for days. I should've done more for you."

I stare at her now. Beck was here and he was out of it, and she didn't do anything? I want to punch her for that. But then again, what could she have done?

"You're sure there wasn't a girl?" Beck asks again, and his voice has lost all confidence. His shoulders are slumped.

"Very sure. I'm sorry."

Beck nods and thanks her. I feel her watching us as we walk back to the door, and when my hand is on the handle, I turn back.

"Whatever you did for my son," I offer, "thank you."

She nods again, and her eyes are soft and I can tell she's a mother.

She did something kind for my son, although I might never know what. Not unless Beck chooses to tell me.

Outside, Beck crouches on the curb, kneeling as though he is catching his breath.

"Honey," I start to say.

"I just need a minute," he croaks. That's when I know. He truly didn't believe us about Angel, not until now, not until this moment.

"Take all the time you need," I answer him softly. I wait in the driver's seat, trying not to fuss over him. It's a while before he finally stands up and drops into the passenger seat.

He looks straight ahead, his skinny hand clutching his leg. He's utterly deflated.

"Are you okay?" I ask him gently.

"No. I don't understand this. She was so real, Mom. I . . . I don't know how to process this."

I hug him tight, and after he pulls away, he looks at me, his eyes red. "Can you take me one more place?"

I'm expecting him to direct me to the abandoned warehouse where he had been living, but he doesn't. He asks to go to Lake Michigan.

My car noses in that direction, gliding down the road.

Beck's knuckles rap against his knees and he's anxious.

"Did you love her?" I ask quietly. "The Angel you thought you knew."

He looks out the glass, staring at the trees.

"Yes. But not like she deserved."

I pull into the parking lot of the beach nearest to us. The water is gray and still ice-cold from winter, but Beck is already out of the car, striding toward the edge.

The sand is hard and doesn't give way underfoot as I follow him. I don't know what he's planning, only that he has a single-minded focus.

I'm hovering at his elbow as he kneels to the ground at the water's edge.

"Angel," he whispers. "They're telling me that you were never real."

I don't know how that can be, but . . . God. I'm sorry. I should've loved you enough. I should've loved you better. You were the best friend I ever had. I don't care what was real or not."

My throat chokes up and I put my hand on his shoulder, and I feel his bone beneath my fingers.

"You don't have to worry about this prison anymore," he says. "There is no more pain, no more hate. No one will ever hurt you again. You're free, Angel."

He stands up and remains still, except for the breeze that flutters his hair.

"The day is done," he tells her softly. Tears stream from my eyes as Beck talks to a girl who never was but who still so profoundly affected him.

I wait silently, and when he turns, he doesn't look at me. He heads straight for the car.

"I just want to sleep in my bed one time before rehab tomorrow," he says as I drive home. "Is that okay, Mama?"

He hasn't called me Mama since he was small, and it clenches a knot in my stomach.

"Of course, sweetie," I tell him.

"I'm sorry. For everything."

"You're my son," I finally answer around the lump in my throat. "I'll love you always, no matter what."

"I'm still sorry," he says.

"I know. Me too."

He doesn't ask for what, and I don't explain . . . that I'm sorry for all of the lost moments, for his dad's death, for every bad thing that isn't my fault, but I'm sorry for it all the same. I think he already knows.

"Tomorrow is the first day of forever," I tell him. "You're going to be healthy and strong, and eventually, you're going to be happy again."

"Okay," he answers simply.

"Do you believe it?" I ask, because I can't tell.

He shrugs. "I will."

forty-four

BECK

MY BED IS SOFTER THAN I REMEMBER, AND IT'S HARD TO sleep.

I went to bed earlier than everyone else because I feel weak now, tired. But still, I can't sleep, so eventually, I give up.

I walk softly through the house. Even though it's dark and filled with shadows, they are familiar. I've seen these same dark shapes since I was small, and heard the same loud creaks in the floor. I hear a murmur of voices coming from the kitchen and see a light on over the table. It sounds like Sam and Vinny are still here, and maybe even Kit.

I curl up on the sofa and my thoughts are loud.

My memories are louder.

I remember the crash.

How my phone rang, and how I answered it.

It happened so fast, and the crunch of metal and the screeching noises.

My own screams.

"You okay?"

Kit is in the hallway, his thumbs looped through his belt loops. He's awkward here, yet comfortable. A strange balance.

I shake my head.

"Not really."

"I didn't think so."

He comes in quietly and sits next to me, his legs sprawled in front of him.

"I'll never forget the crash," I tell him. "I'll never forget how it sounded . . . the screeches of the metal or the screaming. I think that was me."

Kit is serious and he watches me, and his big hands fidget in his lap.

"My father's face when I woke up after. I'll never forget it, Kit. I can't get it out of my head. Anyone who says a dead person looks like they are sleeping is a liar. They don't look asleep. They look dead."

"I agree," Kit says finally. "They do. And I'm so sorry you had to see your father that way, Beck. He would never have chosen that."

My lungs feel heavy and hot and the silence is thick between Kit and me, and he takes a deep breath and he's measuring his words.

"You know, I'm struggling with something myself," Kit tells me. "I'm not sure how to deal with the fact that maybe I could've prevented it too."

My head snaps up.

"Oh yes," Kit tells me. "I could've been there. Your dad invited me to go. It's our alma mater, after all. I almost did, but I had an early morning the next day, so I said no. If I had been there, maybe I would've been driving instead of you."

"You'd have never have let that accident happen," I point out.

Kit shakes his head. "You know, my mom used to tell me that everything happened for a reason. She believed that every single thing on earth was planned by God Himself, that nothing was left to chance. If that's the case, then the accident would've happened anyway."

"But why would I get to live?" My voice is strained and high-pitched.

"Because you are supposed to," Kit says simply.

"But I've watched two people die," I protest. "And they were both better people than me. Good, smart, kind. I'm not. The first chance I got,

I ran away and hid and spent two months high out of my mind. If I hadn't met Angel, maybe she wouldn't be dead right now either. And please don't tell me that she wasn't real. I just don't want to hear that right now."

Kit wraps his arm around my shoulders and squeezes.

"I don't know why things happen. I don't know why your father's seat belt malfunctioned. But what I do know is this: You can't waste this chance. You've got to live your life hard and fiercely. You've got to live for Angel and for your dad."

"I'm going to try," I tell him, and I love him for saying that about Angel. "It's hard, though. I want to use even now."

And I do. I feel the want burgeoning up from my belly into my thoughts, and every time it rears its head I try to suppress it, but I'm afraid that sometime, someday, I won't be strong enough.

"You can beat this," Kit tells me, and he sounds so sure. "I know you can."

We're quiet and the minutes stretch, and finally I turn to him. "I don't know where to go after this. Do you . . . do you think I can still go to college? Maybe I can still play football. I mean, after rehab. Do you think I can?"

Kit levels a stare at me. "Kiddo, I think you can do anything you put your mind to. You've always been that way, and you always will. You can do this."

I exhale and nod. My dad always called me kiddo too, and hearing it now makes my chest warm.

"Thank you, Kit," I tell him sincerely. "Truly."

He nods, and I change the subject.

"Can I borrow your phone? Mine broke, and I'd like to text Elin."

Kit is surprised, but he doesn't hesitate. "Of course." He pulls it out of his pocket and hands it to me.

"Your father was proud of you from the moment you were born," he says and looks straight into my eyes. "He'd be so proud of you for taking the step to go into rehab tomorrow. I know it."

My eyes are hot now and they sting, and Kit leaves me with his phone.

Can you come back over? I text her. *This is Beck, btw.* She'd been here earlier, but I miss her.

I'll be right there. She doesn't even hesitate.

I leave Kit's phone on the chair, and I'm waiting for Elin on the porch steps when she arrives twenty minutes later.

She's in pajamas, but she's here.

My arms close around her, and she smells like sunshine and strawberries, just like I remember.

"I've watched two people die, Elin," I say, and my voice trembles a little. "I don't think I'll ever be the same."

"I doubt you will be," she agrees. "No one would. But I love the person you are, Beck. The person in here." She touches my heart and I close my eyes.

"I'm sorry that I blamed you," I tell her finally. "For calling. That wasn't right. It wasn't your fault."

"And it wasn't yours," she answers. "It was a terrible twist of . . . something. Fate? Tragedy? I don't know. It was an accident."

"I know." And I do. "My brain knows it. I just have to get my heart to understand now."

"Are you happy to be home?" Elin asks, and her voice is oh so soft.

I nod. "Yeah. But I'm leaving tomorrow."

"I'm proud of you," she says, and her hand wraps around mine. "You're so brave."

"What if I'm not strong enough, though?" I ask before I can filter my words. "What if I can't do it?"

Elin is already shaking her head. "You can do anything," she says stoutly. "You always have, and you always will."

"Will you come visit me? I'll understand if you don't want to. I'm sure rehabs aren't pleasant places."

She rolls her eyes. "I'll be there every chance I get."

We chat for a while longer, before she kisses my cheek.

"You're going to be amazing tomorrow," she says. "We're all behind you, Beck."

She leaves to drive back to her normal life and I'm left with my fucked-up one. But that's no one's fault but my own.

I almost crawl back into bed, but then . . . then . . . I remember something.

Something my father said when I was dead for that minute.

Did you ever listen to that CD I gave you?

I feel the sudden urge to do it. To hear his voice. He went to all the trouble of making it for me. The least I can do is listen.

I pad down to the den and find where I'd hidden it between the pages of a book on the top shelf of the bookcase. No one knows how it survived the crash, but it did. It seems almost as though I'm *meant* to hear it.

I pop it into the CD player and press play.

My dad's voice instantly fills the room.

I know you want to sleep in, Beck. But before you reach for the snooze button, remember this:

You want to be the best, and the other players do too. They won't press snooze. The best players are already up, and they're already running, their feet on the floor.

I want you to get out of bed and remember that you are the best of the best. You breathe in challenges, and you spit out wins. You do not accept failure, and you fight for what is yours.

You've got work to do, Beck. So get up, and head out. You're going to sweat, and you're going to hurt, you may even bleed, but you'll get stronger and stronger, and soon, no one will be stronger than you.

A hot tear escapes my eye as I listen. My dad had made this because he knew I hated to get up so early to work out. He meant for it to be motivation, but he had no idea how I might use it now . . . for something far more important than football.

It will motivate me to live.

*There's the right way to do things, son, and the easy way. You
will take the right way. You will work and sweat and bleed,
and you will win. The easy way out is not YOUR WAY. Your
way is hard and less traveled, but your way is the best way.
Your way is the way of winners.*

*You are strong, and you are fierce. You will get up today, you
will rise, and you will do it again and again. You will take one
step then another. You are your own biggest opponent. Your
own biggest challenge.*

You will not defeat yourself.

You can do anything you put your mind to.

Remember what you're fighting for.

Put on your armor and wear it every day. Give it all you've got.

You can run faster.

You can throw harder.

You are a fierce warrior.

You can do this.

*So shake the sleep from your eyes, and put your feet on the
floor.*

It's time to fight for what's yours.

The CD ends and the room is quiet. All I can hear is my breathing
and my heartbeat. One beat. Two beats. Three. My dad was talking
about football.

But I'm interpreting it differently now. Maybe Kit is right. Maybe
things happen because they are supposed to. Maybe my dad was supposed to make this CD.

He thought he was talking about football.

But he wasn't.

He was talking about my life.

I have to fight for my life.

And this time, I will win.

epilogue

THE CEMETERY IS SILENT BUT FOR THE CHIRP OF THE BIRDS. I'm not sure why cemeteries are so peaceful and reverent, but they are. Even the trees are hushed, as though anything else would be disrespectful.

I stand in front of my father's black stone and stare down at his name.

Matthew Beckitt Kingsley.

I lay the flowers down on the marble and sink into the grass, running my fingers along the inscribed letters. The day of his death, October 12.

"It's beautiful here," Elin observes, her arm linked through mine.

She called me every day I was in rehab, after that initial first week. She's buoyed me up, talked me down when I was upset, and been there throughout every minute. Just like my mom, Sam, Kit, and Vinny. They all have. They visited every visiting day and called me every night.

Today, I came here to share a victory with the one person who couldn't do those things.

"I made it through rehab, Dad," I tell him. "I'm clean now. I've been clean for a hundred and thirty-four days."

It's a long time, but I don't want to focus on that. I want to focus only on today, because today is all that matters. I can't get cocky. I can't slip. I slide my hand into my pocket and run my fingers over my Narcotics Anonymous medallion. It is always in my pocket now, next to Devin's green good-luck marble.

"So now I'm going to go to a halfway house," I continue bluntly. From beside me, I hear Elin suck in her breath. I know she doesn't really want me there, living among addicts. But I *am* an addict. I have to come through the stages, just like everyone else. I have to put in the work, go through the steps, and most importantly, I can't lie to myself about what I am. It's the only way I'll truly recover.

And now, it's time to live in a halfway house and put the pieces back together. I'm already looking better. I've put on weight and my face has filled back in. My skin is a normal color instead of gray. I feel more like myself.

"Don't worry," I tell my dad. "I'm still going to go to college. I'll start in the fall. And . . . I've decided to go to Notre Dame. I'm going to try for a walk-on spot on the football team. Maybe I can still get that scholarship."

I wait, even though he's not here to react. If he were, he'd be crowing and doing a victory dance.

"And don't worry, Mr. K," Elin says. "I've gone ahead of him and felt out all the local spots. I've lit some candles for you in the grotto too."

It's me sucking in my breath now. I haven't told anyone about my vision of my father in the grotto. I don't know if they would believe me, but even if they did, it's still so personal, so *mine*.

When I do move onto campus, I'll be in that grotto a lot. I know it already.

"So I just wanted to give you the good news in person," I tell the headstone. I know my dad isn't here, but this is the best place to come to talk to him. Wherever he is, I feel like he hears me. "Everyone is okay, by the way. Mom, Kit, the kids. Anna-B hasn't wet the bed in a while, which is good. Devin won the county spelling bee. He goes on to the state contest next. Oh, and Mom decided not to take the settlement. She's going to fight it. She doesn't want another car to kill someone else the way you died. The money would've been nice, but the lawyer thinks she'll win. So we just have to be patient. We all miss you, Dad."

I leave out that I think Mom and Kit will end up dating. I'm sure Dad already knows.

I kiss my fingers and press them to the stone, and then Elin and I stand up and stroll through the grassy lanes.

My gaze roves over the rows of stones, the colorful pinwheels spinning in the breeze, the flowers, the trinkets. I love how people come and try to breathe life into a place that is full of death.

We walk in comfortable silence and turn down another lane.

As we do, my attention is drawn to a stone at the end of the row. It's white and glimmers in the sunlight, an angel statue perched on the side, its wings drawn up protectively, standing watch for all of eternity.

For some reason, I'm drawn to it. And as we grow closer, I look again.

The letters are visible now to me, and they are clear as day in the sun.

SARAH GREENE.

The date of her death was October 12. The day of my accident.

I freeze and stare at the grave. It's sparse, with no decoration, no visitors. But the sole guardian angel stands, and I think it weeps.

"What's wrong?" Elin asks quickly, because I'm not moving a muscle. My feet are frozen; my heart is stuttering.

Can it be?

I close my eyes and I am in that car again, before it was wrecked and twisted. I am behind the wheel and I look up from my phone, into the headlights shining into my face. Behind the light, there was a face, something I hadn't allowed myself to remember until now. It was a girl's face, a girl with short, spiky hair and wide, startled eyes. When our cars collided and rolled, blackbirds had exploded from the ditches into the night sky.

Angel.

I find myself kneeling on the ground in front of the white angel now, and my hand rests on the stone.

I feel the warmth now, radiating into my hand and my face and my arm. It was her. The whole time it was her.

Sarah Greene.

I close my eyes and envision her admonishing me for ever doubting her. She'd stare at me with her eyebrow lifted. *You get it now, King?* She'd ask.

I take a deep breath. Yeah, I get it.

She believed in me every step of the way. She always did.

You can do this, King, she would say. *You've got this.*

And I do.

author's note

Dear Reader,

If this story felt authentic to you, that is because it *is*. My son is a re-covering addict.

Loving someone with an addiction is a heavy burden to carry. At times, you feel alone, as though no one else could possibly understand. And most of the time, no one can, unless they've walked this particular path themselves.

My twenty-two-year-old son, my firstborn, my Gunner, was a cheer-ful little boy, his smile like sunshine, his charm enough to talk himself in and out of mostly everything. He was bright, he was bursting with potential, and he was beautiful. He was rambunctious, he was all boy, playing with lizards and turtles and snakes from the yard. His favorite show was *The Land before Time*, and he wanted to be a zoologist when he grew up.

Then, as a teenager, he changed. He became a shell of his former self, his mood mercurial. He lied to himself, and to us, told us that nothing was wrong, that his disinterest in school was because he was bored. That was a lie.

The truth came out soon enough.

He had started out huffing aerosol cans in secret, and that progressed to other things, like methamphetamine and heroin and pretty much anything he could get his hands on. The Addiction hooked into him with sharp talons. I address it in capital letters, like it is *a thing*, because it is. Addiction is a palpable monster. It grabbed my son, and it wouldn't let go, and he didn't want to let it.

It dragged him down, and we all went with him.

Loving someone with an addiction is like being on a terrible roller coaster that you can never get off of. Like Beck, Gunner went off the grid. He slept on couches, in garages, in parks, under bridges. He called me in the middle of the night; he called me crying; he called me saying he wanted to die.

He raged. He cried. He soared. He crashed.

People on the outside looking in thought that I should've been able to fix it. That if I FORCED him into getting help, he would've beat the addiction.

That's not the way it works. I put him into rehab multiple times. It didn't take. Because he wasn't ready. He wasn't a minor anymore—he was over eighteen. So I couldn't MAKE him do anything, not even when he was killing himself with that dangerous cycle. The addiction made him someone he wasn't, someone who said awful things, someone who tried to hurt those who loved him, because the only thing that was important to him was feeding that demon inside of him.

It was exhausting.

And then, one night, at two a.m., he called me. I could tell he'd been high, that he'd crashed. He was very, very low. His speech was jumbled, incoherent. Eventually, he said, "Mom, what time is it?"

I pulled the phone away from my ear to look at it.

"Two thirty," I told him.

He didn't answer.

"Gunner?"

He didn't answer.

"Gunner?!"

Still no answer. I could hear some sort of ragged, gurgly sound in the background, and I knew it was coming from his throat. I hung up and tried to call him back.

No answer.

So I did the only thing I could do. I called for an ambulance. I didn't know if he was dying; I only knew, in my mother's heart, that time was of the essence. I waited by my phone, barely breathing myself, until I heard back.

He had overdosed, and the police had found drugs in his house. He was lucky, though. He lived.

This certainly wasn't the worst incident we experienced with Gunner, but it was the one that for some reason turned out to be his catalyst. He was treated and arrested, and he was put into jail. He was eventually released and placed on a list for rehab. Finally, after several weeks, he entered rehab. Again.

All we could do was hope that this time it took. That this was the time he'd want to get better and we could all get off the roller-coaster ride from hell. He told me he wanted to get better, but he was in for the fight of his life. He woke up in the night, in cold sweats and craving needles. The cravings were stronger than he was, he thought. But I knew that wasn't true.

And you know what?

I was right.

He came through rehab triumphant that time. And then he entered a postrehab program, and then a halfway house. He got a job and he put himself back on the path to recovery.

Today, he's still fighting his way back. He got a crappy job and bought a bicycle so he could get a job farther away. Then he got a better job and rides his bike to work every day, through rain and snow. He's determined to be better, and he's doing it. He's been clean for a year. That's huge for him, and it's huge for me as his mother.

In *Saving Beck*, I wanted to show how a series of choices can affect life, how addiction can affect anyone, from any walk of life. Our family is normal, like any family that might live next door to you. If it can happen to us, it can happen to anyone.

According to the numbers provided by the National Institute on Drug Abuse, the rise of drug-related deaths is startling.

- During 2014, 47,055 drug-overdose deaths occurred in the United States.
- In 2015, that number increased to 52,404.
- In 2016, that number became 64,070.

This is a pandemic. It is growing, and it is real. I've lived it—I know. As a society, we have to stop ignoring it and start fixing it. Most of the time, people don't start out wanting to use hard drugs. They slip into it, like a whisper that turns into a roar. We've got to stop labeling and condemning, and start helping.

I know that at times, this book was hard to read. That's because I wanted it to be *real*. I wanted to show what addiction is, and what it can do, without a filtered lens.

Through the ugliness, though, I also wanted to illustrate that while life is full of tragedy and loss, it is also full of hope and redemption.

Where there is life, there is hope. That is something I've learned, and it is something we should all remember.

If you or someone you love is in the midst of drug addiction, know this: You are worthy of hope. You are worthy of help. You are worthy of LIFE. Take the first step today and go to a Narcotics Anonymous meeting. They can help you find a program to get you on your way to recovery.

I have also recently started a Facebook support group called The Anchor Room. In there, you have a safe place to share and listen, without judgment. Find it by searching for The Anchor Room in your Facebook search bar.

You may also call SAMHSA (Substance Abuse and Mental Health Services Administration). SAMHSA's National Helpline, 1-800-662-HELP (4357), also known as the Treatment Referral Routing Service, is a confidential, free, twenty-four-hour-a-day, 365-day-a-year information service in English and Spanish for individuals and family members facing mental and/or substance-use disorders. This service provides referrals to local treatment facilities, support groups, and community-based organizations. Callers can also order free publications and other information.

If you need help, please, please, please ask for it.

Then fight for it.

You are strong enough, and you are worth it.

Live one day at a time, one moment at a time.

Live fiercely.

BOOK
CLUB
FAVORITES

READER'S
GUIDE

saving
beck

COURTNEY COLE

This reader's guide for Saving Beck *includes an introduction, discussion questions, and ideas for enhancing your book club. The suggested questions are intended to help your reading group find new and interesting angles and topics for your discussion. We hope that these ideas will enrich your conversation and increase your enjoyment of the book.*

introduction

When Natalie Kingsley's husband, Matt, dies in a car crash on his way home from a college visit with their teenage son, their happy family life is irreparably damaged. One year later, she's a widow still unmoored by grief, struggling to raise three grieving children who feel as if they have somehow lost both parents.

Her older son, Beck, helps Natalie with daily responsibilities that she can't seem to manage alone. But in private, Beck agonizes over his role as driver of the car the night his father died. Unwilling to accept that a faulty seat belt is to blame, Beck turns to heroin to cope, and he quickly becomes addicted to the temporary escape it offers.

For Natalie and Beck, heroin threatens to endanger the fragile recovery that they have painstakingly achieved. Separately, and together, they must fight for their family's survival.

topics and questions for discussion

1. Describe Natalie Kingsley's condition when she arrives at Mercy Hospital with her oldest son, Beck. What does Natalie's heightened awareness of the private waiting area in the hospital—its sounds, smells, lighting, decor—reveal about her emotional state? How does her husband's recent death intensify her perceptions?

2. "I feel my chest rise off the table, breaking rank from the rest of my body, and I feel myself thrashing against my will, yet it doesn't hurt. . . . I don't know why I'm able to think calmly when my body is out of control" (page 14). How does the author's decision to incorporate Beck's internal monologue into the novel's narrative affect your understanding of his character and his motivations? How would you describe Beck's awareness of his condition and his whereabouts?

3. Compare Beck's relationship with his father, Matt, to his relationship with his mother, Natalie. With whom does he seem most able

to express himself and why? In your discussion, consider examining his parents' individual feelings about Beck's athletic and academic pursuits, his future goals, his girlfriend, and his strengths and weaknesses as a person.

4. "Beck was the one who had been feeding the kids for me; he even paid the utility bill for me yesterday. . . . He couldn't be that responsible and also smoke pot on the side" (pages 66–67). In the aftermath of Matt's death, why does Beck assume the role of co-parent? In what respects do his self-medicating and use of illicit drugs reveal the impulsivity of a typical adolescent, the rebelliousness of one who cannot bear the new burdens imposed on him, or something altogether different?

5. Beck's first experience with heroin leads him to seek out more drugs in a run-down Chicago building populated by drug users he imagines as his "new family." Why does Beck want to leave his family and the comforts of home? To what degree are Beck's family and friends responsible for his drug use?

6. "It's Kit, my husband's best friend, and he's filling the doorway with his giant shoulders. He's a Great Dane in a sea of Labradors" (page 11). How would you characterize Natalie's feelings for Kit? How does Kit's changing role in the Kingsley family following the accident disrupt the stability Natalie has sought to reclaim?

7. How would you describe the sibling dynamic between Natalie and her younger sister, Sam LaRosa? In the aftermath of Matt's accident, what substantive changes in Beck does Sam observe that Natalie is unable or unwilling to acknowledge? To what extent are these changes visible to others close to Beck, like his girlfriend, Elin, and his younger siblings, Annabelle and Devin?

8. How do the present-tense and flashback narratives of Natalie and Beck provide a more comprehensive picture of their family's expe-

rience? Which character's voice or story did you find more compelling, and why? Why do you think the author chose to write the novel using these dual—and at times dueling—perspectives?

9. Discuss the character of Angel and the role she plays in the novel. What does she represent to Beck? How did you react as a reader upon learning that Angel was a figment of Beck's drug-addled imagination? To what extent does Beck's interpretation of Angel—that she was the embodied spirit of Sarah Greene, the other driver, who perished in the car accident—seem persuasive to you? What are some other possible ways readers might understand Angel?

10. How does the premature death of Matt Kingsley impact each member of his immediate family? How does Natalie's grief exacerbate Beck's feelings of guilt for his role in his father's death? If you were a therapist treating the Kingsley family, what would you encourage them to explore as they come to terms with their profound loss? To what extent do you think Natalie and Beck could have taken more preventive measures to avoid Beck's overdose?

11. "People on the outside looking in thought that I should've been able to fix it. That if I FORCED him into getting help, he would've beat the addiction. That's not the way it works" (Author's Note, page 290). How did the author's decision to relate her experiences as a mother dealing with her son's drug addiction affect you as a reader? Why do you think she chose to do so at the end of the novel, rather than in a foreword?

12. *Saving Beck* touches on many complex social issues of our time—including illicit drug use, digital privacy, drug addiction, rehabilitation, adolescent/parent conflict, the consequences of extramarital sex, the death of a parent, distracted driving, vehicular homicide, grief, depression, and prescription drug abuse. Of the many issues the author highlights, which especially captured your imagination as a reader, and why?

enhance your book club

1. Imagine that Natalie is a cherished member of your book club. How might fellow club members support her as she mourns her husband and despairs over the emergency hospitalization of Beck? Members of your club may want to share stories of acts of compassion and kindness they have received during difficult moments in their own lives, or discuss what they wish had been said to or done for them.

2. Over the course of the novel, Beck and Natalie experience many different stages of grief. Have members of your club reflect on losses they and those they know well have experienced. What kinds of healthy activities enabled them to come through these painful moments intact? In what ways does the novel's depiction of grief in the aftermath of the death of a loved one echo their own lived experiences?

3. In its depiction of a high-achieving student from a well-to-do family whose life is nearly destroyed by illegal drug use, *Saving Beck* upends commonly held perceptions that drug addiction happens to people in less stable circumstances. Have members of your club reflect on their own direct or indirect experiences with substance abuse and discuss as a group the current attitudes toward illicit drug use in their wider communities.

4. The catalyst for the plot of *Saving Beck* is a fatal car accident involving substance abuse on the part of one young driver, distracted driving by another, and a potentially faulty seat belt. Ask your book club to defend the author's decision to incorporate these narrative ambiguities into the novel. To what extent does the author's implicit refusal to render judgment on her characters' choices place the burden to do so on the reader? How does the author's use of two narrative perspectives further complicate the reader's assignment of responsibility?